PEGASUS

AND THE ORIGINS OF OLYMPUS

PEGASUS

AND THE ORIGINS OF OLYMPUS

KATE O'HEARN

Hodder Children's Books

A division of Hachette Children's Books

A Catalogue record for this book is available from the British Library

ISBN 978 1 444 91094 0

Typeset in AGaramond Book by Avon DataSet Ltd,
Bidford on Avon, Warwickshire

Printed and bound in Great Britain by
CPI Group (UK) Ltd, Croydon, CR0 4YY

The paper and board used in this paperback by Hodder Children's Books
are natural recyclable products made from wood grown in
sustainable forests. The manufacturing processes conform to the
environmental regulations of the country of origin.

Hodder Children's Books
a division of Hachette Children's Books
338 Euston Road, London NW1 3BH
An Hachette UK company
www.hachette.co.uk

For the abandoned dogs of Greece

1

The light of the Solar Stream pulsed and flashed as she tore through it as fast as she could. She had to get home! But the faster she travelled, the longer the journey became. Obstacles blocked her path, slowed her down. Other worlds called to her. Unseen hands reached for her and pulled her down.

'No,' she screamed. 'I must return before it is too late. Leave me be!'

Breaking free of their grip, she raced through the Solar Stream until at last she made it home. She arrived in the temple and hurtled along its long stone corridors. Her heart roared and her terror grew as she felt the others gathering far from the temple. They were drawing together and merging their powers. She had to reach them. Join them. She couldn't be left behind.

She emerged from the stone temple and dashed into the dense green jungle. She put on more speed as she moved along paths as old as time itself, rushing past the great statues of her people and dodging around the massive trees. This was her home. Her sanctuary. Her world. But they were all about to leave it. To go on.

They had said they would try to wait for her. But when the stars aligned, they would go with or without her.

'Please don't let me be too late . . .' she begged.

'Please! Please!'

Emily's cry awoke her from the terrifying dream and she felt a warm tongue on her cheek. She looked up and saw the magnificent winged stallion, Pegasus, standing at the side of her bed. He was glowing brightly as he stared down at her and nickered softly.

Emily's face was hot and flushed and she was panting heavily as if she'd been in a race. 'I'm OK, Pegs,' she said quietly as she looked up into his large, concerned eyes.

Pegasus nickered again and pressed his face to hers.

'Em!' Her father raced into the room. 'What's wrong? You were shouting and crying.'

She was shaking all over. 'It's just a dream,' she said. 'Ever since we got back from Area 51, I've had the same dream over and over again. It's like I'm someone else and trying to get home before something huge happens. I'm so scared that I'm going to miss it. But as I go through the Solar Stream, things I can't see block

2

my path and something tries to hold me back.' She looked up into his caring face. 'What does it mean?'

Emily's father sat on the bed and pulled her into a tight embrace. 'I don't know, honey. They say dreams come from our subconscious as it tries to work something out.'

'Like what?' Emily asked.

'I'm not sure. But you've been through so much lately. Maybe your mind is trying to digest everything that's happened. Look at how our life has changed. We live here in Olympus and you've got so many powers now. I know they scare you. Maybe that's the cause of your nightmares.'

'Not nightmares,' Emily corrected. 'It's always the same. I'm desperate to get home to some kind of gathering. But I always wake up before I make it there.'

'Home?' he asked. 'You mean New York? Do you want to go back?'

Emily frowned and shook her head. 'No, not New York, and it's not Olympus either. It's a strange place with jungle all around. I'm in a complicated stone temple surrounded by tall statues.'

Pegasus snorted loudly and shook his head. He stepped closer to Emily and stared at her intently. As she gazed deep into his warm brown eyes, Emily saw a vision of a jungle world filled with tall stone statues.

'That's the jungle! Have you been dreaming of it too?'

The strong, white stallion shook his head, pawed the floor and whinnied several times. He turned his head to the door. Then he nudged Emily's father and turned to the door again.

'What is it?' her father asked. 'What are you trying to tell me?'

'He wants you to go somewhere,' Emily explained.

'This time of night?'

After several more failed attempts to get Emily and her father to understand, Pegasus gave up and left the room. He returned moments later with a very sleepy Paelen and Joel.

'You OK, Em?' Joel asked groggily as he stepped closer to her bed. He was just wearing pyjama bottoms so she could see where his new silver arm joined his broad body. It looked exactly like the old one that Vulcan had created for him after he lost his real arm in the fight against the Gorgons. She was amazed at how quickly Vulcan had been able to build it after the Central Research Unit scientists at Area 51 had surgically removed the old one.

Emily nodded. 'I'm fine. I've had that dream again.

4

But then Pegs showed me a place exactly like in my dream.'

Paelen yawned loudly. His hair stood at all angles and his night clothes were twisted and unkempt. He looked at Pegasus and frowned. 'You woke me because Emily was having a dream? What about me? I was having my own amazing dream featuring several water nymphs.'

Pegasus whinnied and shoved Paelen.

'What!' Paelen cried. 'Am I not allowed to dream?'

'Paelen, please,' Emily said. 'Pegasus is trying to tell me something, but I can't understand him. I think it's important.'

Paelen concentrated on Pegasus. 'What is it?'

The stallion nickered several times and shook his head.

'This is very strange,' Paelen said. 'Pegasus says the world you have been describing from your dream is the world you sent him to when you were shot at the CRU facility in the Nevada desert.'

Emily frowned. 'How? I've never been there or even heard about it. Why would I dream of a place I've never seen? And why is it always the same dream?'

Pegasus pawed the floor and whinnied softly.

Paelen looked shocked. 'Really? Why have we not

heard about this when it concerns Emily?'

'What concerns me?' Emily asked.

'Apparently after we returned from Earth, Jupiter had some of his people go to the jungle world to explore it. He was curious why your powers would send things there.'

Emily looked at Pegasus. 'You knew about this and didn't tell me?'

The stallion dropped his head, looking very guilty.

'Pegasus only just found out. Jupiter told him to say nothing as he feared it might upset you. After everything that happened on Earth, he wanted you to spend some quiet time in Olympus and not worry about the jungle world.'

'Not telling me is what upsets me!' Emily shot back. 'Jupiter promised we were going to figure that out together. He shouldn't have sent people there without me.'

Emily's father nodded. 'I agree. There must be some reason why Emily's powers sent you and Alexis, the Sphinx, there. We have a right to be involved in the investigation. I'll have a chat with Jupiter in the morning and find out what's going on.'

'I'm coming with you,' Emily said.

'Me too,' Joel added.

'And me,' Paelen said.

Pegasus nickered and nodded his head. Emily didn't need Paelen to translate. The stallion would be there too.

Sleep would not return to Emily. After her latest dream she didn't really want it to. Instead she and Pegasus slipped silently out of the palace and flew high in the night skies over Olympus.

The stars were shining brightly overhead and cast enough light for them to see. Emily looked down on the night dwellers as they went about their silent lives, working, living and playing only by starlight.

Pegasus landed on their private silver beach surrounding the calm lake. No wind disturbed its surface and it was like a giant mirror reflecting the stars from above.

Emily climbed off Pegasus and walked knee-deep into the cool, still water. She no longer needed her leg brace as her powers had healed her damaged leg back at Area 51. The revelations from her time at the CRU facility still troubled her. She had only confided in Pegasus about what the scientists had said about her. She hadn't even told Joel or Paelen for fear of what they might think of her.

Was she really not alive? They claimed she didn't have physical matter the same way all living organisms do – including the Olympians. And although she had blood and a heart that pumped it around her body, it wasn't needed to keep her going. The scientists believed it was all there because Emily thought it should be.

In her quiet moments, or when she was alone with Pegasus, Emily asked herself the same question time and time again. 'What am I?' But despite his love and support of her, Pegasus had no answers.

'It's so beautiful here,' she sighed as Pegasus joined her in the water. 'Sometimes I wish we could stay here for ever and not worry about all the other stuff. Just you and me and this silver lake.'

Pegasus pressed his head to hers.

She looked up into his beautiful face and combed his long mane away from his eyes. 'Something's changed. I can feel it. I've changed and it really scares me.' Emily lifted her smooth leg. 'Look, there's no trace of the scar. All I had to do was imagine it gone, and it was gone. I sent you and Alexis away without really thinking about it and I destroyed the CRU facility at Area 51 without any effort at all. Doesn't it scare you that I can do all that?'

Pegasus snorted and shook his head, then pressed closer to her.

'Thanks, Pegs,' she said gratefully. 'But it scares me. What if I make a mistake? What if I really hurt someone? I just don't have enough control.'

Pegasus and Emily walked along the silver beach all night. When the dawn started to rise over Olympus, she climbed on the stallion's back and they made their way home to Jupiter's palace.

Flying through her large open window, Emily barely had time to change into her tunic before there was a knock on her door.

'You ready to see Jupiter?' Joel asked as he entered her room.

The winged boar, Chrysaor, was standing beside Joel and nudged his hairy snout into Emily's hand for a pat.

'I'm ready,' Emily said as she gave the boar a good-morning kiss on the head.

They met up with her father in the corridor and made their way along the wide marble steps leading down to the main floor.

As always, there was a lot of activity in the palace as people came and went about their business. Bouquets of unusual, fragrant flowers were being delivered and the statues that adorned the palace were being cleaned by a group of young male satyrs. The half-goat, half-boys saw Emily and Pegasus and greeted them excitedly.

Cupid was at the base of the stairs, chatting with a young centaur. When he saw Emily, his face lit up with a bright smile.

'Oh, great,' Joel muttered to Paelen. 'Just what we need, Cupid here to cause trouble.'

'Good morning, Flame,' Cupid said brightly as he approached Emily and bowed elegantly. He reached for her hand and gave it a light kiss.

'Hi, Cupid. What brings you to the palace?'

'My mother is in a meeting with Jupiter this morning,' the winged Olympian explained. 'I came along hoping to see your lovely face.'

Emily blushed at the compliment. Though her crush on him was long over, he still managed to charm her in an instant.

Beside her, Joel made an exaggerated gagging sound. 'Give me a break, Cupid.'

Paelen was standing on Emily's left. From the corner of her eye, she watched him use his Olympian powers to stretch his arm. While Cupid was distracted with Emily, Paelen's elongated arm slid past her back and then Joel's until it looped around, unseen, behind Cupid.

Emily poked her elbow in Paelen's side, but his hand had already reached Cupid and caught hold of a handful of feathers from Cupid's wings. Paelen gave a mighty pull.

'Ouch!' Cupid cried as his wings flashed open. He spun around to see who had attacked him and didn't see Paelen's arm retracting. What he did see were several feathers falling to the floor.

'Paelen!' Cupid accused. 'I know it was you.'

Joel and Paelen were lost in fits of laughter at the rage on Cupid's face. As the Olympian charged, Paelen called down to the winged sandals at his feet. They had been a gift from Mercury, the messenger of Olympus and now served only him. 'Take me up!'

The tiny wings flashed acknowledgement and then lifted Paelen high in the air over Cupid's head.

'Come down here, you coward,' Cupid roared, jumping up and trying to reach him. 'You know I can't fly indoors!'

'Come and get me, pretty boy,' Paelen teased as he dropped Cupid's feathers one by one.

Emily's father stifled a grin and raised his hands to

11

calm the room. 'That's enough, boys. We've got work to do.'

'But you saw what he did to me!' Cupid cried. 'He pulled out my feathers.'

'I did not,' Paelen teased, still hovering overhead and releasing feathers.

Footsteps on the stairs behind them stopped the argument.

'Good morning, Emily, Pegasus and everyone,' Juno called as she descended the steps. Beside her, her pet peacock fanned open its large tail and a hundred eyes blinked at them in unison.

She looked up at Paelen. 'Have I missed something here?'

Paelen ordered his sandals to land. He bowed before Juno.

'No,' Emily's father said, also bowing. 'The boys were just having a little fun.'

Emily bowed respectfully to the wife of Jupiter. 'Good morning, Juno,' she said. 'Do you think it's possible for us to see Jupiter sometime this morning?'

Juno was much younger-looking than Jupiter and stunningly beautiful. She wore a long white gown of flowing silk that had thousands of pearls woven into the fabric. There was a delicate gold belt tied at her waist and fine sandals adorned her feet. Her eyes were dark chocolate-brown and were the same colour as her hair, which was elegantly styled high on her head and dressed in a ring of pearls.

'Of course, child,' Juno said as she led them across the foyer and into one of the large side chambers. 'He is in here with his council.'

Emily's father stepped forward. 'If he is with the council, we don't want to disturb him.'

Juno paused and smiled radiantly at Emily's father. 'My husband will always have time for you, Steve. You need not ask.' She pushed open the double doors to the council chamber and invited everyone in.

Behind Emily, Paelen and Joel were still chuckling at Cupid as the winged Olympian followed further back and muttered threats.

Jupiter was standing with his two brothers, Pluto and Neptune, as well as an odd assortment of councillors. Among them was the Big Three's half brother, Chiron, the centaur and closest advisor to Jupiter. There was also a giant – so massive in size that his head nearly touched the ceiling of the tall chamber. Yet despite their size, the giants in Olympus were some of the gentlest citizens. A one-eyed Cyclops stood beside the giant talking softly.

Emily looked at the gathering in awe. After all this time in Olympus, she still marvelled at the wondrous assortment of mythical creatures that now formed part of her everyday life.

Across the chamber, Emily spotted Diana with her twin brother, Apollo. Vesta was also there, locked in deep conversation with Cupid's mother, Venus. Hercules was standing further back with his arms crossed over his broad chest talking to Mars, the head of the war council, and looking very disturbed.

Emily had only seen Mars on two other occasions and had never spoken with him. He was tall, handsome and muscular like Hercules, but seemed perpetually angry, with a scowl that always darkened his fine features. Yet despite his angry exterior, Mars was a bit of a heartthrob in Olympus and was often seen out with Venus. His presence in the council room meant something big was happening.

Paelen stood beside Emily and nudged her lightly. 'Vesta is not on the general council, neither is Hercules, Mars or Venus. I wonder what they are doing here.'

'Husband,' Juno called as she strode in, 'Emily and her family would like a word.'

Jupiter looked up and his face lit with a broad smile. 'Of course, of course, come in!'

Since the events at Area 51, where Emily had been forced to challenge Jupiter for the protection of Earth, they had grown closer. It frightened everyone to realize how near they had come to fighting over the fate of the world. They now talked often and Jupiter, Pluto and Neptune had become more like beloved grandfathers than the most powerful leaders of Olympus.

'What may I do for you?' Jupiter asked as he put his arm around Emily.

Before anyone could speak, Pegasus started to whinny.

Jupiter's smile faded. 'You have been having bad dreams?'

Emily described the recurring dream. As she spoke of the jungle world, the other council members crowded around her. When she finished, Vesta turned to Jupiter. 'I believe it is time we showed her what we have found.'

'Indeed,' Jupiter agreed. He swept his arm wide to include everyone. 'All of you, come with me.'

Jupiter led them through a second set of doors into an even larger marble chamber. It was filled with artifacts. Strange items sat on tables and on the floor. But it was the large slate chalkboard in the centre of the room that immediately caught Emily's attention. The board was filled with strange writing and symbols.

'There are millions of worlds along the Solar Stream,' Jupiter began, 'though we have only catalogued a small number of them. But recently, thanks to Emily sending both Pegasus and Alexis there, we have discovered a world at the very start of the Solar Stream.'

Chiron stepped forward, his horse's hooves clicking on the marble floor. 'Until now, we never knew the Solar Stream had a starting point. This is a very exciting time for us. We have much to discover.'

'Are you talking about the jungle world?' Emily asked.

'Indeed we are,' Jupiter said. 'Around this room are just a few of the artifacts we have found there. But among the most interesting was a stone slate mounted on the wall of a large temple.'

Jupiter invited Emily forward to get a closer view. 'We have transcribed the words from that stone slate here. I've had my best scholars trying to decipher it, but as yet, they have failed.'

Emily studied the chalkboard. There was something familiar about the symbols. As she stared at the strange writing, the symbols seemed to blur and swim before her eyes. Suddenly dizziness overwhelmed her and she started to stagger back.

Joel was at her side in an instant. He put his arm around her and steadied her. 'You OK, Em?'

Emily leaned heavily into him. 'I – I'm fine,' she said. 'It's just that . . .' When she looked back at the chalkboard, she sucked in her breath. 'I know this writing!'

'What?' her father gasped.

Emily approached the board. 'I can understand it. All of it.' She pointed to each symbol and started to read aloud.

> *Gentle travellers –*
> *Welcome to Xanadu.*
> *We ask only that you venture here with peace in your hearts and respect in your minds. For ours is the oldest world and much beloved. Yet we offer it to you as refuge. That which is ours is now yours. But be mindful of our home and honour our laws.*
> - *Xanadu must be respected. It will feed you, if you do not abuse it.*
> - *Our ways are the ways of peace. Do not break that peace or we will defend our home.*

- *All life is precious. You will not kill anything here or you will be for ever cast out.*
  We are the Xan, creators of the Solar Stream.
  Guardians of the universe.
  Xanadu is sanctuary.

Emily turned back to Jupiter. The leader of Olympus had his hand over his mouth and his eyes were the widest she'd ever seen them. He looked at her like he was seeing a ghost.

Vesta looked from the chalkboard back to Emily in shock.

'Xanadu,' Diana and Apollo both breathed reverently.

'Is it possible?' Chiron asked softly. His golden eyes were huge and filled with admiration. 'After all this time, we have finally found it?' The centaur turned to Emily and bowed respectfully. 'Thank you, child.'

Pegasus had his head bowed as he stood before her. As did Chrysaor, the giant and even the Cyclops.

'Would someone please let us in on the secret?' Joel asked, confused by the odd behaviour of the Olympians.

Their reactions troubled Emily. They were all looking at her like she was something strange, dredged up from the bottom of the sea.

'What is it?' she asked. 'Pegs, stop bowing and tell me what's going on? What's so special about Xanadu?'

Jupiter righted himself and a reverent smile came to his lips. 'As Earth has its ancient myths about us, we Olympians have our own ancient myths and legends.'

Vesta took over speaking. 'Our oldest legend says that from the time before time, long before the Olympians, and even the Titans, there was Xanadu. It was said to be a precious and sacred place protected by the Xan; a great and powerful race that benevolently ruled the universe. But something happened and the Xan disappeared.'

Diana continued, her face radiant. 'It was because of that legend that we took over as guardians of the Solar Stream. We have been visiting the many worlds searching for the Xan and evidence that Xanadu really existed. This, at last, is the proof we have sought. We have finally found Xanadu.'

'But what does that have to do with Emily?' Her father asked.

Diana put her arm around Emily's shoulder and started to walk her around the room. 'Take a look at these artifacts we have brought back. Do you recognize anything here?'

As they moved from table to table, Emily stared at

the items. They all looked so familiar to her, as though she knew what they were, but had somehow forgotten. She reached for what looked like a dull piece of flat, round metal and recognized its weight and shape. She touched the bottom of the piece and it burst into brilliant light.

'I know this,' she whispered. 'It's used like a flashlight.'

As the light blazed through the room, Jupiter ordered that the doors to the chamber be closed and the windows sealed. He called everyone forward. 'Listen to me. This does not go any further. It would shake the very core of our foundation if Olympians were to learn that the one we have called Flame of Olympus, is not Olympian at all.'

Jupiter knelt down before Emily and dropped his head. When he lifted it again, he reached for her hands. 'Child, I do not understand how it is possible. But it is my strongest belief that you are neither human nor Olympian, but are in fact, Xan.'

2

Emily's mind was spinning as she and Pegasus flew hard and high above Olympus. After Jupiter's announcement, the room burst into excited discussion. Plans were being made to create a permanent access link between Olympus and Xanadu. But the more they talked about the origins of the Flame, the worse Emily felt.

Unable to take any more, she asked to be excused. With Pegasus loyally at her side, she begged the stallion to take her away from the palace. It didn't matter where, just away from the proof that she didn't belong anywhere.

Emily always felt better when it was just her and Pegasus. But this time, soaring high with the magnificent stallion wasn't helping. She felt so lost. Like no one in Olympus would understand how she felt – and then she remembered.

She leaned forward on the soaring stallion. 'Pegs,

can we please go and see Alexis and Agent T?'

Pegasus whinnied once and changed direction. Before long they were passing over a different kind of landscape. It was not as green and blooming as the surroundings of Jupiter's palace. Instead there were fewer trees in an area of smooth golden earth. The terrain turned rocky with high sharp mountain ranges. A few buildings dotted the area, but it was basically isolated. Up ahead, Emily saw a tall, lush, willow tree standing alone and looking strangely out of place in the desert-like area.

It had been a long time since Emily had visited the ex-CRU agent. After Jupiter saved his life and turned him into a beautiful willow tree, he was planted in Olympus and lived with Alexis, the Sphinx.

They had built a large platform in the branches of the tree for Alexis to live on. Now Alexis rarely left it and hadn't been seen in Jupiter's palace in ages.

The moment they touched down and approached the willow, the slender branches started to quiver and wave.

'Emily, Pegasus, hello! What a lovely surprise.'

Agent T's voice was light and leafy, but it was there. In the beginning, it had disturbed Emily that he had been turned into a talking tree, when he didn't even have a mouth. But somehow, in Olympus, everything was possible.

Emily slid off the stallion's back and approached the tree trunk. She gave it a greeting pat. 'Hi Agent T.'

The leaves seemed to laugh. 'Emily, I am not Agent T any more, as I am no longer a CRU agent. I'm not even human. Surely by now you can call me Tom.'

'She will never learn,' called Alexis from her platform high up in the thicker branches. 'But as you are here, you might just as well come up.'

Emily stroked Pegasus's neck. 'I'll be back in a bit, Pegs.'

She climbed up the rope ladder and crawled on to the sturdy platform. The Sphinx's lion legs were curled underneath her human upper body as she lounged on a soft silken pillow pressed up against the tree's side. Her eagle wings were folded neatly across her back.

'What brings the Flame of Olympus to our home?' Alexis asked. 'You are not planning another adventure to Earth, are you? Because if you are, I will not be joining you.'

'Alexis, please,' Tom said. 'Let her speak.'

Emily was stunned at the change in the ex-CRU agent. Since arriving in Olympus, his cold exterior had melted in to a warm and friendly personality. Emily could now see what had attracted Alexis to him. The Sphinx was completely devoted. Nothing could draw her down from his strong branches save an order from Jupiter or Juno.

'Actually, I came to speak with Agent . . . I mean, Tom.' Emily said awkwardly.

'If you must,' Alexis sighed. 'Take a seat.'

Emily had wanted to speak with Tom alone, but Alexis wouldn't budge. The Sphinx was as stubborn and single-minded as she always had been. Emily sat on the platform. She crossed her legs and stared down at her laced fingers.

'What's wrong?' Tom asked. 'I don't need human eyes to see that something is bothering you.'

Emily inhaled deeply. She looked at the smooth bark of the strange willow tree. 'Tom, are you happy?'

'Me?' he laughed. 'You came all this way to ask if I am happy?'

'Are you?'

The tree turned serious. 'Yes, I am. I can honestly say I am the happiest I've ever been.' Tom paused. 'Back when you first entered my life, I cursed you, Pegasus and all the Olympians. I hadn't been content with anything around me, but at least I thought I had a place where I belonged. But after everything we went through together, you showed me how much I was missing. Now, even though I may not be the man I once was, I couldn't be more content.'

'Even though you aren't human any more?'

'Yes, even though I'm not human. Although . . .' he paused.

'What?' Emily asked.

'Well, if I could ask for just one more thing, it would be to have real arms so that I might hold Alexis again.'

'Oh, Tom,' Alexis mewed softly. She rose from her cushion and brushed up against the bark of the tree like a cat does to its owner's legs.

Emily was stunned by the soft, loving expression on Alexis's face. The deadly Sphinx had totally lost her heart to the ex-CRU agent.

'But apart from that,' he continued, 'I am very happy. Why do you ask?'

Emily looked down at her hands. They were starting to tremble. Unable to lift her head, she whispered, 'I don't know who or what I am any more.'

Alexis tilted her head to the side. Her piercing green eyes bore into Emily. She sat down beside her and put a large paw over Emily's hands. 'What is wrong? What troubles you so?'

Emily fought back her emotions. 'Back in the beginning, when I first entered the Temple of the Flame and changed . . .'

'You sacrificed yourself for us. Because of that, you saved Olympus and we will always be grateful to you.'

Emily nodded but wouldn't look up. 'It was hard to get used to the changes in me, but everyone here was so kind and made me feel like I was one of you.'

'You are one of us,' Alexis said.

Emily looked into the Sphinx's beautiful face. 'No, I'm not.'

'What do you mean?' Tom asked.

'Jupiter said not to tell anyone yet. At least not until we are certain. But if I don't talk to someone soon, I'm going to go crazy.'

'You can trust us,' Alexis said. 'Tell us what is wrong.'

Emily looked from Alexis to the trunk of the tree and started to speak. She told them of the recurring dream and ended with the revelations of the morning where she could read the language of the ancients.

'That was actually Xanadu you sent me to!' Alexis said breathlessly. 'And you are Xan?'

Emily sniffed and nodded. 'That's what Jupiter says.'

26

'I don't understand,' Tom said. 'What's so special about Xanadu? We had that name on Earth too. It was an ancient city in China and I think it was even a 1980s roller-skating movie.'

'You knew of it because of us,' Alexis explained. 'We often spoke of Xanadu when we visited your world. But it is so much more than an ancient Earth city.' Alexis explained to Tom what she knew of the Xan and then looked at Emily in complete awe.

'See!' Emily said. 'That's what's driving me crazy.'

'What is?' Tom asked, shaking his leaves. 'I couldn't see what happened.'

'Suddenly everything's changed.' Emily stood up and walked over to the trunk of the tree and leaned her forehead against it. 'Jupiter bowed before me this morning. So did his brothers and even Pegs.' Emily looked back at the Sphinx. 'And now even you are looking at me differently. I don't want that. I want to be one of you. Not treated like I'm some kind of ancient queen. I'm the same person I was yesterday. But now everyone who knows is treating me differently. It was hard enough when everyone called me the Flame of Olympus. But at least then, I was part of you. But if I'm really Xan, what am I part of? Who am I?'

'You are Emily,' Tom said.

27

'But I'm not even alive,' Emily moaned.

'What do you mean?' Alexis said. 'Of course you are alive.'

Emily shook her head. 'That's not what the CRU scientists told me.'

The tree sighed heavily and its leaves drooped. 'Ah yes, the CRU, of course. I might have known they would still be causing you grief. What lies did they tell you?'

'It's not lies. It's the truth. When I was at their laboratory in Area 51, they ran tests on me. They said I don't even exist! I have no cells and no physical matter. I'm not alive, I'm not dead. I'm nothing but contained energy that imagines itself alive.'

'Ridiculous!' Alexis spat.

'I understand now why you came to me,' Tom said gently. 'You asked if I'm happy. You meant, am I happy now that I am no longer human but a tree. My answer is still the same. Yes I am. I have changed in ways I could never imagine. We both have. But despite all the changes, in essence we are still who we were before. Perhaps we're even better than before. I was never a kind man and never cared for anyone. Now I know what it is to love and to be loved. What we are

28

physically is only one small part of who we are. And, Emily Jacobs, whether you are a human, the Flame of Olympus or Xan, you are still you. I doubt anything could ever change that.'

'But if people find out I'm from Xanadu, they'll treat me differently.'

'First off,' Tom said seriously, 'you are not from Xanadu. Perhaps your powers are. But you are still a girl from New York City. You were born there and went to school there. And secondly, if people discover that you are part Xan and treat you differently, just show them that you are still Emily. They will soon learn. Look how you felt when you first saw me as a tree. Don't think I didn't notice how you looked at me. But eventually you got over that and now I am just Tom to you. Or at least, Agent T. You are what you believe you are, Emily. You have family and friends who love you. What more could you want?'

Emily threw her arms around the trunk of the tree and pressed her face to the bark. 'Thank you, Tom,' she said gratefully. 'I knew you'd understand.'

The leaves around her quivered. 'I do, Emily. And I am always here if you need to talk.' Suddenly the tree burst out laughing. 'Besides, it's not like I've got anywhere to run to!'

3

Stella Giannakou packed her travel bag, muttering to herself and complaining because she couldn't stay in Athens while her parents went to the new find at Cape Sounio. She was almost sixteen and could take care of herself. She didn't need anyone to stay with her while her parents were away. But they wouldn't listen. So she was once again forced to go with them on yet another dig.

Her parents were the archaeologists, not her. So why did they insist on dragging her away with them? Stella had spent most of her life travelling all around Greece while her parents moved from one ancient site to another, trying to unravel the past.

To Stella, history was boring. The only thing that interested her about the past was the myths. But despite being Greek and living in the land of the ancient stories, her parents didn't believe in them. All they cared about was digging in dirt and finding pieces of broken pottery.

'Stella, please hurry. We're ready to go!' her mother called from downstairs.

'Then go,' she mumbled to herself. 'Leave me here. I don't want to see some stupid old broken pots anyway. It's my holiday too, you know.'

'You heard your mother,' her father shouted, anger rising in his voice. 'Finish packing and get down here. We leave in five minutes.'

Stella threw the last of her clothes in the bag. She looked at the stack of engineering books on her bedside table and then over to the project she was building. She was trying to design a new kind of wheelchair that would make life easier for those who needed them, like herself.

She had planned to spend her spring break working on the project. Now all she could look forward to was watching her parents digging in the dirt and pretending to be excited when they found a chip of pottery or the toe from some broken old statue.

Seated in the back of the car and surrounded by her parents' tools and camping supplies, Stella looked out of the window at the grey water of the Aegean Sea. They were leaving Athens and heading along the coast to Cape Sounio.

Being February, Greece was in the middle of winter. It wasn't overly cold, but it was dull and grey. The sky above was filled with scuttling clouds that promised a long day of rain.

'Why do we have to stay there?' Stella complained. 'It's not that far. We could drive home at night. It would be so much easier for me.'

Her mother turned from the front. The expression on her face showed that she was growing tired of the argument. 'I told you before, Stella, we will be working long hours. Your father will be too tired to drive all the way back to Athens each night.' She sat forward in her seat. 'I don't know what's wrong with you. You used to love coming on digs and camping on site.'

'That was when I was a kid. Before the accident, when I could get around on my own without help,' Stella spat. 'This is your dream, not mine. I don't want to be an archaeologist.'

'Well, what do you want to be?' her mother demanded.

'An engineer,' Stella fired back. 'I want to design new things to make people's lives easier, not spend my time digging in the dirt and finding old junk. It's boring!'

A heavy silence filled the car as it drove steadily

towards the Temple of Poseidon at Cape Sounio. It was only yesterday they'd received the phone call saying part of the rock face at the temple had collapsed down into the sea and some items had been revealed. That one phone call had ruined Stella's school holidays.

Rain started to fall as the car made its way along the narrow winding roads of Cape Sounio. Finally her father turned along the path that led up a tall hill and drove towards the temple's parking area. The site was now closed due to the find and red-and-white tape covered the entrance area. A warning sign was posted in the parking lot which said the ground around the temple was now unstable and that the ancient site would be closed until further notice.

'Let's get up there and see what's happening before we unload,' her father suggested as he opened the door.

Stella could see the growing excitement in his sparkling dark eyes. He may have had greying hair and beard, but suddenly, her father looked very young. He always did when there was something new to discover.

Saying nothing, Stella lagged behind her parents as they made their way to the top of the hill that overlooked the sea. It was at the very top that they would find the Temple of Poseidon. Stella had been a young girl the first time she'd been here and had marvelled at the

33

stories surrounding it. The Athenian hero, Theseus, had left to go to Crete to fight the Minotaur in the Labyrinth of King Minos. And when his father, King Aegeus, had thought his son had died, he came to the temple and threw himself into the sea far below. That was why the sea was now called the Aegean.

Those stories had always interested Stella. But now, as she made her way to the temple, all she would see was a bunch of old broken-down columns and the echoes of an ancient people who had spent years building the temple to a sea god that didn't exist.

Her mother turned back to look at her and sighed. 'Would you try to show some interest?'

'But it's boring . . .'

'Just try.'

Up ahead was the small wooden booth where tourists would normally buy their tickets to go to the temple. It had now been turned into a meeting place. Other archaeologists were gathered there. These were all people her parents knew and most worked with them in the Acropolis Museum. In fact, Stella knew most of them as well.

'What did you find?' her mother asked a museum colleague.

'We're not sure,' George Tsoukatou answered. 'At

this point, we can only see a small portion. But we did find this . . .' George handed over a clear plastic bag containing a delicate silver-bladed dagger. It looked almost new and not like it had been in the ground for thousands of years. The blade still looked sharp and the marble of the handle was unpitted. There was a beautiful green jewel on the top pommel.

'This is beautiful,' Stella's father said, receiving the dagger from his wife.

'That's just the appetizer,' George answered. 'Wait till you see the main course.' He led them the rest of the way up the hill. As they walked the rain came down heavier.

'It's this weather,' George explained. 'All the rain is breaking away the rock face. It's still quite far from the temple itself, but in the next few years, we may have a problem.'

Further up the high hill, they rounded a bend. Despite her anger, seeing the Temple of Poseidon rising high in the stormy sky stirred something deep within Stella. She couldn't deny that the tall mottled marble pillars on the smooth base were still awe-inspiring.

It wasn't quite as amazing as the Acropolis or the Temple of Zeus in Athens, but here, with the Aegean Sea crashing on all three sides of the rock face, hundreds of metres below, it did have its own enchantment.

Staring at the temple, Stella hadn't been aware that her parents had moved away. Finally her mother's voice called her from her reverie.

'Stella, come over here. See what else has been found.'

Her parents and George were standing away from the temple and closer to the edge of the cliff. She saw the fresh break in the solid rock and knew if she dared to approach the steep edge, she would see the broken pieces far below.

Where the rock face had broken away, a pit had opened. There, with the rain pouring down, her anger at her parents fled. Stella could see the sharp corner of what looked like a large golden box poking out of a sheet of solid rock.

'How did they do it?' her father was asking. 'Look at the sides. That box is embedded in solid rock. How did they get that thing in there?'

George shrugged. 'I have no idea. But I'm sure we'll find out soon enough.'

4

Preparations were well under way for the permanent portal to Xanadu. When Emily and Pegasus arrived in the artifact chamber, they stood back, watching the activity. Jupiter and his brothers were supervising the construction of an archway that would keep the direct Solar Stream access to Xanadu open.

Chiron was chatting with other centaurs and handing out instructions for the investigations of the Temple of Xanadu.

Emily saw her father walking with Diana, carefully inspecting items retrieved from the jungle world. Joel, Paelen and Chrysaor were at another table going through the artifacts and trying to guess their use.

'Em, are you all right?' Her father put down a strangely-shaped object when he noticed her. 'You left here so quickly, I couldn't find you.'

'I know, but I had to get away. I went to speak with Tom.'

'Did it help?'

Emily nodded. She looked back to where Jupiter was supervising the final stone in the archway. 'But I'm still a bit freaked out by everything.'

'Me too, hon,' he said. 'But Emily, whatever we discover, it doesn't change a thing. Maybe part of you does come from the Xan. But no matter what, we'll get through this together, just like we always have.'

Those were the best words in the world to her. 'You bet we will,' she said gratefully as she put her arms around him.

Never one to be too sentimental, Diana cleared her throat loudly. 'Emily, now that you are feeling better, would you take a look at some of these artifacts?'

'Hey Emily,' Paelen called. He was putting an odd-shaped leathery garment on his head. 'I think this is a hat. How do I look?'

Emily took one look at Paelen with his silly, crooked grin and the ridiculous makeshift hat and she burst out laughing. She walked over and pulled down the brim. 'That's better. Now I'm sure the water nymphs will love you in that!'

Emily pulled the hat down further on Paelen's head. But as she clung to the item, sudden flashes shot across her mind. She gripped the brim tighter and closed her eyes.

Emily stopped laughing. She pulled the hat from Paelen's head and walked over to one of the tables where she placed it upside down. Emily waved her hand over the top. Moments later, it filled with fresh, sweet ambrosia cakes.

'Ambrosia cakes, my favourite!' Paelen cried as he reached into the hat for a cake and stuffed it whole in to his mouth. 'Delicious! Thank you, Emily,' he said, spraying crumbs all over her.

'Wow!' Joel said. 'How'd you do that?'

'I don't know.' Emily looked at the odd hat. 'But when I touched it, I knew it could produce food.'

She poured the ambrosia cakes on the table and inspected the hat. The inside was clean, with no trace of the sticky Olympian food. She carried it over to Pegasus.

'What would you like most, Pegs?'

Pegasus touched the hat-like thing and then nickered. Emily put it back on the table and waved her hand over it. Like before, it filled with food. This time, it was the stallion's favourite, chocolate ice cream with bits of sugary breakfast cereal.

'This is so cool!' Joel cried. He caught hold of the

hat and poured out the ice cream for Pegasus. 'My turn.' He held the hat before him and said, 'I would like some cheese ravioli in tomato sauce, smothered in grated Parmesan, with thick garlic bread on the side.' He then held it out to Emily.

Emily waved her hand over the opening. Once again, it filled with a portion of Joel's order, including the garlic bread.

'What is this?' Diana asked as Joel removed his piping-hot lunch. 'How does it work?'

'I really don't know,' Emily admitted. 'I just knew it was for food. So the bearer would never go hungry when they travelled.'

'We sure could have used that in Las Vegas!' Paelen said as he devoured his third ambrosia cake.

Emily looked around at all the other items on the tables and frowned. 'It's so strange. I kind of know what these things are, but really can't remember.'

Jupiter, Pluto and Neptune looked at the odd assortment of food. Jupiter reached for an ambrosia cake and tasted it. He nodded approvingly. 'This is ambrosia. Very fresh and very pure.'

Neptune stuck a finger in Pegasus's ice cream and sampled his first chocolate. 'This is very good indeed,' he said grinning at his son. 'What a wonderful device.'

Diana neatly folded the hat until it was no bigger than a deck of cards. 'It was written that the Xan crossed the cosmos. This would be the most efficient way of transporting food supplies. Very simple and very neat.'

She handed it to Emily. 'This, my child, is yours.'

Emily took the food-hat and slipped it into her tunic pocket as Joel leaned closer to her and whispered, 'Now we can have all our favourites from back home.' He flicked her playfully on the tip of her nose. 'Including all the marshmallows you can eat!'

'And chocolate bars,' said Paelen.

'And potato chips,' Joel suggested.

Emily smiled at her friends and turned to Pegasus. 'Pegs, you can have all the chocolate ice cream that you want.'

The stallion whinnied excitedly and nodded his head. He nudged Emily playfully.

'And vegetables,' her father added. 'You kids are going to eat well if it kills me!'

In the front of the chamber, Jupiter, Neptune and Pluto were standing before the completed archway. 'Everyone, stand well back, we are about to turn the Solar Stream.'

Jupiter addressed his brothers. 'All together!'

Pegasus escorted Emily to the back of the chamber

as everyone gathered to watch. The Big Three joined hands and raised them in the air. Suddenly the entire room burst into life with the blazing light of the Solar Stream. The air around them crackled and whooshed with roaring energy. Fierce winds whipped Emily's hair as she tried to see the Olympians, but all she saw was blinding light and the faintest trace of the three large outlines standing before the new marble archway.

Moments later, the bright light and roaring energy pulsed and pulled back as though it was being sucked into the arch and contained by it.

Then, it was gone.

'Well done!' Jupiter cheered, patting his brothers on the back. He combed back his tousled grey hair and turned to the others. Emily could see his face was bathed in sweat, as were the faces of Neptune and Pluto.

'That does clean out one's attic!' Neptune cheered, shaking his head.

Everyone in the room applauded, while Pegasus nickered loudly and trotted up to his father. Emily stood back with her friends. She asked Paelen, 'Is that how they would have destroyed Earth?'

Paelen nodded. 'There are none more powerful than when the Big Three unite their powers.'

'Wow,' Joel said. 'It's one thing to hear about it, another to actually see it.'

'It's terrifying,' Emily muttered.

Together they walked towards the arch. Now that the Solar Stream was closed, it looked exactly the same as it had before.

'How does it work?' Emily's father asked.

'It's very easy,' Jupiter said. 'And you do not have to be Olympian to use it, Steve.' The leader of Olympus waved his hand closer to the arch and the Solar Stream opened again, only now the light was contained within the marble ring.

'All you need do is step close to it and it will open. This is a direct route to Xanadu only. It will not take you anywhere else.'

'But what about from there to here? How do we get back?' Joel asked.

'A good question,' Neptune said. 'We will shortly go to Xanadu to build the same thing and link them together. It will be a permanent tunnel between the two worlds.'

Jupiter clapped his hands together. 'First, our builders will take their supplies through and build the arch at the other end.' He pointed to his brothers. 'Then we shall go to seal the Solar Stream in place.'

He turned to Emily. 'After that, my dear child, it will be time for us to take you home.'

'But Olympus is my home,' Emily cried.

At her alarm, Pegasus nickered and came closer to her.

'Of course it is,' Jupiter corrected. 'Nephew, calm down,' he said to Pegasus. 'I was speaking historically. Of course Olympus will always be Emily's home, you know that. But if she is indeed Xan, that must be part of her home too. We cannot deny her her origins.'

That calmed the stallion as he pressed his head to Emily.

'Thanks, Pegs,' she whispered gratefully, putting her arms around his neck. She turned to Jupiter. 'When will it be ready for all of us to go?'

'First thing tomorrow,' Jupiter said. 'We will summon you when we are ready.'

As Emily, Pegasus and her friends filed out of the room, Emily looked back at the arch. That portal might hold the answers to the source of her powers. But as she looked at all the odd items in the room, a good part of her really didn't want to know.

5

It was late the next morning when Jupiter called everyone back to the artifact chamber. Pluto and Neptune were on Xanadu and were waiting for them.

He also instructed everyone to bring extra clothing and bedding. The journey to Xanadu was a long one and they would be spending several nights there.

They gathered before the arch in excitement. Jupiter stepped forward and raised his hand to the portal. When it burst to life, everyone filed into the Solar Stream.

The journey was longer than Emily could have imagined. Travelling within the power of the Solar Stream, time could not be measured, but she was sure it had to be well over a full day.

Pegasus was beating his wings as they moved, but it wasn't really necessary. To her left, Diana, Apollo and her father travelled without the use of wings or any other flying method. She smiled as she watched her father with his arms outstretched, looking like Superman.

Speaking and being heard within the roaring of the Solar Stream was next to impossible. With nothing to do, and unable to talk to anyone, Emily leaned forward on Pegasus's strong neck and let the rhythmic beating of his wings lull her into a deep sleep.

She emerged from the stone temple and dashed into the dense green jungle. She put on more speed as she moved along paths as old as time itself; rushing past the great statues of her people and dodging around the massive trees. This was her home. Her sanctuary. Her world. But they were all about to leave it. To go on.

They said they would try to wait for her. But when the stars aligned, they would go with or without her.

'Please don't let me be too late . . .' she begged. 'Please!'

Around her, the jungle was alive. All the creatures she knew and loved wished her well and offered their heartfelt farewells.

'Not much further,' she cried. 'Please wait for me, I am almost there.'

But even as she forced more speed she could feel the power of the others building. They had waited as long as they could. But the stars above were aligned. They could wait no longer.

'No!' she howled as she felt their energy converging. 'Wait for me! I'm coming with you!'

She pressed on, struggling to reach the gathering. As she burst through the trees, she arrived at the appointed place. Before her, stood her people. Arms raised, their powers merged, until they finally released themselves into the cosmos.

'No!' she cried. 'Please don't leave me . . .'

'No!' Emily roared.

She awoke to the urgent, frightened whinnies of Pegasus and could feel the stallion nudging her. She was lying on a cool damp floor in a dark place. The only light came from Pegasus as he glowed brilliantly in the darkness. From all around was the sound of dripping water echoing, as if she was in a large, hollow chamber.

She was panting heavily as the residue of the dream remained with her. 'Dad? Joel?'

The only sound in the dark chamber was from Pegasus as he anxiously pawed the stone floor.

'Pegs,' Emily reached up to him, 'what happened?'

Emily climbed to her feet and gazed around. Even with the stallion's glow, she couldn't see much beyond where they stood. 'Where are we?'

Pegasus snorted and shook his head. Once again,

Emily wished she could speak his language. 'I don't understand.'

The stallion caught hold of her hand in his mouth. His grip was light despite his powerful bite as he led her forward. After a few metres he stopped before a wall. In the glow of the stallion, she could see words carved in a stone slab mounted there.

To get a better look, Emily raised her hand in the air and summoned the Flame. Fire burst from her palm and drove back the oppressive darkness. She sucked in her breath. It was the same message from the chalkboard in Jupiter's palace.

Emily traced her fingers along one of the lines and read aloud. ' "Welcome to Xanadu." Are we on Xanadu?'

The stallion nodded his head several times.

'How did we get here?' she asked. 'And how do we get out?'

Pegasus snorted and nudged her. He fluttered his wings and dropped them to invite her to get on his back. Emily climbed up and held her hand high like a torch. They were in a spacious chamber. It was empty except for the writing on the wall. Across from them was a large open doorway.

As Pegasus passed through it, Emily asked him to stop. She shook her head, trying to focus on a too distant memory. 'I know this place. I can't explain it, but I get the feeling I've been here before.'

She could feel the muscles in the stallion's back tensing as his wings pressed tighter against her legs. It was as disturbing to Pegasus as it was to her. 'I don't know how I know this, but if you turn to the right, at the end of the corridor there will be a tall set of steps.'

Pegasus snorted and nodded his head. He trotted down the corridor. As Emily had predicted, they reached some steps.

'Go to the top and then turn left.'

As Pegasus followed each instruction, Emily became more and more convinced she had been there before. It was all so familiar. Despite the many passages and long corridors, they didn't make a wrong turn.

Before long, they reached the surface level and were passing through an archway that led into a dense, green jungle. The air was sweet and warm and full of the sounds of insects, birds and other wildlife. There was a sun shining brightly above and casting a patchwork quilt of shadows on the ground.

'*Xanadu . . .*' Emily breathed in a voice that was hardly her own.

This was the place she had seen time and time again

in her dreams. But it was not exactly the same. The jungle had grown much closer to the temple and the familiar paths were now overgrown and unrecognizable.

Pegasus paused and then turned to the left.

Emily was stunned to see three large military helicopters sitting on the ground beside the temple. Long stringy vines were already crisscrossing the vehicles as the jungle claimed them for its own. These had been some of the helicopters that attacked her and Pegasus at Area 51. Instead of destroying them, her powers had sent them here. The pilots had been returned to Earth, but the helicopters remained.

'This is where I sent you before, isn't it?' Emily asked.

Pegasus nodded his head and nickered.

'How did we get here?'

As they looked around, Pegasus's ears pricked forward and he whinnied. He burst into a gallop. Pushing through the trees, they soon came upon an open encampment.

'Pegasus, Emily!'

Relief washed over her as she saw Pluto running towards them, his cloak billowing behind him like a sail.

'What are you doing here?' He helped her down

from Pegasus. 'Are you all right? How did you get here? The portal to Olympus is on the other side of this clearing. Where did you come from?'

This was the most excited she'd ever seen him. Pluto was always the calmest of the Big Three. 'We're fine,' she said. 'We came from the Temple of Arious.'

Neptune and several other Olympians quickly approached.

'The temple of what?' Neptune asked.

Emily frowned. 'Arious.' She looked at Pluto. 'How did I know that?'

He scratched his head and shrugged. 'I really do not know. That is just one more mystery we must solve.'

Emily and Pegasus explained as best they could what had happened and how she had known the way out of the temple.

'So the others are still in the Solar Stream?' Neptune asked.

'I think so.'

'Considering how long it takes to get here from there, we still have a bit of a wait.'

The Olympians got back to work setting up the camp. Emily and Pegasus stepped away from the group.

'I know I've been here before,' she insisted. Everything around her was so painfully familiar. Even the smell of the dense greenery meant something to her.

Around them were strange-looking trees with oddly-shaped leaves. When she touched a leaf, she knew to turn it over. There was a large caterpillar-like bug clinging to the back. It was several centimetres long and had brightly-coloured fur. When it noticed her, it stood up on its many back legs and peered intently at her.

Emily reached out to touch the bug, but Pegasus nickered, nudging her hand away.

'It's all right, Pegs,' Emily said softly. 'I know he's not dangerous.'

Emily let the caterpillar run on to her hand. Holding it up, she recognized the species. The name was just on the tip of her tongue. But the more she tried to remember, the harder it became.

'Hello,' she finally said as she gently stroked the caterpillar's soft fur. 'See Pegs, he won't hurt us.' Emily paused and looked around at the countless trees, shrubs and flowers. 'Nothing here will hurt any of us.'

As she and Pegasus returned to the others to show them the insect, they became aware of a change in the jungle. Sounds stopped and the area became eerily silent.

Pluto looked around. He raised his hand, preparing

to use his deadly powers to defend the group.

'*No, Pluto, please do not,*' Emily said softly, in a strange and distant voice. '*This is a world of peace. You must never use violence here. They know I have returned.*'

'Who are you?' Neptune asked gently.

'*I am . . . I – am . . . the last.*'

Emily staggered and seemed to come back into herself. She looked at the others as they stared at her oddly.

Neptune put his hand on her shoulder and leaned closer to her. 'Child, what was the last thing you said?'

Emily pointed at the insect on her hand. 'I found this pretty little caterpillar and told Pegasus he wouldn't hurt us.' She frowned. 'Then we came over here to show you.'

'You said nothing else?' Pluto asked.

Emily shrugged. 'No. Why do you ask?'

'It is not important,' Neptune said reassuringly. 'So what have you found there?'

Emily looked at the curious faces around her. There was something they weren't telling her. She held up the insect. 'Isn't he beautiful?'

Neptune leaned in closer. 'He is an amazing little fellow.'

There was a loud rustle in the jungle behind them.

Pegasus whinnied as everyone turned. A massive beast was forcing its way through the greenery. It was like nothing they'd ever seen on Olympus or Earth.

It was big. Very big. At least twice the size of an elephant – but it looked nothing like an elephant. It had two large, heavy heads that moved independently on long thick necks and was walking with many legs, almost like a centipede. But this was no insect; it was an animal with light purple fur.

Other smaller animals and insects followed behind the huge creature and brightly-coloured birds flittered and followed from above. As before, Emily somehow recognized the beast and knew there was no danger. Despite the fact that it towered above her, the creature approached and dropped its massive heads to the ground.

'Be careful, Emily,' Neptune warned.

'It's OK. She's the Mother of the Jungle.' Emily stepped up to the purple creature and fearlessly stroked one of its heads. 'I'm so sorry that I don't remember your name. But I do remember you. This is Pegasus of Olympus,' she said, introducing the stallion. 'Come, meet everyone. They mean you no harm.'

As Emily and Pegasus walked back to the others, the creature raised her two heads and followed behind.

Small birds landed on Emily's shoulders and the stallion's back as they moved.

The stunned Olympians came forward to greet the Mother of the Jungle.

Pegasus snorted. He nudged Emily gently.

Neptune translated. 'My son says you may not remember this world, but it seems its many occupants remember you. There is no doubt now that part of you came from here.'

Emily reached up with her free hand and stroked the stallion's beautiful face. 'I know,' she said softly. 'I just don't understand *how* I know. Or if I'll ever remember.'

'I am certain that eventually you will recall more,' Neptune said. 'But for now, do not trouble yourself. Let the memories return in their own time.'

Emily remained with Pegasus and the Mother of the Jungle while the others finished building their camp.

'Can you understand her, Pegs?' Emily asked.

The stallion snorted and shook his head.

'Me neither,' she agreed as she stroked the Mother of the Jungle. Emily closed her eyes and listened to the returning sounds of the jungle. The memories were there, just beyond her reach. But the harder she tried to grab them, the further away they slipped.

As the long day passed and three moons rose above

them in the sky, everyone gathered around a fire to await the arrival of Jupiter and the others. With the coming of night, Emily found herself becoming more restless. There was something about the moons and the stars behind them that troubled her.

'I'm going for a walk,' she announced.

Pluto shook his head. 'I do not believe that is a wise idea. We have only just arrived here and do not know this world. There may be dangers lurking, especially at night.'

'*There are no dangers here*,' Emily responded in the strange voice. '*I must find my way back.*'

Then, unaware of what had just happened she said, 'I just need to clear my head. We'll be OK.'

'Let her go,' Neptune said. 'She must seek her own answers. Pegasus will be with her; she is in no danger.'

Pluto finally agreed. 'But do not be too long.'

Since her arrival on Xanadu, more and more animals, birds and insects had approached Emily and remained with her. As she and Pegasus walked together into the dense jungle, there was a parade of unimaginable creatures moving with them. Emily tried to shoo them away, but they refused. Even the Mother of the Jungle was bulldozing her way behind them.

With one hand held high and the Flame burning brightly like a torch, Emily walked beside Pegasus. 'I feel like I'm going crazy, Pegs,' she finally admitted. 'It's like I'm not myself any more. Like there are two people in me. I'm afraid I am going to disappear.'

The stallion stopped. He stared into Emily's eyes. Soon a vision of them soaring over the skies of Olympus filled her mind and eased her troubles.

'Promise me, Pegs,' she said softly, 'that no matter what happens, whatever we discover here, we'll always be together.'

Pegasus bobbed his head and then nuzzled Emily's neck. There was something about the stallion that always made her feel better. An unbreakable bond between them that let her know they could endure any hardship, as long as they faced it together.

As they pushed deeper into the dense jungle, the strange feeling of familiarity returned to Emily, stronger than before. Somehow she knew she was on the same trail from her dream. She bent down and started to brush away greenery and dirt from the ground beneath her. After a few minutes, she reached a stone path; the same stones from her dreams.

'I *have* been here before,' she said softly. She lowered her burning hand to show Pegasus. 'Look, these are the stones that make up the trail. They lead to the gathering place. We must go this way.'

Further along, dense leaves and vines completely blocked the way. Emily was reluctant to use her powers in case she accidentally set fire to the jungle. But as she was considering turning back, the Mother of the Jungle made strange, loud noises. Her two heads bobbed as her massive bulk shoved the greenery aside. She took the lead and let her huge body clear the trail, as though she knew exactly where Emily wanted to go.

Emily looked at Pegasus, shrugged and started to follow. After some time, the jungle thinned. She looked up and could see the canopy of stars shining above them as the three moons shone brightly in the night sky.

With the Mother of the Jungle blocking the way ahead, neither Emily nor Pegasus were prepared for what came next. After a few more metres, the creature stepped aside and they were faced with a stunningly beautiful and calm lake. Its dark surface reflected the stars like a perfect mirror. 'It looks just like our silver lake back on Olympus!' gasped Emily.

Closer to the shore, they discovered it wasn't a lake at all. Bending down, Emily held up her flaming hand and saw it was an unbelievably large sheet of smooth black glass.

'Look, Pegs, it's made of glass.' Emily took a cautious step forward and stepped out on to the surface. 'It feels really thick too.'

Pegasus followed Emily out on to the lake of glass. He neighed nervously as his hooves slipped on the smooth surface.

'I wonder what it's for . . .' Emily held up her hand and the Flame rose higher and brighter. As it did, she saw that the glass lake went on for at least a kilometre, maybe more.

Behind them, the Mother of the Jungle grunted, howled and made strange clicking sounds. She was bobbing her two large heads up and down.

'What is it, Mother?' Emily returned to the huge beast. There, several metres from the outer edge of the glass lake, she saw a much smaller piece of glass. She bent down and touched it. It didn't go as deep as the lake and had many tiny cracks in it.

A chill passed through Emily as she inspected the small circle of glass. There was something about it that disturbed her greatly. She snatched her hand back and stepped away.

'I don't like it here. This is a very sad place. Let's go back to camp.'

Emily looked up into the dense, dark jungle.

Suddenly she didn't want to walk through it again. There was no danger, but there was a great sadness and a lonely feeling hanging in the air.

As if sensing the same thing, Pegasus snorted then dropped a wing to invite her up on his back.

'Oh, thank you, Pegs.'

Before climbing on to the stallion, Emily gave the Mother of the Jungle a pat on each head. 'I don't know if you can understand me, but we are going to fly back to the camp.'

Getting into the air was difficult for Pegasus as he couldn't get a good grip on the glass beneath him to run. After two near falls, Emily told him to stop.

'Pegs, I'm going to lift us up so you don't have to run on the glass.'

The stallion nickered as Emily closed her eyes and concentrated on what she wanted to do. Since returning to Olympus from Area 51, she had been working with her teacher, Vesta, to learn to use her new powers.

Soon they were both lifted gently off the ground. Beneath them, the Mother of the Jungle raised her two heads and howled mournfully.

'We're going back to the camp!' Emily called.

Once they were high enough, Pegasus opened his wings and took over. As he climbed steadily into the sky, Emily peered down on the dark jungle. It seemed to go on for ever. Before long, other flying creatures joined them in the sky. Pegasus whinnied in protest as they tried to get closer. But no matter what he did, the birds refused to go.

When they touched down in the camp, Emily explained what they had found, though she didn't mention the feeling of sadness she felt there. She agreed to show the Olympians the glass lake when the sun rose.

Just as they settled down for the night, the portal to Olympus flashed to life. The Solar Stream opened and Jupiter charged through, followed closely by Emily's father, Diana, Joel, Paelen and many others.

'Are they here?' Jupiter demanded as he charged into the camp. 'Emily! Pegasus!'

Pegasus was the first to answer as he whinnied loudly.

'Thank God,' Emily's father cried when he saw her. He scooped her up in his arms. 'I saw you disappear! I thought I'd lost you.'

'We all did,' Diana added. 'You were gone in an instant.'

'I'm fine,' Emily quickly said. 'We're both fine.'

Joel hugged her tightly. 'What happened to you?'

Emily could feel Joel trembling. She realized he had been truly frightened for her. 'I'm OK, Joel, don't worry,' she said softly. 'I don't really know what happened. One moment I was asleep, the next I was waking up in the temple with Pegs.'

'Do not do that again!' Paelen scolded. 'You nearly scared the life out of me. We all thought you had vanished for ever.'

'I'm sorry, Paelen.' Emily grinned as she ruffled his hair. 'Next time I'll bring you with me.'

'There won't be a next time,' Joel insisted.

Jupiter checked on Emily again. 'I doubt this will be the last time we witness your powers surfacing. They are increasing. I just hope you learn control over them.'

'Me too,' Emily agreed.

Soon everyone was seated together around the fire. Goblets of nectar were handed out while Emily used her strange hat-like device to summon snacks for everyone – including a large supply of marshmallows for roasting over the fire.

More than half the night had passed in this way, before everyone settled down to bed.

It felt like Emily had only just closed her eyes when she heard the sound of Paelen screaming.

She sat up and saw the bright sunshine filtering down through the leaves and the sounds of the jungle increasing to greet the new day.

'Help!' Paelen cried as he tried to rise. 'I am being eaten alive by a monster!'

The Mother of the Jungle was standing over Paelen. Both its heads were sniffing and licking him with long, wet purple tongues.

Emily was the first over. 'Paelen, it's OK,' she laughed, kneeling beside him. 'I'm sorry, Mother. He means you no harm and doesn't understand.' She patted the two heads. 'You just surprised him.'

Jupiter approached. 'What is this?'

'Mother,' Emily said respectfully, 'this is Jupiter, leader of Olympus.' She turned to Jupiter. 'This is the Mother of the Jungle. I still can't remember her real name or how to understand her, but she is one of the oldest living creatures in this world. I don't know how I know this, but she is very special. We must always protect her.'

The newcomers greeted the Mother of the Jungle and each took their turn stroking the smooth purple fur of the creature's heads.

'Of course,' Jupiter agreed. 'We will do everything we can to ensure her safety.' He turned on Paelen and pointed a threatening finger, 'You will be nice to the Mother of the Jungle or you will answer to me!'

'I did not do anything!' Paelen cried. 'It was she who attacked *me*.'

Paelen climbed to his feet shakily. As he did, the Mother of the Jungle took a step closer and gave him another long, wet lick.

'She really does like you!' Emily laughed.

As a second large, wet tongue swept up his chest and face, Paelen scrunched his eyes shut and mumbled miserably, 'Why is it always me?'

6

Stella watched her parents help set up the small camp at the tourist booth. There was a lovely resort hotel not far away and Stella had suggested they stay there. But her parents said no. With the precious silver dagger that had already been found and the golden box in the pit, they couldn't risk leaving the area unprotected.

There was also a spacious restaurant and tourist shop at the base of the temple which had also been suggested for use as a camp, but it was considered too far from the find.

Stella busied herself working in her tent. This was one request her parents had granted: that she was allowed her own tent instead of sharing with them. When she finished making up her bed, she returned to the site and was surprised by how far the dig had progressed. The golden box was now almost a quarter of the way out of the rock wall and one whole side of it was now on display.

'Stella, come and look. I think you'll like this,' her mother called.

Her father helped her down into the pit while her mother pointed at the exposed box. 'See someone you know?'

There were carvings in the smooth gold surface. Stella's eyes flew wide when she recognized three large figures standing together. 'Zeus!' she cried. 'That's Zeus, and there's Poseidon and even Hades!'

Her father nodded. 'Now, is archaeology still boring?'

Stella knew better than to touch the side of the ancient box, but her fingers ached to trace the outline of the three Olympians. 'Not now,' she agreed. 'I want to see more.'

'Soon,' her mother promised as she worked to free more of the box. 'With luck, we should have it out of here in the next few days.'

The rainy weather was quickly forgotten as Stella watched her parents and the other archaeologists at work. They had all agreed to keep things quiet until they better understood what they had found.

But by the third day, word had leaked out that 'Zeus's Treasure Chest' had been discovered at the

66

Temple of Poseidon at Cape Sounio. Crowds gathered and the press waited for news and to take photographs of the ancient golden box.

As more and more people arrived, the police had to be called in to help secure the dig. Tourists were trying to get on to the site to see what had been found. There was even fear that there may be an attempt to steal the treasure.

Waiting above the pit with her mother, Stella watched her father working with George and another archaeologist to free the last corner of the gold box. The harder they worked to free it, the more questions arose. The box hadn't been buried. Somehow, it had been sealed in a solid sheet of rock. Yet despite the best testing tools and equipment, no one had any idea how it had been done.

'Once more,' her father grunted. 'Nice and gently, we don't want to damage it.'

Stella held her breath as the three strong men struggled to free the heavy box from its rock prison. But when the final edge came away from the rock base, with the blowing rain making everything slippery, it fell out of the men's grip. The box slid along the receiving table until it flew off the edge and hit the stone floor with an explosive crash. Landing on its side, the lid of the box sprang open. There was a brilliant, pulsing flash and, for an instant, everyone was blinded.

When Stella could see again, she looked down into the pit. The golden box was open. Peering inside, she and everyone else at the dig were shocked to discover there was nothing inside the ornate box except a very large, very heavy, round rock.

7

Emily couldn't get the glass lake out of her mind. She recalled the sick feeling of sadness that had overwhelmed her and wondered if the others would feel the same.

After breakfast, while Chiron led the others into the temple to start their research, Emily and Pegasus took Joel, Paelen and Chrysaor to the glass lake.

Despite Paelen's protests, the Mother of the Jungle stayed close behind him making soft mewing sounds. 'Can you please tell her to leave me alone?' he asked Emily.

The huge beast was looming above him as her two wet tongues licked him.

'I don't think I can, Paelen,' Emily said, fighting back laughter. 'She seems pretty devoted to you.'

'Ah, how sweet,' Joel teased. 'Paelen has a pet.'

'It is not funny!' Paelen protested. 'She is large enough to squash me if I make her mad. But if I do not say something, she is going to drown me with her tongues.'

'But Paelen, you need a special friend,' Joel continued, laughing. 'Emily has Pegasus, I have Chrysaor . . .' He looked at the winged boar and Chrysaor nodded his head. 'And now you have the Mother of the Jungle!'

'But—' Paelen started.

Emily patted the Mother of the Jungle. '*You could not ask for a better friend, young Paelen. Brue will never let you down.*'

'Brue?' Joel asked.

Emily staggered and started to fall. With lightning-fast reflexes, Joel caught her before she hit the ground.

'Em, what's wrong? Are you all right?'

His big brown eyes were full of concern as he held her. Emily shook her head. 'I'm fine. I just went a little dizzy.'

She looked at the large purple creature in surprise. 'I remember! Your name is Brue and you are the very last of your kind. Your world was destroyed when your sun went super-nova. The Xan brought you and the other survivors here.'

Emily paused and looked around at the jungle as though seeing it for the very first time. 'Xanadu is a sanctuary,' she repeated softly from the words on the temple wall.

She looked at Joel and Paelen and shouted, 'Xanadu is a sanctuary! I do remember! The Xan used to bring species here if they were in danger or their world was dying. This entire planet is filled with survivors of disasters.'

'Like a wildlife refuge?' Joel asked.

'Exactly!' Emily cried. 'The Xan brought all they could here. And when they ran out of space they just made it bigger.'

'They could do that?' Paelen asked in wonder. 'They had the power to enlarge their world?'

Emily nodded. 'And if a species couldn't survive the atmosphere or environment here, they created an enclosed continent that mimicked their world so they could. Not too far from here is one of those regions. We couldn't survive there, but many others do!'

'How powerful were they?' Joel asked.

'Super powerful,' Emily replied. 'I think even more powerful than the Olympians.' She looked up at the Mother of the Jungle and sighed. 'By the time the Xan got to her world, almost everything was dead except for Brue and a few other smaller animals. All the vegetation and water was burned up and they were dying. The

Xan saved them and brought them back here to live.'

Paelen turned back to the large creature and stroked her two heads. 'I am so sorry that you are the last of your kind. You must be very lonely.'

Brue gave no indication that she understood Paelen's words, but she mewed and pressed her two large heads to him.

'What else do you remember?' Joel asked.

Emily frowned and looked around. 'Nothing. Things just come to me in waves. I can't reach the memories.'

'Then don't try,' Joel said. 'Just take us to what you wanted to show us.'

They continued through the jungle along the path until they reached the glass lake. They marvelled at how the bright blue sky above them was perfectly reflected on the surface.

'Cool!' Joel said as he stepped on to it. He ran for several metres then stopped and slid even further. 'It's like a giant skating rink, but without the cold!'

Emily and Paelen joined Joel and soon they were laughing and tackling each other – sliding on the surface and playing like children. Pegasus, Chrysaor and Brue remained on the shore, reluctant to step on to the slippery surface.

'It's a lot more fun when you are here!' Emily laughed. 'This place was really creepy last night. Especially that small piece of glass over there.'

Emily led her friends to the small circle of cracked glass. Even in the bright daylight with her closest friends at her side, Emily felt a chill when she looked at it.

Pegasus was first to notice and nickered softly. He nudged her away from it.

'What's wrong?' Joel asked. 'You look like you've seen a ghost.'

'I don't know,' Emily replied. She was stroking Pegasus, but was unable to draw her eyes away from the small patch of glass. 'This means something really important. It scares me.'

Pegasus whinnied and Chrysaor joined in.

'They both believe it is best if we leave here,' Paelen said. He looked around. 'I agree. This place is not good for you.'

With the mood broken, they returned to the camp, where Jupiter greeted them. 'I am glad you are back, I was just coming to get you. There is a lot more writing on the walls of the temple and we need your help to understand it.'

While they made their way to the temple, Emily

told Jupiter what she remembered of the Xan and how Xanadu really was a sanctuary.

'Brue,' Jupiter repeated as he stroked the Mother of the Jungle, 'you will not be alone any more. Our own myths tell us the Xan were a great and benevolent race,' he told Emily. 'With what you tell me of this place, I can see that it is true. It also explains why you sent Pegasus and Alexis here. They were in grave danger from the military at Area 51. Your instincts took over and you sent them to a place of safety, to sanctuary.'

Pegasus nickered softly and bobbed his head up and down. He then nudged Emily gently.

'He is thanking you for protecting him at Area 51.'

Emily put her arms around the stallion's neck. 'You don't need to thank me, Pegs. To be honest, I really thought I'd killed you. Sending you here was an accident – a good one, but still an accident.'

There was something about the temple that called to Emily. Part of her was curious to find out what it was, but another part wanted to run as far from it as possible. Pushing her doubts aside, Emily followed Jupiter. 'This is the Temple of Arious,' she explained. 'I can't remember who Arious was, but I do know she was important.'

'I wonder if we'll ever figure it out,' Joel said. 'I mean, you and all of this? What does it mean?'

Emily shrugged. 'I really don't know.'

They walked into the temple and stood in the spacious entranceway. Long corridors ran in several directions as well as the stairway that Pegasus had used the night before.

'Wow,' Joel said, 'this place is massive.'

'It is also very dark,' Paelen commented. 'Emily, would you turn on your Flame?'

Jupiter nodded. 'That is a good idea. At least until Apollo, Diana and Steve return. They are making torches for all of us.'

'*We do not need them*,' Emily said softly in a voice that wasn't her own. She walked, as if in a dream, to a wall and placed her hand on a raised carved stone. '*Illumination.*'

Suddenly the entire temple was filled with bright light. There was no apparent source, but every wall was glowing. With the entrance brightly lit, they saw multiple carvings in the language of the Xan.

Emily shook her head and looked around in shock. She turned to Joel. 'How did you turn on the lights?'

'Me?' Joel said. 'I didn't do anything. It was you.'

'No it wasn't.'

Pegasus pawed the floor and snorted. He nudged Emily.

Paelen said, 'Emily, it was you. Do you not remember?'

She looked desperately from Paelen to Pegasus. 'Was it really me? I don't remember. What does it mean?'

Pegasus pressed his head to her and nickered.

Paelen translated. 'He believes the longer you are here, the more memories from your previous life as a Xan come forward. The person you were is mixing with the Emily you are. There is going to be some confusion as you two come together.'

Emily wrapped her arms around the stallion's neck and pressed her face to him. 'But what if I lose myself, Pegs? What if that other person is stronger than me and I disappear completely?'

Pegasus whinnied and pounded the ground with his hoof.

'He will not let that happen. He will protect you, even if it means protecting you from your previous self,' said Paelen.

'We all will,' Joel added, putting his hands on her shoulders. 'Emily, I don't understand any of this either. But no matter what, I promise we won't let anything happen to you. Xan or not, you are still our Emily.'

Emily was grateful to her friends, but still frightened. Something was stirring deep within her, as if waking from a long slumber. When that something woke fully, would she be strong enough to survive?

'Now,' Joel said, 'how about we look around?'

Emily tried to push her fears aside as she and the others explored the temple. Before long, her father joined them.

'This place is amazing,' he mused. 'It seems to go on for ever.'

'It may well do so,' Jupiter said. 'I believe for today we will just take a quick tour. Then tomorrow, Emily, I hope you will work with the scribes to start translating the writings.'

Each and every chamber they entered was filled with secrets and messages. Strange items were scattered everywhere as if the owners had just gone out for a bit and planned to return. Yet by the layers of dust over everything, they had lain undisturbed for hundreds, if not thousands, of years.

They spent most of the day in the temple and had only explored the tiniest portion of it. When they returned to camp, they found that Mercury had just arrived through the portal to the Solar Stream.

The blonde messenger was breathing heavily as he ran up to Jupiter. 'Juno has taken very ill,' he reported, gulping air. 'She has asked for me to bring you back.'

'Ill?' Jupiter repeated in alarm. 'How? What is wrong?'

'I do not know,' Mercury panted. 'But she is not the only one. Ceres, Venus and Minerva are also ill. We found Vesta collapsed in the Temple of the Flame.'

'Vesta?' Emily cared deeply for her teacher. It was because of Vesta that she now had Pegasus in her life. She owed her everything.

'I came as fast as my sandals could fly me,' Mercury continued. 'But the journey was long. I fear for what we will return to.'

Jupiter called his two brothers forward. 'Neptune, Pluto, come. We must return to Olympus immediately.'

'I'm coming with you!' Emily insisted.

Jupiter shook his head. 'No, child. We do not know what we are facing. You must remain here. Work with Chiron and his team. Try to discover what you can about your past and your powers. I am sure this is nothing.'

The centaur approached Emily and placed a hand lightly on her arm. 'Stay with us, Emily. There is much work to be done here. I'm sure everyting is fine.'

Chiron said the words, but his eyes expressed something else. He wasn't alone. There were exchanged looks passing between him, Jupiter, Neptune and Pluto. They were all deeply concerned.

'My brothers and I will return when the crisis has ended,' Jupiter said. 'For now, please remain here and continue with your investigations.'

Emily stood back with Pegasus as Mercury and the Big Three slipped through the portal to the Solar Stream. It would be a long journey back to Olympus and an even longer wait to find out what was wrong.

Emily turned to Pegasus. 'In all the time before time, have you even known any Olympian to become sick?'

Pegasus snorted, pawed the ground and shook his head. Emily didn't need a translator to understand. No one in Olympus had ever been ill before. Wounded, yes, on occasion. But never ill.

'I have a bad feeling about this, Pegs,' Emily said as she leaned in closer to the stallion.

8

The journey along the path was endless. All the animals and insects were wishing her well, but were grieved that the Xan were leaving.

'Not much further,' Riza cried. 'Please wait for me, I'm coming.'

But even as she forced more speed, she could feel the power of the others building. They had waited as long as they could. But the stars above were aligned. They could wait no longer.

'No!' she howled as she felt their energy converging. 'Wait for me! I am almost there!'

Riza pressed on, struggling to reach the gathering. She burst through the trees and arrived at the appointed place. Before her stood her people; arms raised, their powers merged, until they finally released themselves into the cosmos.

'Wait!' she cried. 'Please don't leave me . . .'

She was too late.

Her people had merged themselves into one great blinding flash and released themselves. It was as it should be. They had ruled long enough and had earned their rest. It was time to let the younger ones take over.

Standing at the edge of the gathering, she watched her people go. Rainbows of pure energy flashed across the night sky, blocking out the stars and moons. Powers divided joyously and scattered across the universe.

Then they were gone.

Beside her, Brue, the Mother of the Jungle, raised her two heads and howled in lonely mourning at the passing of the Xan. Brue turned pain-filled eyes to her, begging her to stay.

'I cannot be the last,' Riza said. 'Forgive me, Brue, I must try to follow.'

Riza summoned all her powers. Perhaps it would not be too late. Perhaps she could still reach her people and join them on their new journey. She knew what she had to do. She just prayed her single powers were enough.

Raising her hands in the air, Riza did as she was taught to do. She opened herself and released her powers to the cosmos . . .

'No!' Emily howled. She woke, panting heavily as the memories of that terrible night came flooding back.

Pegasus was beside her. He licked her face while

everyone else in the camp gathered around.

'Dad?'

'Em, you're safe,' he said, putting his arms around her.

Emily started to shiver. 'I remember what happened.' Her eyes landed on Brue, who was towering over Paelen. 'They all died . . .'

'Who?' Diana asked, kneeling before her. 'Emily, who died?'

'The Xan.' Emily was overcome with sadness as she remembered everything that had happened on this world so very long ago. She pulled out her special sea-green handkerchief and dabbed at the tears that threatened to fall. The handkerchief had been a gift from Neptune – to collect and store her tears before their powers could do any harm.

'I was there,' she spoke slowly as it became clear in her head. 'I watched them go. They were tired of their endless existence. They said it was time for the younger ones to take over so they could move on. They gathered together and merged their powers and released themselves into the universe.'

'You were with them?' Diana asked.

Emily shook her head. 'No. I was late getting back. Something happened, I can't remember what. By the time I arrived at the temple, the moons and stars had aligned and everyone was already at the gathering place. I tried to get there on time, but I couldn't.' Emily dropped her head. 'They left without me.'

'Em,' her father said gently, 'that wasn't you. You're my baby girl, born and raised in New York City. Those are just memories from someone else's life.'

Emily raised her eyes and looked at her father. 'No Dad, it was me. Somehow it was.' She looked over to the Mother of the Jungle. 'Brue was there. She saw it all. She begged me to stay so she wouldn't be left alone. But I couldn't. I couldn't be like her, the last of my kind.'

'What did you do?' Joel asked. 'Em, what happened?'

Emily sniffed and searched his handsome face, finding strength in the warmth of his gaze. 'Joel, do you remember that glass lake?'

When he nodded, she continued. 'That is all that remains of the Xan. When they released themselves into the universe, their bodies and the ground beneath them melted into thick glass.'

'We were skating on bodies?' Joel cried in shock and disgust. Suddenly he understood more. 'Wait! That small circle? The one on the shore all by itself, that was you, wasn't it? That was your body?'

Emily nodded. Then her voice changed, and sounded as though someone else was speaking directly through her mouth. '*I did not want to be left alone. I tried to follow, but I did not have their collective power. I released myself the same way they did, but it would not work. Instead I destroyed my body and sent what was left of me flaming through the Solar Stream.*'

'Who are you?' Emily's father asked. 'Who is speaking and where is Emily?'

'*I am Riza, the last Xan. Emily is here with me. We are one.*'

Diana nodded in blinding comprehension. 'Riza? That was you who crashed on Olympus!'

'Of course!' Chiron added. 'It all makes sense now. Alone, you were not strong enough to join the others and disperse properly. Instead you somehow crashed on Olympus right before the war with the Titans. It was you, the last Xan, who made it possible for us to defeat them and restore peace. You shared your powers with us. We are part of you!'

Emily nodded. '*But it was not just Olympus. I became fragmented. Other parts of me were scattered to other worlds along the Solar Stream. Most of my memories are gone. I cannot remember my early life or my family. That Flame-shard is still missing. I carry only bits and pieces of myself.*

'*Yet despite being separated, I remained conscious and aware. I remember Vesta coming to me and taking the heart of my powers away. She fragmented me further, when all I wanted was to be whole again.*'

Diana reached for Emily's hands and lowered her head. 'I am so very sorry. Had we known, Vesta would never have done that.'

Beside her, Pegasus nickered and pressed his head to her. Emily reached up and stroked his beautiful face. '*Do not be sorry. If she had not done it, I would still be just the Flame. Unknown and unheard. Existing in lonely misery. But because she put my heart in a human girl, it gave me a chance to live again. And I have lived, many, many lives. Passing from one girl to another until, finally, the "I" that was the human Emily went into the Temple of the Flame and we merged together.*'

Emily looked down at her hands and took over speaking. 'I am still Emily, but I am also Riza.'

'Riza,' her father repeated softly. He pulled her into a tight embrace and whispered in her ear. 'Listen to me, Em. I don't care if you are still my Emily or Riza. I love you – both of you. And you are not alone. There may be no more Xan, but you have a family and people here who care for you.'

'Oh Dad!' Emily cried as she threw her arms around

85

him. 'We love you too!'

'We Olympians are so very sorry that Riza was left behind,' Diana told her. 'But we are so very grateful to the Xan for making us the people we are.'

'Yes,' Apollo agreed. 'And we will gladly continue the work the Xan started so very long ago.' He stood. 'I must return to Olympus to tell the others what we have learned. We must celebrate the discovery of Xanadu and show our gratitude to Riza.'

'You don't have to do that, Apollo,' Emily said. 'We aren't any different than before. Please, can't things stay the way they are?'

Apollo bent down and kissed Emily lightly on the forehead. Like his sister, he had dark hair and brilliant blue eyes and was incredibly handsome. Emily blushed at his attention.

'I must share this, Emily. It is far too important – this is part of our heritage too. Also, I need to find out what is happening with the others. If I leave now, I should be back tomorrow.'

'Let him go,' Diana said. 'Apollo is right. This is monumental news, Emily. It must be shared. Olympians must be told that we are part of the Xan.'

They stood around the archway and watched Apollo open the Solar Stream and disappear.

'How are you feeling?' Joel asked Emily when Apollo was gone.

'We're fine,' Emily said. 'We feel kind of weird, but we'll be OK.'

'You'll be OK when you stop saying "we",' Joel said. 'You are Emily. You look like Emily and you talk like Emily. Even if Riza is in there with you, you are more Emily than her.'

'I agree with Joel,' Paelen said. 'You are Emily. I could never call you anything but that.'

Beside her, Pegasus snorted and nodded his head.

'You too, Pegs?' Emily said.

Once again, Pegasus bobbed his head up and down.

Emily smiled at her friends, but knew they could never understand how she had changed. She wasn't just Emily any more. She was also Riza.

'Of course I'm still your Emily,' she said reassuringly. 'But if I say some strange things, you're just going to have to accept it.'

Paelen laughed and punched Emily playfully. 'So there will be no difference. You are always saying strange things!'

9

They spent the next day in the temple. Though Emily had recovered a few scattered memories of the Xan, Riza's personal life was still a mystery. Walking through the temple, she was as surprised by the discoveries as everyone else.

They soon found that each chamber was dedicated to a specific world the Xan had visited. It was like sections of a library that held books on different subjects, with each section supplying details of the people and life-forms the Xan discovered, including their requirements for continued survival.

'Simply fascinating,' Chiron said excitedly, as he asked Emily to do translation after translation.

Some chambers described worlds where nothing was needed. The Xan quietly visited them to ensure everything was all right, but did not do anything. Other chambers spoke of bringing the survivors of dying worlds to Xanadu and the work involved in creating an environment suitable to sustain their lives.

'This is amazing,' Emily's father said as Emily read information from the wall of a new chamber. 'What an extraordinary people the Xan were. Look at all the work they did for so many worlds. I wonder if we will find a chamber describing Earth.'

'Or Olympus,' Paelen added. 'Did the Xan know about us?'

Emily nodded. '*We did,*' she said in the strange, gentle voice they now knew was Riza's. '*We visited both your worlds many times.*'

Emily's father shook his head in wonder. 'The Xan were the guardian of so much.'

'It's just like the Olympians today,' Emily said. Pegasus was standing close at her side as she stroked his strong, warm neck. 'Pegs, you go to other worlds along the Solar Stream and watch over the people.'

'Not like this,' Paelen said. 'Compared to what the Xan did, we do nothing.'

'Especially you, little thief,' Diana teased. She approached Emily's father. 'Steve, come with me, I have something to show you.'

Emily and her friends continued to look around. 'This place is so cool!' Joel said. 'I wonder how big it really is.'

'Do you think we might be able to visit some of the different regions the Xan have created here?' Paelen asked.

Emily shrugged. She walked up to one of the walls in the chamber and rubbed her hand along the writing. 'It says that we can visit this people's continent. But I've seen warnings in other chambers to stay away.'

'Why?' Joel asked.

'I'm not sure,' Emily said. 'We'd have to read all the details. Maybe those continents are dangerous.'

'*No,*' Riza corrected aloud, '*not dangerous for us. But for some, the inhabitants do not know they have been moved. We must not contaminate them.*'

'Riza?' Paelen said, speaking to her directly.

'*I am here, Paelen. We both are.*'

'Can Emily come back please?' Joel said uncomfortably.

Emily smiled. 'Joel, I never left. But Riza wanted to tell us something.'

'This is getting too freaky!' Joel said. 'No offence, Riza, but it's going to take some time to get used to you being in there.'

'*No offence taken, Joel,*' Emily said with Riza's voice. '*But understand this. I have known you as long as Emily*

90

has. We have no secrets between us. I was with you at Area 51 when we kissed.'

'You did *what?*' Paelen shot an accusing look at Joel.

'Hey, that was private,' Joel said, his face turning red. 'It was between Emily and me.'

'*And me,*' Riza said, laughing softly.

Paelen looked from Emily to Joel. 'Is there something you two want to tell me?'

Emily blushed. 'Not really.'

'Yeah, let's just keep exploring,' Joel said gruffly as he stormed out of the chamber.

They were back at camp excitedly discussing their findings when the arch of the Solar Stream came to life. Apollo appeared. They knew something was wrong as soon as they saw him.

'Father is gravely ill and he has asked for Emily. I fear he is dying.'

'What?' Diana cried and rushed over to her brother. 'That is impossible! Father only just went back.'

'I know,' Apollo agreed. 'It is happening very quickly. Many Olympians are taking ill, including Pluto and Neptune.'

At the mention of his father, Pegasus reared. He whinnied and threw his head back.

'What's wrong with them?' Emily's father demanded.

'Father will not say. Only that I am to bring Emily home immediately. He said that Olympus is in grave danger. He has ordered those Olympians here to remain here. He does not want you infected.'

Diana leaned forward and peered closely at her brother's face. She reached out and touched the hair at his temples. 'Apollo, your hair is going grey.'

He nodded. 'So is everyone's in Olympus. That, and much worse. We are all ageing rapidly.' He turned to Emily. 'We have no time to spare; please hurry.'

Pegasus protested loudly and reared again.

'No, Pegasus, you must remain here,' Apollo said. 'No one is immune to this. It is affecting the older Olympians fastest, but none of us are safe. Father believes Emily, Steve and Joel will be safe to return as Aunt Maureen remains unaffected.'

'I am not staying here,' Diana insisted, 'not while Father is ill. You know you cannot stop me, Apollo. So stand aside.'

Apollo dropped his head, knowing there was no stopping his headstrong sister. 'Father asked all Olympians to remain here.'

'Then Father is about to be disappointed!' Diana

shot back. She looked at the others in the camp. 'Those who do not wish to return are welcome to stay here with no judgments made against you. But I for one will not.'

Chiron shook his head and pawed the ground with a hoof. 'I will not remain here while Olympus is in danger.'

No one in the camp followed the orders to stay on Xanadu. One by one, they charged through the portal into the Solar Stream.

10

Jupiter lay in his bed. His skin was dry and leathery and he was deathly pale. He looked like he had aged a thousand years since Emily had seen him last. His grey beard was white and thin and his eyes were sunken in a face too wrinkled to recognize.

'Father!' Diana pushed past Emily and ran up to Jupiter's bed. 'What has happened to you?'

The leader of Olympus opened his eyes wearily. They were covered in a white film; he was completely blind.

'Emily,' he rasped, 'I must speak with Emily.'

'I'm here,' Emily said softly. Pegasus was behind her and reluctantly followed her up to the leader's bed. He neighed and shook his head, greatly disturbed by the sight of the leader of Olympus looking so frail.

Emily reached for Jupiter's hand. 'I'm right here. Please let me heal you.'

'You cannot,' Jupiter said. 'I am not ill. I am old.

We are all growing old. Not even your powers can stop the ravages of time.'

'No, Father, do not speak,' Apollo soothed as he crowded in. 'Save your strength.'

Jupiter shook his head and strands of thin, white hair fell from his rapidly ageing head. 'I have no strength left, as I have very little time left. Apollo, I am dying. My beloved Juno passed but moments ago. Vesta and Ceres have also gone. I will join them soon. Neptune and Pluto will follow me.'

Emily's hand flashed up to her mouth. 'They're dead? But that's not possible! You're Olympians, you can't die!'

Pegasus whinnied in misery as he pawed the marble floor of Jupiter's chamber.

Diana looked desperately around the room. 'What is happening? Why are you ageing?'

'It is not just me,' Jupiter struggled to say. 'You too, my precious daughter, have started to age.'

'How?' Emily's father demanded. 'What has changed? Is it Xanadu? Is that world infecting you?'

'It is not Xanadu,' said Jupiter. 'It is the Titan's final revenge. After all this time, they have won the war – unless Emily can stop them.'

'Me?' Emily gasped.

Jupiter struggled to sit up. It took both Diana and Apollo to help him into a seated position.

'Listen to me,' Jupiter said in a fading voice. 'Long ago, long before Olympus was how we know it now, there was a great war.'

'Yes, Father,' Diana said gently, 'you defeated the Titans.'

Jupiter nodded, but then shook his head. 'We almost failed. It was in the height of the battle. With our powers matched against each other, neither side could defeat the other. The war raged on and on. All we were achieving was destruction. Olympus was in ruins, Earth was almost destroyed and many worlds are gone now because of us.

'Finally, we were able to raise an army strong enough to take on my father, Saturn.'

'Your father!' Emily cried. 'The leader of the Titans was your father?'

Jupiter nodded. 'It is a very long and complicated story. I have no time left to tell you.'

'I've studied the myths. I can tell Emily about the war with the Titans,' Joel offered. 'But what happened? What did Saturn do?'

'He and the Titans created a new army. They called them the Shadow Titans. They outnumbered us by

96

many thousands. They were difficult to destroy or even stop. But that was not the end of it. The Titans also created a devastating weapon capable of killing us and ending the war.'

'I never heard any of this,' Apollo said. 'It is not written anywhere.'

Jupiter shook his head. 'No, we kept it secret. It happened long before you and Diana were born. Before all that we now know. It was from the dark time.'

'What was the weapon?' Emily asked.

'It was a large stone. It held the power to strip us of our abilities and to rapidly age us – to death.'

'What?' Diana cried. 'That is monstrous.'

'Wait,' Joel said, shaking his head, 'this doesn't make sense. If Saturn was your father, surely the weapon would affect him and the other Titans as well. To use it against you would have been suicide.'

Jupiter shook his head. 'No, my father was as clever as he was evil. He found a place to hide, free from the effects of the weapon. He and the other Titans fled there and left it to the Shadow Titans to distract us while they had volunteers prepare the weapon.'

'What happened?' Diana pressed. 'Father, how did you defeat them?'

Jupiter dropped his head and his eyes closed.

'Father!' Diana cried, shaking his arm. 'Father, wake up!'

Jupiter opened his eyes.

'How did you stop the weapon?' Diana repeated.

Jupiter paused, struggling to remember. Then he nodded. 'The weapon, yes. Before it could be launched against Olympus, Neptune, Pluto and I struck first. We entered their camp and before the weapon's powers could destroy us, we secured it in a golden box created by Vulcan. We then embedded it in a sheet of rock and buried it deep in the ground. And there it has lain undisturbed for all this time.'

'Why didn't you destroy it?' Emily asked.

Jupiter sighed. 'We could not. It stripped us of our powers and was killing us as we drew near. We were fortunate to even survive the encounter. But then, we were still very young and powerful.'

Diana sucked in her breath. 'You faced the weapon directly?'

'We had no choice. But it aged us greatly in a very short time and we lost many of our powers. However, we did manage to secure the weapon before it destroyed everything. After that, with the Titans still in hiding, we were finally able to defeat the Shadow Titans.'

Emily leaned closer. 'It aged you? Is that why you and your brothers look older than everyone else?'

Jupiter nodded weakly. 'It was the price we paid for winning the war.'

'So what has happened now, Father?' Apollo asked. 'Why are we all ageing?'

Jupiter sighed. 'The box has been opened. I can feel it. Its deadly powers are seeping through the Solar Stream. Soon it will finish the job it was created for. It will destroy Olympus and kill everyone here.'

'No!' Joel cried. 'No, we won't let that happen. If the box has been opened, we will close it again! Maybe this time we can even destroy the weapon. Tell us, Jupiter. Where did you hide it? Where was it buried?'

Jupiter struggled to remain awake. 'Where we fought and won many battles against the Titans,' he mumbled softly. 'On Earth. We buried the box far from Olympus in a place where humans built a temple to my brother, Neptune – though they knew him as Poseidon. It is in a place you call Greece . . .'

11

It was late in the day. Emily stood beside Pegasus and clung to the stallion tightly.

'I just can't believe he's gone.' Emily's words were so soft, they were barely audible. 'Jupiter is really dead. After facing everything from the CRU, it was the Titans that finally killed him.'

Pegasus pawed the floor, whining. Neptune was gravely ill and being tended by the ageing Sirens and his merman son, Triton, at the bottom of the sea. He could not survive the journey to the surface, so Pegasus did not have the opportunity to say goodbye to his father.

Pluto, leader of the Underworld, had also passed earlier that day. With the oldest Olympians now dead, the younger ones were showing signs of rapid ageing.

Emily and Pegasus were standing in the artifact chamber, watching the long line of grieving Olympians being evacuated to Xanadu. They hoped that the effects of the Titan weapon would be weaker there, as it was further away from Earth.

'Please go now, Pegs,' Emily begged, holding the stallion tight. 'I promise I'll be there as soon as I can. I just want to make sure that those who can leave do.'

She looked into the stallion's eyes and could see the effects of the weapon already taking hold. They weren't as bright as before and his wings drooped. The smooth hair of his mane and tail was growing coarse and brittle. Emily hadn't told him, but she had already found several of his feathers on the ground.

Pegasus snorted and shook his head. He would not leave without her.

'Please,' she begged again, 'staying here is killing you. You must go!'

But Pegasus refused to leave her side.

Joel was having the same problem with Paelen. His hair was turning grey and his back had developed a hunch. He was becoming hard of hearing, but refused to leave Olympus without them.

'I told you to go!' Joel yelled at Paelen.

'No,' Paelen shot back, 'and you do not need to shout at me!'

'Yes I do!' Joel screamed. 'It's that or I pound my message into your thick skull! You can't stay here. Now

101

go through the Solar Stream before I throw you through it, you old goat!'

'Who are you calling a goat?' Paelen challenged.

'You!' Joel yelled. 'Look at you, you're a mess. And your sandals are losing their feathers. If you won't go for yourself, go for them.'

Paelen looked down at his sandals. They were ageing as fast as he was. Their little wings dragged along the floor and were now almost bald of feathers. Finally he and Chrysaor surrendered to Joel's threats and agreed to go to Xanadu.

Emily gave Paelen a tight hug. She was shocked by how thin and frail he had become in such a short time.

'We'll be right behind you,' she promised. 'Dad and my Aunt Maureen are already on the other side waiting for you. I'm sure Brue will be glad to see you again.'

'Oh, wonderful,' Paelen said sarcastically. 'Now I *really* want to go back there, to get drooled on by that great hulking beast.'

'Stop being so grumpy,' Emily said. 'You are lucky that Brue cares for you.'

'Why do I not feel lucky?' Paelen muttered.

'Because you're an old goat!' Joel snapped. 'Now go!'

'I should be here helping you,' Paelen complained. 'I am not an old man, you know.'

'No, you're not,' Emily agreed, 'but Dad needs you on the other side. There are a lot of older Olympians who need help getting settled.'

'All right,' Paelen surrendered, 'but do not be long or I will come back for you.'

'We won't,' Emily promised. She was finding it impossible to watch her dear, sweet Paelen age by the minute. He was far too young to be so old!

Emily stood back with Joel and Pegasus as Paelen and Chrysaor joined the line feeding through to the Solar Stream. Elderly Diana stood on one side of the portal while Hercules was on the other. The hero of Olympus hadn't escaped the ravages of the weapon. Even though he was half human, he was still ageing rapidly.

'This can't be happening.' Joel's haunted eyes took in the room of ageing Olympians. 'Not after everything we've been through.'

'We've got to stop it, Joel. We can't let that weapon kill everyone.'

'I know,' Joel agreed. 'Just as soon as we get everyone to Xanadu, you and I will go to Greece and find it. We'll destroy it before it kills everyone.'

As they stood watching the line feeding through the portal, Cupid approached slowly.

'Well?' Emily asked. 'What did she say?'

Like Pegasus, Cupid's wings drooped and the sheen had left the feathers. His hair was long and grey and wrinkles now coursed along his once beautiful face. He shook his head. 'She refuses to leave Tom.'

Emily turned to Joel. 'I asked Cupid to go to Alexis and tell her what has happened and that we are evacuating Olympus.'

'You knew she wouldn't leave him,' Joel said. 'She is devoted to him.'

'I know, but I had to try. Thank you for trying too, Cupid. I know it was a long flight for you.'

Cupid shrugged. 'It was my last. I cannot fly any more. My wings will not carry me.' He opened a wing to show many missing and tattered feathers. Even with her healing touch, Emily could not grow them back for him. 'I am grounded, just like an ordinary human.'

Emily was glad Joel let the insult go. 'Go to Xanadu, Cupid,' she said sadly. 'You might be safe there.'

The winged Olympian nodded his head and joined the line to the portal.

* * *

Emily, Joel and Pegasus were soon alone in the artifact chamber. Emily walked over to a window. The sky was clear and brilliantly blue, but no one was flying. Anyone with wings was now grounded by age.

Down on the ground, elderly Olympians shuffled along the beautiful cobbled streets. Around them, trees lost their leaves and flowers wilted and turned black.

Olympus was dying.

'So many are refusing to leave,' Joel said sadly as he looked at the people and animals below.

'Olympus is their home. They can't bear to leave it.'

Emily looked at Pegasus in disbelief. The stallion's head was hung low in grief.

'Come on, Pegs.' She kissed him on the muzzle. 'You can't stay here any longer.' She looked back to the window. 'None of us can.'

12

It was night in the jungle world when Emily, Joel and Pegasus arrived on Xanadu. Many small camp fires burned as the survivors of Olympus settled down to rest. Emily saw her aunt moving between sleeping people. She was carrying a jug of water and looked exhausted. Since she started living in Olympus after the Area 51 incident, her aunt had spent most of her time locked in the libraries doing research. She always said it would take a disaster to pry her out of them. She had been right.

'Em!' her father called. He approached the archway. Diana was with him. Her once beautiful dark hair was now coarse and peppered with grey. Yet despite her older age, she was still a stunning woman.

'Is that everyone?' Chiron asked, peering past Emily. His chestnut-coloured hair was also greying and his horse's body was bent and crippled.

Emily nodded. She looked at the gathered Olympians

and realized just how few had evacuated Olympus. 'Not many came.'

Diana shook her head. 'I am not surprised. We are all loyal to Olympus.' She dropped her head. 'I chose to stay, but your father was stubborn and refused to allow me. He threatened to carry me if I did not promise to come.'

Emily put her arms around the tall, proud woman. 'I'm glad, Diana. I couldn't bear to lose you.'

Diana returned the hug and kissed the top of Emily's head. 'I am sorry, child, but you must still face that loss. The effects of the Titan weapon have taken time to get here, but they have now reached Xanadu. I am still ageing. We all are.'

Joel's eyes were locked on Paelen as their friend cared for an elderly giant. Each step he made was stiff as if he was in terrible pain. The Mother of the Jungle was walking carefully behind him, whining and doing what she could for him.

Chrysaor was beside Joel, trying to get his attention. The hair on his snout was gone and his face was so wrinkled that it was impossible to see his eyes.

'I can't stay here,' Joel said angrily. He bent down to the boar's level and stroked his bare snout. 'I can't watch this happening to you.' He looked up at Emily.

'We've got to go to Greece right now. We'll find and destroy that stupid weapon once and for all.'

Emily had been thinking the same thing and nodded. 'Diana, please tell us how to open the Solar Stream to Earth.'

Beside her, Pegasus nickered and pawed the ground.

'No, Pegasus,' Diana said, 'you cannot carry them to Earth. You are not strong enough.' She looked down at the boar. 'Neither are you, Chrysaor.'

'Pegs, you can't come back to Earth with us,' Emily said sadly. 'That's where the weapon is. It'll kill you.' She stroked his face and pressed her forehead to him. 'Please, you promised we'd always be together. Stay here and live. We won't be long.'

On the other side of the clearing, Diana showed Emily and Joel how to use the two blue jewels that opened the Solar Stream.

'Father made three of these for emergencies, back when the Nirads first invaded Olympus.' Diana sighed sadly at the mention of her father. She handed one each to Emily and then Joel.

'I used the third jewel to go to Earth the first time we met in New York. Unfortunately I lost mine at those wretched stables where we took the carriage for

Pegasus. I have no doubt the foul, greedy owner found it and most likely had it made into a ring. When this is over, I must go back there to retrieve it and to rescue those poor horses. No animal should be forced to work like those unfortunates – New York City is no place for horses . . .' Diana's mind seemed to wander.

'How do they work?' asked Joel, drawing her back to the present.

Diana focused again. 'You just hold it up and clearly state your destination. The Solar Stream will open and you walk through.'

Emily looked down at the beautiful blue jewel and prayed it would lead them to the Titan weapon. It was now critical. Poor Diana was fading away.

Beside her, Pegasus was looking worse. He no longer noticed the increasing bald patches on his wings or the trail of white feathers he was leaving behind.

Emily picked one up. 'Do you see this feather, Pegs? I'm taking it with me. So you'll be beside me the whole time. We'll still be together.' She hugged the stallion tightly, not wanting to let him go. It tore at her heart to leave him behind.

As she said goodbye to her father, he held her close. 'Be careful . . . And Em,' his voice dropped. 'Don't be afraid to use your powers. You can't let anyone stop you. Especially the CRU, if they are involved in any of this. Do what you must to destroy that weapon.'

Emily nodded as her eyes landed on Paelen. He was trying his best not to show the pain he was in. But all the bone-stretching and manipulation had taken a terrible toll on his ageing body. He was filled with painful arthritis as his misshapen joints swelled. It was only because Brue was standing behind him and supporting him with one of her large heads that he was able to stay upright.

'Come on, Em, we've got to go,' Joel said impatiently.

Emily looked at him and saw the genuine terror on his face. So often Joel tried to keep his emotions locked deep inside. But there was no hiding this. Olympus had become his home and the Olympians his family. Joel was losing them and it was tearing him apart.

Emily gave Pegasus a final kiss and a quick hug to Paelen. 'You'd better be here when we get back.'

'Where else would I be?' Paelen shouted irritably. 'Las Vegas is gone.'

As everyone stood back, Emily held up the jewel.

'Take us to Earth – Greece and the Temple of Poseidon!'

13

After six days on site, the rain finally stopped. Despite their amazing discovery, the archaeologists had found nothing more than the large gold box and silver dagger. Those items had already been taken to the Acropolis Museum in Athens for testing and dating.

Stella, her parents and George had remained at Cape Sounio to keep looking for clues to explain how they had become embedded in the rock. But after days of digging and searching, they were still no further ahead.

As the sun set after yet another long and fruitless day, they returned to their tents. For the better part of the afternoon, her mother had been trying to call her colleagues at the museum without success.

'I don't understand it; Stavros is still not answering his phone.' Stella's mother closed her phone. 'Neither is Anya. I keep getting the same message at the department's switchboard saying I should call back later.'

Stella's father was busy typing his notes on his laptop. 'They are probably being inundated with calls from the press, asking about the treasure chest. Look how the reporters are still at the bottom of the hill waiting to see what else we find. I checked this morning, there are even more down there. I'm sure Stavros and the others have turned off their phones so they can work.'

'Perhaps,' Stella's mother said as she started to prepare their dinner.

Stella waited until after the meal for the best moment to talk to her parents. 'Can we please go home now? You are both needed at the museum and there isn't anything else to find here. All the good stuff has been taken to Athens.'

'Don't be so impatient,' her father said. 'You cannot race archaeology. There is always more to investigate. Besides, you don't have to be back at school until Monday. You'll be staying here with us until then. After that, we can all go back to Athens together.'

'Monday?' Stella cried. 'But that won't give me any holiday at all!'

'This find could be the biggest of our careers. Who knows what else we might discover.'

'But what about me?'

'Stella, you're fifteen,' her mother said tiredly. 'When you are older you can go where you want, when you want. Until then, you will do as your father and I say. We will go back to Athens on Monday.'

Stella gave up. She knew there was no point arguing. There was nothing more she could say or do to change her parents' minds. Once they got started on something, they didn't stop.

She left their tent and tried to calm down. It was far too early to go to bed, but there was little else to do here. Beside her parents' tent, George's tent glowed with light. He usually stayed up late, writing down notes and doing research. She considered speaking to him, but talking to George was like talking to her parents. All he ever thought about was finding things from the past.

'One day,' Stella muttered angrily as she turned on her torch and wheeled her way up the hill towards the Temple of Poseidon. 'One day I'll be old enough to do what I want and you won't be able to stop me! I'll go so far away from here and these stupid digs you'll never see me again. Then you'll be sorry you forced me to stay.'

At the top of the hill, she looked at the marble pillars of the temple. There was no moon, but the starlight was shining on the cream marble, making the temple look like it was made of giant's bones.

A rope barrier encircled the temple to keep tourists from climbing up into the ancient monument. Stella lifted the rope and passed under it. Her parents were top archaeologists so that gave her the right to go where most other people couldn't. But when she stopped before the first tall step into the temple, she heard a whoosh and felt a powerful wind. A blinding light flashed right in the centre of the temple.

Stella raised her hands to shield her eyes against the bright light. Two dark figures were moving within it. With a scream locked deep in her throat, she realized they were heading right for her.

14

Emily and Joel emerged into complete darkness. It always took a few moments to adjust from the brilliance of the Solar Stream.

When Emily could see again, she was stunned to find a girl in a wheelchair at the base of the steps no more than a couple of metres from her. She was holding a flashlight and her mouth was hanging open in shock.

'I think we've got trouble,' Joel muttered.

The sound of Joel's voice seemed to startle the girl. She dropped the flashlight and turned the wheelchair to roll away. But the wheelchair caught on some larger rocks and tipped to the side. The girl fell and cried out as she hit the rocky surface.

'C'mon,' Joel cried. 'We can't let her tell anyone we're here.'

They caught up with the girl in moments. Her eyes were filled with terror. She was speaking quickly, but not in a language they could understand.

'It's all right,' Emily said. 'Don't be afraid. We're not going to hurt you.'

'Can you understand us? Do you speak English?' Joel asked.

The girl looked from Emily to Joel and landed on his silver arm. 'Are you . . . gods?' she stammered.

'You do speak English!' Emily said.

'I learn it at school,' she said with a thick Greek accent.

'Are you hurt?' Joel asked. He squinted and tried to see the girl's cut knee. 'Em, we could use some light here.'

Emily held up her hand and summoned the Flame. It burst from her palm and caused the girl to gasp and try to drag herself away.

'I promise we're not going to hurt you,' Emily said. 'I'm Emily and this is Joel. Who are you?'

'St . . . Stella.'

Holding up her hand, Emily could see the girl wasn't much older than her. She had cropped dark hair and eyes as black as night. She was able to move her upper body, but her legs remained still. Emily saw that the girl's knee was bleeding, but she didn't show signs of feeling it.

116

Stella's eyes were locked on Emily's flaming hand. 'You *are* gods!'

'No, we're not,' Joel said. 'It's a long story, but we don't have time to explain. Are you hurt?'

Stella shook her head. 'I am paralyzed from the waist down. I don't feel anything.'

Emily righted Stella's wheelchair while Joel lifted her up and placed her gently on the seat. 'Can you tell us if this is the Temple of Poseidon?' he asked.

'That is the temple.' Stella raised a shaking finger at the ancient monument behind them. 'You just came from it.'

Joel turned back and looked up at the columns of the temple. 'Good. It's got to be somewhere around here.'

Emily raised her hand higher and increased the flame. 'Jupiter didn't tell us where to look. It could be anywhere.'

'Jupiter?' Stella repeated softly. 'Do . . . do you mean . . . ?' she stuttered, and paused. 'Are you saying, Zeus – he is the one who sent you here?'

Emily nodded.

'He is real?' Stella asked, her voice barely audible. 'Does he truly live on Mount Olympus with all the other gods?'

'No, not Mount Olympus, but another world called Olympus,' Emily explained. 'When the Olympians first visited Earth long ago, they came to Greece. They told the ancient people of their world and, because of that, the Greek people named their tallest mountain after them, but it's not the same place.'

Emily paused. 'I know this may be impossible to believe, but I promise you, they are very real. Only they're in trouble. We've come here to find something that is hurting them.'

Stella's eyes kept passing from Emily's burning hand to Joel's arm. 'They are real,' she kept repeating. 'They are real . . .'

'Yes, and they're dying,' Joel said.

Emily gazed around and saw the glow of the tents further down the hill. 'Joel, look, people are camping here.'

'Nuts!' Joel cursed. He focused on Stella. 'What are you doing here? Are you really camping at a temple?'

Stella shook her head. 'No, my parents are archaeologists. Part of the cliff broke away over there and an artifact was discovered embedded in the rock.'

'A golden box?' Emily asked.

Stella's eyes grew big. 'Yes, you know of Zeus's Treasure Chest?'

118

'Are you the one who opened it?'

'Me? No. It was heavy and it fell. The box opened by itself and there was a flash of light. Then there was nothing inside but a big rock.'

'You saw the rock?' Emily cried. 'Where is it?'

'Gone.'

'What do you mean, gone? Gone where?'

'The others took it and the box to the Acropolis Museum in Athens.'

'Dammit!' Emily's fury rose. She ran to the cliff edge, raised her hands in the air and released two powerful blasts of Flame at the sea far below. 'Why?' she howled to the dark sky. 'Why couldn't it be here?'

'Em, calm down!' Joel cried. 'Don't lose control, you know what can happen if you do! We'll just go to Athens and destroy it there. This is only a small delay.'

Emily turned on Joel. 'But we're losing precious time. You saw how bad Paelen was. And Pegs. As long as that box is open it's killing them.'

Stella rolled up to Emily and bowed her head reverently. 'You *are* a god!'

'No, I'm not,' Emily said angrily. 'I'm just upset! And stop that, I don't want you or anyone ever bowing to me.'

'But you must be gods. I have seen your pictures.'

119

'Pictures? Where? Who are you?' Joel caught hold of Stella's arm with a silver hand.

'You're hurting me,' Stella cried. 'Please, let me go.'

'Joel, let her go,' Emily said. She turned to Stella. 'How do you know us?'

'From the pottery in the Acropolis Museum,' Stella explained. 'There is an amphora with paintings of you with Zeus and the other gods.'

'What's an amphora?' Emily asked.

'It is a two-handled pot,' Stella explained. 'There are many at the museum. I know of at least two from more than 500 BC with pictures of a girl who shoots fire from her hands. The colour is faded, but there were traces of blue in her eyes.' She peered closer at Emily. 'Your eyes are blue.' She gestured to Joel. 'There is a boy with her. He has a strong arm made of metal, just like yours.'

'If it's on ancient pots, it can't be us,' Emily said. 'We were never here in the past.'

'But it is,' Stella insisted. 'The girl looks just like you and is dressed the same.'

Emily looked down at her Olympian tunic. 'No, Stella, it wasn't us.' She gazed around. 'Tell me, how far is it to Athens? We must go there to destroy that rock.'

'You cannot,' Stella said. 'It is in the museum. There is too much security. You will not get in.'

'Oh yes we will,' Emily said. 'Trust me, nothing can stop us.'

'Except maybe transport,' Joel added. 'I've never been to Greece before. I have no idea where Athens is from here.'

'Athens is easy,' Stella said, pointing down the hill. 'You just follow that road.'

'You know how to get to Athens?' When Stella nodded, Emily continued, 'Good. You are going to take us there.'

'What? But my parents are here. I will get into trouble. And I have to be back at school on Monday.'

'I'm sorry, but this is too important. The lives of the Olympians are at stake. You are going to take us to the Acropolis Museum and show us that rock.'

'But I can't.'

'Oh, yes you can,' Emily said firmly. 'You can and you will. You don't have a choice.'

'Em,' Joel said softly, crooking a finger at her, 'can I speak with you for a moment please?'

'Stella, stay here,' Emily ordered as she walked away with Joel.

After a few paces, Joel stopped. 'Emily Jacobs, have

121

you lost your mind? You're talking about kidnapping that girl!'

'Not kidnapping, just borrowing,' Emily said.

'But she's in a wheelchair,' Joel argued.

'So?' Emily said. 'Just because she's in a wheelchair doesn't mean she can't help. We'll just take it with us.'

'But—'

'Joel, listen to me,' Emily said. 'Pegasus is dying. So are Paelen, Diana and all the others. They are dying because of that rock. We don't have time to waste getting lost in Greece. Stella knows the way to Athens. We need to get there. She knows the museum. That is where the rock is. We don't have any choice.'

As Emily and Joel argued, Stella started to wheel away.

Emily saw her out of the corner of her eye and raised her hand in Stella's direction. Stella squealed as her wheelchair was lifted off the ground and delivered back at Emily's side.

'I'm really sorry, Stella,' Emily said, turning to the girl. 'But people I love are dying because of that rock at the museum. All we're asking is that you help us get there so we can destroy it. I promise we'll let you go afterwards and you'll never see us again.'

'And if I refuse?' Stella said fearfully.

Emily leaned closer. 'You've seen my powers; you can't refuse. Nothing, not even you, is going to stop me from saving Pegasus!'

15

'Are you sure you want to do this?' Joel whispered as he walked behind Stella, pushing her wheelchair down the hill.

Emily nodded. 'We don't have a choice. Even if we used the Solar Stream to get to the museum, we still don't know the way in, or what the rock actually looks like. Stella has seen it. We've got to take her with us.'

She was walking beside Stella and could see her trembling and knew she was the cause of it. She just wished she could make her understand what was at stake.

As they drew nearer to the campsite, Emily leaned in closer to Stella. 'For everyone's protection, you will not say one word when we go past the tents. In just a few hours we'll make sure you are safely back here without anyone ever knowing what happened. Do you understand?'

Fear remained on Stella's face as she nodded. 'I understand.'

Emily exchanged a glance with Joel. She could see that he still didn't agree with the plan, but Emily couldn't see any other way.

It was surprisingly easy to get past the tents. But what Emily hadn't expected was the number of parked cars further down the hill. There was a crowd of men and women standing around, smoking.

Emily leaned down to Stella. 'What's going on here? Who are those people?'

'It's the media. They heard about the golden treasure chest. They are all waiting here to see what else my parents will discover. During the day, the police are here to keep them back. They should be here at night too, but it looks like they are gone.'

'The media?' Joel said. 'You mean, like newspapers and photographers?'

Stella nodded.

'Em, are you thinking what I'm thinking?'

'I sure hope not,' Emily said. 'If the CRU were to find out about this . . .'

Further conversation was cut short when they noticed one of the journalists looking in their direction. He stamped out his cigarette and started to walk towards them.

'Em,' Joel warned.

Emily looked desperately around. They had already been seen and there was nowhere to go. 'Nothing is going to stop us, Joel,' Emily said grimly. 'Even Dad agreed I should use my powers if I have to.'

'No!' Stella cried. 'Please do not hurt them. I swear I will help you. But you must not kill them.'

Emily had no intention of hurting them and she was about to say so when Joel quickly shook his head. 'All right then, Stella,' he said. 'Help us out of this and they will stay safe.' He looked at Emily. 'You push Stella and I'll stand behind you to hide my arm. We can't let them see it.'

Emily took a position behind Stella's wheelchair while Joel stood further back. They moved forward to meet the man who was walking towards them. Emily could feel her nerves bunching up in her stomach. It made the Flame deep within her rumble.

The man was of slender build and very tall, dressed in casual dark clothes and an open long black coat. He looked to be in his mid-thirties, with dark curly hair and ice-blue eyes.

Stella was the first to speak. She addressed the man in Greek, which made Emily all the more nervous. She could be telling him anything and they would never know. While they spoke, the man kept looking at Emily and Joel. There was something in his eyes – something almost predatory. Behind him all the other journalists stopped talking and were looking in their direction.

Warning bells were going off in Emily's head. She balled her hands into fists, preparing to summon the Flame. But after a few minutes, the man speaking with Stella smiled and nodded his head.

Stella looked up at Emily. 'He's a reporter. I told him you two are here for publicity. That your costumes are to celebrate the discovery of Zeus's Treasure Chest and that you are just trying them on in preparation for tomorrow.'

Emily smiled back and nodded her head. 'Yes, yes, we are,' she said.

'You are American?' the reporter asked in broken English.

Emily nodded. 'My father is one of the archaeologists. He thought it would be fun for us to dress up.'

The reporter nodded. 'But are you not cold in that light clothing? It is not warm out here.'

Both Emily and Joel shook their heads. 'No, we're fine.'

Emily's heart nearly stopped when the reporter reached out to shake her hand. She reluctantly returned the handshake. But when he reached for Joel, Emily shook her head. 'My friend doesn't shake hands,' she quickly said. 'He's afraid of germs.'

'Germs?' the reporter said. 'I do not understand.'

Stella quickly translated and the reporter's eyes lingered on Joel for several heartbeats. Finally he smiled again. 'OK, OK, see you later.'

'Yes, OK, fine,' Emily agreed, nodding and still grinning. 'See you later. Have a good night.'

They watched the reporter heading back to the group.

Stella looked back at Emily and Joel's tunics. 'If you are going to spend any time in Greece, you must change your clothes. We do not dress like that any more.'

'We're only going to be here a short time,' Emily said. 'As soon as we destroy that rock we'll go.'

Stella directed them towards her parents' car. 'I do not have the keys and there is no one to drive it.'

'I can drive,' Joel said.

'And I can open it,' offered Emily. At the driver's side, she placed her hand on the lock. She concentrated and thought 'Open'. Moments later, they heard a click and the door opened.

'That's a neat trick,' Joel said as he lifted Stella out of her wheelchair and helped her in to the front passenger seat. 'I just hope it works to get the engine going.'

They stored Stella's wheelchair in the back and Emily used her powers to start the car engine. Joel put the car in gear and drove out of the parking area, past all the reporters' cars and out on to the main road.

The journey started in silence, only broken when Stella gave Joel directions. 'What happened to you?' Joel finally asked her. 'Were you always paralyzed?'

Stella shook her head. 'No, it was an accident when I was eight. I went on a dig with my parents to Delphi. I wandered off and fell down into a pit. I landed on a rock and broke my back. I've been paralyzed ever since.'

'I'm sorry,' Joel said.

Stella shrugged. 'I am used to it now. But because of the accident, my parents won't let me do anything or go anywhere without them. They do not think I can take care of myself. I did not want to come on this dig, but they would not let me stay home alone.'

'At least you've got parents,' Joel said softly. 'Mine died in a car accident. If it weren't for Emily and the Olympians, I'm sure I would have ended up in prison.'

Emily sat in the back, listening to Joel and Stella. She pulled out Pegasus's feather and spun it in her fingers. 'Hold on, Pegs,' she whispered softly. 'Just hold on.'

'Are you talking to that feather?' Stella asked.

Emily nodded and gazed lovingly at it. 'It belongs to Pegasus. He is very sick.'

'Pegasus?' Stella said. 'The flying horse?'

'He's not a horse,' Emily barked. 'He's Pegasus!'

'Sorry!' Stella said quickly. 'I do not wish to make you angry.'

Emily sighed heavily. 'No, I'm sorry I yelled. I'm just frightened. Before the gold box was opened, Pegasus and I would fly everywhere together. Now, because of it, he's very ill. A lot of Olympians have died and the few survivors are dying.'

'How can this be?' Stella asked. 'I still do not understand. The gods are immortal. How can a simple rock be so dangerous?'

'It's not a simple rock,' Joel answered as he drove the car along the empty rural Greek roads. 'It was a weapon created by the Titans.'

'The Titans!' Stella repeated. 'They are real too?'

'They were,' Emily said. 'Jupiter defeated them. But right before he did, the Titans created a weapon that could destroy the Olympians. Luckily, Jupiter and his brothers got to it first and sealed it in the gold box. It has remained undisturbed all this time.'

'Until we found it,' Stella mused. 'What happens after you destroy it?'

'We don't know,' Joel answered. 'The survivors are old and sick. I hope by destroying it, we will reverse the damage. If not, then even if we do destroy it, we may be too late to save them.'

Joel had said the words that Emily had been dreading. She'd thought the same thing herself time and time again. Could the damage be reversed? And if it could, what would happen to the survivors?

It was approaching midnight when they reached central Athens. Like any big city, there were a lot of cars on the main roads, but not on the inner, smaller routes.

'This place is crazy,' Joel complained as he manoeuvered the car through the quiet streets. 'I thought driving in New York was bad, but Athens is impossible! How can anyone get a car down these narrow streets?'

'My father does not have a problem,' Stella said.

'Your father must be crazy,' Joel muttered.

As Stella directed them to the Acropolis Museum,

Joel turned down a particularly narrow road; he miscalculated the width and smashed into a parked car.

'My father's car!' Stella cried.

When they inspected the damage, they saw that the entire side was caved in.

'What am I going to tell him?' Stella groaned.

'Nothing,' Joel said. 'He'll think the car was stolen. We'll use another car to get you back to the temple.' He looked around the area. 'But it's too dangerous to leave it here in the street.'

'I've got it,' Emily said. She stretched her right arm in front of her towards the damaged car – it lifted off the road, over the top of the parked cars and then it was lowered on its side to the narrow pavement. 'Let the police try to figure out how it got there.'

'I am in such trouble,' Stella sighed.

'Not as much as the Olympians,' Emily said. 'Take us to the museum.'

Joel once again took the position behind Stella's wheelchair as they made their way through the deserted streets of Athens.

Apartment buildings, shops and boutique hotels lined the way. It almost reminded Emily of New York. But the comparison ended when she became aware of graffiti on all the buildings and closed shutters of the shops. It seemed there wasn't a single doorway or wall that had escaped the street artists' spray paint.

Another difference was the calm feeling of the place. Despite it being the middle of the night, the few people they passed on the street gave them friendly greetings and smiles instead of the suspicion that was built into all New Yorkers. Of course, Emily reasoned, it could be their Olympian dress that caused all the smiles.

Somewhere along the way, Emily became aware of a large chocolate-brown dog following them. When they stopped, the dog came straight up to Emily, wagging its tail and wanting to be petted.

Emily knelt down and stroked the dog's pretty face. 'You look just like my mum's dog, Mike. Go home now, I'm sure your family is missing you.'

'He has no home,' Stella said. 'That red tag on his collar means he is a street dog. He has been abandoned. The government has veterinarians who treat them. But it is the public who feed them.'

Emily looked at the red tag. It had a date and serial number on it. 'Who would do that? He's so sweet.'

'Look around you, there are lots of abandoned dogs in Athens. Sometimes pets grow too large and people release them to the streets. Just leave him and he will go away.'

Emily became aware of the other dogs sleeping in doorways or wandering the streets. 'Are they all homeless?'

Stella nodded. 'It is normal. There are dogs everywhere. Cats too.'

'Normal?' Joel said. 'It's not normal to abandon pets on the street. That's awful.'

'We have always done it,' Stella said.

'That doesn't make it right,' Emily said. She gave the dog a final pat. 'I'm so sorry, I wish we could take you with us,' she said to the dog. 'But you can't come where we're going. Stay here.'

But the dog refused to leave and continued to follow them.

'Just ignore him,' Stella said. 'He will leave eventually.' She made Joel stop pushing her chair and pointed up. 'There is the Acropolis.'

Emily and Joel gazed up to the top of a tall hill rising out of the ordinary city streets and graffiti-covered buildings. They drew in their breath at the amazing sight.

The Acropolis was actually a series of several ancient temples built closely together at the top of one of the highest points in Athens. Spotlights shone brightly on the white marble, showing off the large monument.

'How many buildings are up there?' Joel asked softly.

'A lot,' Stella said. 'The largest is the Parthenon – the temple to Athena. Behind it is the temple of Poseidon, and at the very front, you can see the temple of Athena Nike. It's really tiring to climb up all the stairs to get there, but worth it. Even with all the scaffolding.'

'My mom always dreamed of seeing the Acropolis,' Emily said. 'She used to show me pictures of it from books she collected. It's so beautiful.'

'But it really looks out of place here in the city,' Joel said. 'Down below, this could be New York. But the moment you look up and see it, you know you're in Greece.'

Emily frowned. 'Joel, doesn't the Parthenon remind you a bit of Jupiter's palace with all those pillars?'

Joel nodded. 'Only Jupiter's is much, much bigger. And it doesn't have all that construction scaffolding around it . . .' his voice tapered off and he looked away.

Emily dropped her head and felt a pain tearing through her. 'I still can't believe he's gone.'

'Who?' Stella asked.

'Jupiter,' Emily said sadly. 'I told you, he died a couple of days ago. So did his brothers, his wife, and my teacher, Vesta.'

'So Zeus is truly dead?'

'His name was Jupiter!' Joel shouted angrily.

'In Greece, we call him Zeus, not Jupiter,' Stella challenged. 'You are here now, so you must also call him Zeus.'

'It doesn't matter what we call him, he's dead!' Joel shouted. 'They're all dead! And unless we destroy that weapon, the survivors will die too. C'mon, let's go!'

They travelled the rest of the way in silence with the dog trailing behind. Before long, they came upon the museum. The building was large and strangely shaped, made of glass, steel and concrete.

'They designed the museum to look like a modern version of the Parthenon,' Stella explained.

'That's supposed to look like the Parthenon?' Emily said. 'It doesn't look anything like it!'

'Some say it does,' Stella defended.

Emily's heart pounded harder, knowing that the rock that was killing all the Olympians was locked deep inside that building. 'How do we get in?'

Stella led them around the building. 'In the daytime when the museum is open, visitors go in through those front doors,' she said, pointing at the high glass front of the building. Tall pillars ran the length of the building and the ground leading up to the entrance was covered in thick glass panels. Emily peered down through one of the panels and saw a lighted archaeological dig running deeper under the building. At any other time she might have been interested. But now, all she cared about was getting in and out as quickly as possible.

'Visitors can walk on the glass,' Stella explained. 'They can follow what the archaeologists are doing and finding.' She moved towards the side of the building. 'When the museum is closed, we go in through the side, here.'

They followed the building around. Up ahead was a set of heavily secured doors. Stella held up her hand. 'This is the way into the research area. My parents enter from here.' She indicated a security box with a number pad and swipe terminal. 'But you need a special code, pass-card and keys. I don't have those.'

'We don't need them,' Joel said. 'Em, can you open the doors or shall I force them?'

'It might have alarms – I'll do it.'

Emily approached the doors and released the Flame from her hands, directing it into a laser-like beam to burn a large round hole in the centre of the solid security doors.

Stella stared in complete shock. 'How do you do that?'

'I don't have time to explain,' Emily said. She passed through the hole and used her powers to lift Stella's wheelchair.

The dog followed them into the building. 'He should not be in here,' Stella said. 'The rules say no animals allowed.'

'We've just broken in – it's not the time to start caring about rules,' Emily said. 'Just take us to where they would keep the rock.'

Stella glared at the dog, but led the group through the maze at the rear of the Acropolis museum. 'My mother's office is on the lower level. There is a lift on the other side of the building. We go this way. I want to show you something.'

They entered the general public area of the main level of the closed museum. The primary lights were off, but each display cabinet was lit to show the contents. They walked past some of the museum's older exhibits.

'Here.' Stella stopped her wheelchair before one of the lighted cabinets. 'I told you I had seen your picture before.'

Emily and Joel peered at the terracotta amphora with the ancient black, cream and orange artwork. Despite the cracks and seams from where breaks had been mended, there was no mistaking the image on the front. It was the profile of a girl in an Olympian tunic. She was holding up her hands and shooting flames at tentacled monsters. Standing directly behind her were two men. One was a tall, muscular young man holding a spear. Emily's eyes landed on his right arm. It was torn open, the mechanical insides on display.

'Joel, look!' Emily said. 'That really does look like your arm.'

'It can't be!' Joel said. 'But look at the fire from the girl's hands. That really could be you. How is this possible?'

'I don't know.' A chill ran through Emily as she studied the ancient pot. Then her eyes landed on something else and her breathing stopped completely. Beside the girl figure on the pot was a large dog. It was snarling and baring its teeth at one of the monsters. The dog was chocolate-brown, apart from its right front leg, which was white.

'Joel, look.' Emily pointed from the pot down to the dog. 'Look at his front leg. You don't think . . .'

'No, it's impossible. There's got to be some mistake.'

'There is no mistake. It is you,' Stella insisted. 'I knew it the moment I saw you. I can take you to the other amphora to show you with Zeus and Poseidon.'

Emily shook her head. 'No, I don't want to see any more. I just want to destroy that rock and go home.'

Stella led them through the darkened museum. From the main public area, they entered a freight elevator.

Stella pushed the bottom button. 'This is where they store some of the pieces that will go on display later. My mother's office is at the end. Beside that is the workroom where she dates and restores pottery. Her assistant, Stavros, came back here a week ago with the golden box and the rock. They should be in there.'

As they made their way down the long hall, the dog slowed and started to let out a low, rumbling growl.

'Something's wrong,' Emily said.

'He is just a silly street dog,' Stella said. 'There is nothing here.' She approached the workroom and pushed open the door.

All of a sudden the lights flashed on. The room was filled with at least ten men dressed in black suits, all holding up weapons pointed directly at them. In the centre of the room stood the same reporter from the temple at Cape Sounio. He smiled smugly as he stamped out a cigarette.

'Emily Jacobs and Joel DeSilva. What took you so long to get here?'

16

Emily raised her hand to fire a blast of Flame. Beside her, the dog lunged for the closest man by the door and caught hold of his arm. The agent struck him with his gun butt and knocked him, stunned, to the floor.

'Stop!' the fake reporter shouted. He fired a warning shot into the ceiling before turning the gun on Joel. 'I know we can't hurt you, Emily. But Joel is still human. So is your new friend, Stella. I can shoot them in a heartbeat. Now drop your hands.'

'Who are you?' Joel demanded.

The man leaned casually against one of the work tables. 'Oh, I think you already know who we are.' His eyes settled on Joel's silver arm. 'It didn't take the Olympians long to replace your arm. I never saw the other one, but I heard it was a masterpiece.'

Joel looked down at his new arm. 'You're with the CRU.'

'Good guess, you got it in one,' the agent teased. 'I'm Agent B.'

'You're not Greek,' Stella accused.

'No,' the agent said. 'I'm British. But I had you fooled, didn't I?'

'British?' Emily repeated. 'I thought the CRU were an American organization.'

'You foolish girl,' Agent B said in his deepest English accent. 'We are a world-wide organization. Bigger than any one government. You should know that by now.'

Beside them, the dog began to stir. When he sat up, he growled.

'Shoot it,' Agent B casually ordered.

The nearest agent pointed his weapon at the dog. But before he had a chance to pull the trigger, Emily had knocked him backwards with an invisible force. He smashed against a wall unit filled with pieces of restored pottery. They all crashed to the ground in a heap.

Emily knelt down by the dog and glared up at Agent B. 'You try anything and you'll be sorry.'

'It's a street dog, Emily,' Agent B said contemptuously. 'There are hundreds of them in Athens. You've got bigger problems to worry about than that filthy animal.'

Emily raised her hand and fire flashed in her palm. 'I'm warning you. You hurt him again or anyone here and I won't hold back. Remember what I did to Area 51.'

For an instant, fear flashed in the agent's clear blue eyes. 'Calm down, Emily. No one is going to hurt anyone here. Put your Flame away, we just want to talk.' He walked over to one of his men, undid the tie at his neck and tossed it to her. 'Just tie up your friend and keep him under control.'

'Take it easy, Mike,' Emily said to the dog as she attached the tie to his collar. 'They won't hurt you again.'

When Mike was restrained, Emily returned to Joel's side. 'What are you doing here?' she demanded.

The agent shrugged. 'Do you think you're the only one who knows the significance of that golden box? When we discovered what it could do, we knew you'd have to come for it. From the moment you arrived at the temple, we've been watching you.' He chuckled softly. 'That was a clever move with the car on the pavement. But I'm afraid we've had to remove it. We can't have the local police asking too many questions.'

'I don't understand.' Emily said. 'How did you know about the box?'

'We're the Central Research Unit. If someone sneezes, we know about it.'

Emily's heart pounded in her chest. They were losing precious time. Pegasus's life was depending on her and she didn't have time to play games with the CRU. She summoned the Flame again and raised her hand threateningly. 'We don't have time for this. Just hand over the box and we'll go.'

Agent B shook his head. 'You can kill us, Emily, but it won't change anything. The box isn't here.'

'Where is it?'

'Gone.'

'Gone where?'

The agent was in no hurry as he started to explain. 'The moment that box was opened at the Temple of Poseidon, it killed all the clones we'd had stored around the world. No matter what we did or how we tried to protect them, they all died.'

'There were more clones?' Joel asked in astonishment.

'Of course,' the agent said. 'Come now, Joel, don't be naive. You really didn't think the CRU would put all its eggs in one basket? They were created at the Area 51 facility, but then moved on. We had over two dozen in our UK facility alone. Unfortunately, due to the

144

death of all the clones, the entire programme has been mothballed.'

'However,' Agent B continued, 'it wasn't a complete loss. After a bit of investigation, we learned about the golden box discovered here in Greece. At first we thought it was the box itself. It really is a piece of art – I'll have to show it to you sometime. We've moved it to one of our facilities in the States. That and the archaeologists who found it.'

Agent B focused on Stella. 'Actually, Stella, your parents and George Tsoukatou are on their way there right now.' He paused and checked his watch. 'They should be landing in a few hours.'

'No!' Stella cried. 'Who are you?'

Agent B pretended to be hurt. 'Emily, you didn't tell Stella who we are and about all the fun we've had together?'

Emily's nerves were ready to snap. 'Where – is – the – box?' she said. 'Tell me now before I lose my temper!'

'Calm down, Emily, I'm getting to that,' Agent B said. 'After some testing, we discovered that the box itself wasn't the prize. The real treasure was the rock inside. When we saw what it did to our clones, we wondered what it might do to real Olympians. So we took the last of the blood from Diana and Paelen and exposed it to the rock. Do you want to know what happened? It was destroyed – turned to dust. Poof – and it was gone!'

Emily felt a heavy lump form in the pit of her stomach. The CRU knew what the rock could do. They now possessed the Titan weapon.

'Where is it?' she demanded. 'What have you done with it?'

'Us?' Agent B said innocently. 'We haven't done anything with it. When we realized what it could do and how dangerous it was, we decided we didn't want anything like that on our planet. So we sent it away.'

'Where?' Emily shrieked.

The agent crossed his arms over his chest and smiled smugly.

Emily suddenly realized he was playing for time. The CRU were planning something. Maybe he was waiting for back-up. 'Tell me right now, or I swear you'll regret it!'

'I told you to calm down before you blow a gasket,' the agent continued. 'You really are quite impatient. But let me tell you something funny. When Pegasus first arrived in New York, our agents found a strange little blue jewel in the stable where you stole that carriage. No one thought much of it at the time. After

146

all, they did have bigger problems, with the Nirads running amok in the city. But then, quite by accident, our scientists discovered its secrets.'

Emily looked desperately over to Joel and could see he was thinking the same thing. The agent was too calm. Too in control and filled with his own self-importance.

'What did you do with the rock?' Joel demanded.

'The only thing we could do. We used that strange little blue jewel to send it back where it belongs,' Agent B paused and smiled cruelly.

'We sent it to Olympus.'

17

'What?' Emily spat. 'You didn't!'

'We did,' Agent B said. 'Not too long ago either. From early reports, there were no survivors. Earth will not have to worry about the Olympians coming here again. You are all that remain of those ancient people.'

'No!' Emily cried. 'You couldn't. You just couldn't. Not even the CRU would destroy an entire race . . .'

'We could and we did,' the agent said. 'It's over, Emily. You have no choice but to join us now. What we started at Area 51 will continue. Without the Olympians around to distract you, we can work together. Before long, you and I will be the closest of friends.'

'Never,' Emily uttered.

'We'll see about that,' Agent B said. 'Now come along, there's transport waiting outside the museum to take us to London. Together we will bring order to this troubled world. And you, my dear Emily, you will be the ultimate weapon against those who oppose us.'

'Ultimate weapon?' Emily whispered. 'You think of me as a weapon?'

The agent nodded. 'What else are you but an Olympian weapon? From the reports I've read, you're not even alive.'

'No!' Emily insisted. 'I'm not a weapon. I'm a person. Do you hear me? Not a weapon!'

Learning about her origins with the Xan, watching Jupiter and the others die, seeing her beloved Pegasus ageing by the moment and finally learning that the CRU had used the Solar Stream to launch the weapon against Olympus – it was all too much.

Something in Emily snapped.

'I AM A PERSON!'

Emily threw back her head and roared as her body temperature climbed higher than she had ever felt it. She had never known such fury before. Even when the Gorgons threatened everyone she loved, she had been able to keep control. But hearing what the CRU had done was more than she could take. Flames shot wildly from her hands, her eyes and her mouth as her powers surged and she lost all control.

Wild fires flashed around the room, shooting up through the ceiling, through all the levels of the Acropolis Museum and high into the night sky above Athens.

Emily's furious burning eyes turned on the CRU agents. One by one, they blinked out of existence. Behind her, she heard Joel calling her name and begging her to stop. But Emily couldn't stop. More agents burst into the room and opened gunfire. But not one bullet touched her or Joel, Stella or the dog. The Flame was unleashed and free. But for all the damage it was doing to the museum and Athens around it, it was protecting those she cared for.

Her emotions were too raw and too wild to contain the maelstrom of the Flame. Pain that she had kept locked deep inside was all coming out now. She could feel her powers spreading out, incinerating the museum and beyond.

'Emily, stop!' Joel cried.

But Emily could not stop.

'Riza,' Joel shouted, 'please stop Emily before it's too late!'

Deep within, Emily felt Riza calling to her and struggling for control. *'Let it go, Emily,'* Riza told her. *'Let the hurt and pain go! There is another way, I promise you. You are still too young for all these powers. You do not understand what you can do. Please, do not destroy this world. Pull it back. Pull the power back.'*

Riza's words cut through her rage. 'Destroy the

world?' What did she mean?

She focused on Riza's calm tone and found a moment of clarity to cling on to. She began to steady the power coming from deep within her and slowly regained control. She soon managed to pull her powers back into herself.

Emily collapsed to her knees, panting heavily. As her senses cleared, she could smell thick, choking smoke and hear the sound of breaking glass, groaning structures and roaring flames.

'We're surrounded,' Joel cried, wracked by coughing. 'There's no way out!'

They were trapped in an inferno. Flames were still burning wildly around them as the museum went up in a huge fireball. But her powers were surrounding and protecting them.

Joel pulled out the blue jewel from his tunic pocket and held it up. 'Olympus!' he choked. 'Take us to Olympus!'

The Solar Stream opened and cut a path through the roaring flames. Joel caught hold of Stella's wheelchair and started to move. 'Come on,' he yelled. 'Before the whole place comes crashing down on us!'

18

They emerged from the Solar Stream into the heart of Olympus. Joel released Stella and fell to the ground, coughing and gasping for air. Stella was barely conscious and slumped in her wheelchair. Mike lay down beside them, panting heavily.

Emily watched Joel struggling to get his breath and realized she was fine. Yet the others were all suffering and trying to breathe.

'Joel?' Emily knelt down beside him. 'Are you OK?'

He was still coughing as he sat up. 'Just need air.'

'What happened?'

He looked at her in disbelief. 'Are you serious?'

Emily could only recall fragments of the past few moments. Agent B saying they had launched the Titan weapon on Olympus and how they planned to use her as some kind of ultimate weapon. Then she remembered the pain. The unbearable, searing pain of loss and then, finally, uncontained fury.

'I nearly destroyed the world . . .' Emily whispered. She looked down at her trembling hands. 'I couldn't stop it. I nearly destroyed the world and I just couldn't stop!'

She began to rock back and forth as she realized what had happened. 'I can't do it any more,' she cried. 'Please, someone, take these powers away from me!'

From deep within her, Emily felt Riza's calm presence hovering near. *'I am so sorry, Emily. But I cannot. The powers of the Xan are yours now. But you can learn to control them. I promise you can.'*

Joel was by her side. 'It will be OK, Em,' he said softly, holding her now. 'We're all safe. You didn't destroy the world. You pulled it back before it went too far. You do have control.'

'No I don't!' Emily cried. 'It was Riza. She stopped it, not me.'

'It was both of us,' Riza called.

Emily clung to Joel as though he was the only life raft in a raging sea. 'Don't let me lose control again . . .' she whispered into his chest.

'I won't,' he promised softly and squeezed her tighter. 'I'll always be there to help you, Em, no matter what.'

Joel held Emily until her trembling calmed. As she

took deep cleansing breaths, he smiled at her gently. 'Better?'

Emily nodded.

'Then come on. Let's look around and see if there's anyone left alive.'

Emily gazed around sadly and became aware of the painful silence. Not even the wind blew.

The marble buildings of Olympus were still intact, beautiful and untouched. As were the tall statues lining the roads and all the other art around them. But there was not a single living thing left alive. The trees were all dead. The grass beneath them was gone. Only dust remained.

'It's all gone,' she said softly. 'The CRU really did it. They destroyed what was left of Olympus.'

'Please, those men have taken my family. I must go back.' It was Stella, now fully awake, looking shell-shocked.

Emily felt the weight of responsibility resting heavily on her shoulders. She knew how Stella felt. Emily's own father had been a prisoner of the CRU not so very long ago. She nodded. 'We will, I promise. They won't have your parents for long.'

Joel nodded. 'But we need to look for survivors first.'

Mike came up to Emily, wagging his tail. 'Don't

worry, you're coming too,' she said softly, patting his head.

They made their way to Jupiter's palace. Suddenly the dog cocked his head to the side and the hackles on his back rose. He started to growl.

Emily knelt down beside him. 'What is it, boy?'

The low rumbling growl continued as Joel stopped to listen. 'Wait, I think I hear something too. It's coming from inside the palace.'

They headed towards the back entrance of Jupiter's palace. 'Wait here,' Emily said to Stella, handing her the dog's lead. 'We'll be right back.'

They climbed the stairs and cautiously approached the open doors. Inside was a large group of men pulling off what looked like bulky white spacesuits. Others, still in their white suits, were descending the marble stairs into the grand foyer. They removed their helmets. 'All clear on the upper levels,' one man reported. 'We found where the Jacobs family and DeSilva live, but there is no sign of the father or aunt. They're not here. Is it possible they died with the others?'

'I don't think so,' the commander on the main floor said. 'They're human and the weapon is harmless to us. It's more likely they're in hiding. Take a team and tear this place apart. We need them as hostages to control the girl.' He turned to another of his men. 'Agent S, call all the units. Let them know the air is breathable. Have them meet us back here at base. We need to coordinate the search for Emily's family.'

Turning to another he said, 'Agent T, get back to Earth and start sending the development teams, trucks and equipment. Tell command Olympus is ours. The CRU can start setting up operations from here.'

Inside the large foyer, another man emerged from the council chamber. 'Hey Captain, in here! You aren't going to believe this. There's another room filled with strange stuff and there's an arch that opens the space tunnel.'

Emily and Joel looked at each other. 'Xanadu!' Joel gasped.

'No,' Emily whispered. 'We can't let them use the portal to find Xanadu. We've got to destroy it.'

'How?' Joel asked. 'Look at all the men in there. I bet there are even more scattered around here. What are we going to do? Kill them all?'

Emily shook her head and walked down the stairs to Stella. 'No way! I won't use my powers against them. Not after what happened at the museum!'

'Then we are going to need a distraction,' Stella offered calmly. 'Emily, you must use your powers, but

156

not directed at them. Destroy something big that will call them out of there. Then we can capture them.'

Both Emily and Joel looked at Stella in shock.

Stella frowned. 'What? Just because I'm in this wheelchair doesn't mean I'm stupid. You promised to save my family and you are going to keep that promise. Even if it means you use your powers again.'

'She's right,' Joel agreed. 'We only need a few seconds to get in there. Then we can destroy the portal to Xanadu and use our jewels to get away.'

They crept further away from the palace and peered up to the highest level of the left wing. 'Up there.' Emily pointed. 'Our apartment, it's on the other side of the palace. If I destroy it, we should have time to get into the artifact chamber before they find us.'

'Do it,' Joel said.

Emily raised her hands and pointed at the beautiful structure that had once been the home she shared with her father, Joel, Paelen and Pegasus. All her favourite things were in there, all her best memories born there.

'Forgive me, Jupiter,' Emily said sadly as she released a powerful stream of Flame. It shot up into the same bedroom window she and Pegasus always used during their night flights.

Commanding her powers, she imagined them

swirling around her bedroom like a tornado. Letting the Flame build and build, it turned into a ferocious, self-contained fire storm. When the swirling flames overflowed out of the window, Emily let go. 'Now!'

A massive explosion tore the roof off and blew out the entire side of the elegant building. Tall, sparkling while marble columns crashed to the ground and the whole palace shuddered.

'Amazing!' Stella cried.

The sound of loud voices seemed to come from everywhere as soldiers and CRU agents ran to investigate the explosion. They came from the dead gardens, from the buildings around the palace and all over the area. The scientists within the palace itself ran out and followed the others.

'Look how many there are!' Emily cried. 'It's too many to capture!'

'Forget them,' Joel called. 'Let's move!'

Keeping hidden behind a long row of statues, they carried Stella's wheelchair up the stairs and entered the evacuated palace. Making it to the artifact chamber, they saw scientific equipment had been set up before the arch.

'They weren't wasting any time!' Joel said. 'Destroy it now, before they come back.'

Joel pushed Stella to the back of the room as Emily faced the arch. It had only been built a few days ago, but already, it seemed like an eternity. She raised both her hands and released her powers directly at the portal.

The moment her powers touched the arch, the Solar Stream opened. In that same instant, the marble stones exploded and flew into the open stream of light. Without the arch to contain its power, the Solar Stream started to pulse and swell. It expanded to fill the room.

Suddenly the tables of artifacts from Xanadu flew across the chamber and were sucked into the Solar Stream. The slate board with the writing of the ancients followed.

Mike's lead was wrenched from Joel's hand and he flew, howling, into the heart of the Solar Stream. Stella's screams followed as she was sucked in. Joel reached for Emily as she tried to use her powers as protection, but the force of the Solar Stream was greater.

'No!' Emily cried as she and Joel were lifted off the floor and pulled into the powerful blazing light.

19

Every other time they had travelled within the Solar Stream, it had been a contained and managed flight. This time, Emily, Joel and what appeared to be the whole of Jupiter's palace, was tumbling madly through it without any control.

As the moments ticked by, the palace structure began to come apart. Huge chunks of wall, roof and column spun madly around them. Emily used her powers to deflect most of the fragments, but they were still being struck by large pieces of marble, statues and furniture.

'Emily,' Joel shouted, still clinging to her, 'do something before it kills us.'

'What?'

'Use your powers, stop us—' Joel had not even finished speaking when a large chunk of wall struck him in the head. Knocked unconscious, he became limp in Emily's arms.

'Joel!' Emily cried as she felt him slipping away from her grasp. She closed her eyes and concentrated harder than she ever had in her life. 'Xanadu!' she shouted. 'Get us to Xanadu!'

Emily and Joel were suddenly slammed against a stone floor.

Emily rolled over, panting heavily. 'Thank you.'

She sat up. They were in a dark and cool place. The smell of damp moss filled the air and reminded her of the Temple of Arious. Lighting one hand, Emily saw the familiar stone walls of the temple. She reached for Joel with the other. 'Joel, talk to me. Are you OK?'

Joel moaned. He had a deep, bleeding gash on his forehead and his nose was broken. Emily reached out and touched his face to heal his wounds.

He sat up slowly and gazed around. 'Where are we?'

Emily said, 'I think we're back in the temple on Xanadu. I didn't have much time to concentrate.'

'That was insane,' Joel said, rubbing his head. 'It felt like half of Olympus came through with us. I never realized the Solar Stream was so powerful.'

'Me neither,' Emily agreed. Suddenly she remembered. 'Stella and Mike are still in there! They'll be crushed. I've got to go back and get them!'

Joel pulled her back down. 'Emily, calm down. They went through before the Solar Stream sucked in the palace. They're ahead of it. If they keep moving, they'll be fine.'

'And what about when they arrive?'

After a moment, Joel understood. 'It's all coming right behind them. The palace and all that debris are coming here!' He rose quickly and reached for Emily's hand. 'C'mon, we've got to get to the arch before it kills everyone!'

When Emily and Joel emerged from the temple, they stopped short. Her father and aunt stood with the CRU agents from the museum. Further back, the Olympians were eyeing the agents as if they were ready to pounce on the men at any moment.

'Dad!' Emily and Joel ran up to him. Her eyes landed on Agent B and her temper flared. 'What are you doing here?'

The agent's dark curly hair was a mess and his face looked dirty and singed from the fire. He smelled of smoke. 'I'm wondering the same thing,' he said shakily. 'I don't know whether to thank you for saving us from the fire, or to shoot you for trying to kill us.'

Emily raised her flaming hand. 'Just try it!'

'No one is going to shoot anyone here,' her father ordered. 'We heard cries and found these men in the temple. Did you send them here?'

'Not by choice,' Emily said furiously.

Diana, Apollo and Chiron were standing back. 'Will someone please tell us what has happened?' Diana said. 'Emily, did you destroy the weapon?'

Emily shook her head. Then her eyes landed back on Agent B. 'No, we didn't because *he* already sent it to Olympus!'

Everyone turned to Agent B.

'It wasn't me,' Agent B challenged. 'I was assigned to capture Emily and Joel, that's all. It was the others in command who did it!'

'It does not matter who did it,' Chiron said as his hooves pounded the ground in rage. 'You have destroyed our people and our home. How did you do it? How did you get the weapon to Olympus?'

Agent B crossed his arms over his chest and refused to speak.

Emily glared at him. 'The CRU found Diana's jewel in New York and once they figured out how to use the Solar Stream, they sent the weapon to Olympus. We just came from there. It killed everything. People, animals, plants, even the insects are gone. Now the

CRU are setting up bases and have claimed Olympus for themselves.'

'No!' Diana said. 'It is my fault. Our world is dead because of me. If I had not lost my jewel, they could not have taken Olympus.'

'No, Diana,' Emily's father said as his hard eyes fell on the CRU agents. 'It's their fault. Not yours.'

'We did what we had to, to protect Earth,' Agent B said. 'You Olympians are a deadly infection. We had to cut deep to save our world!'

'Don't you start with that!' Emily shot back. 'I've heard all about the CRU's plans from Agent P.S. back at Area 51. You are going to take over the world.'

'Change the world,' Agent B insisted. 'For the better.'

'Change it or take it over, it's all the same!' Emily shot back. 'But we won't let you do it! Do you hear me? We're going to stop you!'

'Emily, calm down,' her father said. He looked at his sister. 'Mo, would you and the others take the agents away before Emily really loses her temper?'

Maureen nodded. 'Good idea.' She and several ageing Olympians moved forward to collect the CRU agents. 'I think it's about time you saw all the damage you've done to these people. You are all going to help us take care of them.'

Emily noticed that, in the time they had been gone, Diana and the others had aged even more. Diana's hair was now white and thin. Deep age lines cut across her face.

Emily's eyes scanned the area fearfully. 'Where's Pegasus?'

A whinny from behind let her know that Pegasus was there. She turned and what she saw made her gasp. Pegasus's back sloped deeply and his wings hung down at his sides as he walked slowly towards her. But he whinnied excitedly and called to her.

'Pegs!' Emily ran up to the stallion and embraced him tightly. 'Olympus is gone. The CRU have taken it!' She pressed her face into his warm thick neck and was grateful that at least he was still alive.

Paelen was being supported by Brue as he approached Joel. His hair was grey and he was even more hunched over. 'What happened to you?' he asked loudly. 'You are covered in blood. I knew I should have gone with you. You cannot be trusted on your own!'

'You couldn't have stopped this.' Joel spoke loudly enough for Paelen to hear. 'I was hit by a piece of Jupiter's palace. It's in the Solar Stream and on its way here right now.'

165

'What?' Emily's father cried. 'Jupiter's palace is coming here?'

Emily and Joel explained everything that had happened from the point when they left Xanadu and travelled to Earth to when they returned.

'We didn't realize how powerful the Solar Stream was,' Emily said. 'If we had stayed in it, we'd have been killed. I'm just glad my powers worked and got us back here.'

Chiron shook his head and muttered softly to himself. The hair on his horse's body was now white. The top of his head was bald, his face heavily wrinkled and his upper man's torso sunken.

'This is bad – very, very bad indeed,' he said. He started to pace the area. 'I told Jupiter building a permanent portal would be disastrous. The Solar Stream is too powerful, too dangerous to be contained. But would he listen to me? No. After all, who am I? Just his half-brother – why should he listen to anything I had to say!'

'Chiron, stop,' Diana said. 'What is happening?'

The centaur shook his head. 'It is far more than just the palace coming here. In destroying the arch at the other end, Emily destroyed the containment field. There is nothing to stop the Solar Stream from sucking in the whole world. Olympus is now on a collision course with Xanadu.'

'What?' Emily cried. 'No, that's not possible.'

Chiron nodded. 'It is not only possible, it is what is happening. If the Xanadu arch opens, what is left of Olympus will come smashing through it.'

'Emily, you must destroy the arch,' Apollo cried. 'Right now, before it all gets here.'

'But Stella is still in there,' Emily argued. 'I can't. Not until she and the dog are safe.'

'It's too dangerous,' Chiron insisted. 'Stella must be sacrificed for the good of Xanadu.'

Emily shook her head. 'I won't do it. Not until Stella is safe. It's because of us that her parents have been taken by the CRU. I promised her I would save them, and I will.'

Pegasus whinnied and nodded his head.

'Your faith in Emily is admirable, old friend,' Chiron said to Pegasus. 'But I do not agree. Emily must destroy the arch now.'

Joel shook his head. 'Stella and the dog were sucked in before everything else. They'll arrive before the rest. If we clear the area around the arch and wait, the moment they come through, Emily can destroy it.'

'No, no, no,' Chiron insisted. 'You are gambling

with the lives of everyone here. The risk to Xanadu is too great.'

'*All life is precious, Chiron.*' Riza spoke softly from Emily's mouth. '*We can do this. All will be well. Stella and the dog will survive and Xanadu will be safe.*'

'Riza, are you sure?' Emily's father said.

Emily nodded. 'We both are.'

Paelen tutted and muttered, 'I still do not like it when you do that, Emily.'

For the rest of the night, those that could work shifted those who could not move away from the arch. The CRU agents had been stripped of their weapons and forced to help with the move.

When the area was clear, Emily stood beside Pegasus stroking his neck.

'I'm so scared, Pegs,' Emily admitted. 'My powers keep growing, but not my control over them.'

She told the stallion of her loss of control at the Acropolis Museum and her fear that if Riza hadn't stopped her, she would have destroyed Earth.

Pegasus pressed his head to her.

There was little Pegasus or anyone could say or do that would ease Emily's troubled mind. They could never understand how she felt. Or how she could feel the power's strength increasing. What was she turning into? She hated to even consider it, but was she becoming what Agent B had called her – a weapon?

All night they waited, prepared for Stella's arrival at any moment.

'Remember what Chiron told you,' Emily's father said. 'The moment Stella and the dog come through, no matter what condition they're in, you ignore them. Fire everything you've got at the arch. If all goes well, it will close the Solar Stream before everything else gets here.'

Agent B shook his head. 'I think the centaur was right. It is too dangerous to wait for the girl. Emily, you must destroy that thing right now. Your sentimentality will get us all killed.'

Emily raised a threatening finger to the agent. 'Don't you dare tell me what to do; I am this close to showing you how I feel about you and your men!'

'Em, calm down,' her father said as he put his arm around her. 'Ignore him. Just concentrate on what you need to do. Don't let anything distract you.'

Emily nodded. Neither had the heart to say what would happen if she failed. They already knew. The entire debris field, which could actually be all of Olympus, would tear through the arch and destroy Xanadu.

'Get ready,' Diana warned.

Everyone gathered closely together. There was no point hiding from the arch. If this went wrong, no matter where they hid, the collision of the two worlds would be catastrophic.

'You can do this, Em,' Joel said. 'We're right behind you.'

Emily looked back at him and Paelen and smiled weakly. She turned back to the arch and waited.

Suddenly the arch burst to life with the blazing light of the Solar Stream. 'Here we go!' Chiron called. 'Emily, fire the moment the girl comes through. Do not hesitate!'

Fear coursed through Emily like an electric current. Her nerves were ready to snap. What if she couldn't save them?

'*Calm yourself, child,*' Riza called softly. '*I am with you. We are one. We will save them together.*'

For the first time since she became aware of Riza's presence, Emily was grateful to her. She took a deep breath and felt herself calming as she waited for Stella.

Loose objects from the artifact chamber at Jupiter's

palace began to fly through the arch, forcing everyone to duck and dive to avoid being struck by the flying objects.

And then came the dog. Mike yelped and howled as he flew wildly through the air. Emily's father lunged forward and caught him mid-air and they tumbled to the ground together. Stella, still in her wheelchair, followed close behind. Her cries filled the air as she cartwheeled through the arch. An elderly giant ran forward and caught hold of her before she slammed into a thick tree.

'Now!' Chiron cried. 'Fire!'

Emily reacted instantly. She released the Flame at the arch, using all the power and control she had. With the blazing light of the Solar Stream still open, the two powers met in an explosive union. Sparks filled the air and the crackling sound of energy was deafening. As Emily fed more power into the Flame, pieces of palace debris continued to shoot through the arch.

'*Push harder!*' Riza called. '*Focus and push. Command the Solar Stream to close!*'

Emily did as Riza suggested. She focused and pushed her powers as hard as she could.

There was a blinding snap and brilliant whoosh.

The marble arch was gone.

The Solar Stream closed.

A cheer rang out. Emily fell to her knees, exhausted from the strain. 'Thank you, Riza,' she panted softly. 'Thank you . . .'

The world around her started to spin and finally went dark.

20

Emily opened her eyes, grateful to see Pegasus settled on the ground beside her. She was lying on a blanket under the shade of a tall jungle tree. The sun was high, so she must have slept most of the day.

'Hi Pegs,' she said softly as she stroked the stallion's neck and soft muzzle.

Mike was on the other side of her with his large head lying on her legs. He whined when Emily looked at him. 'Hey, boy,' she said as she patted his head.

'That dog hasn't left your side since I carried you here,' her father said as he knelt down beside her. 'Joel told me you've called him Mike.' He smiled. 'He does remind me of your mom's dog.'

Emily smiled at the dog. 'That's what I thought.'

'So, how are you feeling?'

'Really tired,' Emily said.

'I don't doubt it after everything you've been through.'

Emily sat up and looked around. The makeshift camp was crowded, with very little in the way of shelters or supplies. She saw Joel with Paelen and Stella. They were petting Brue's two heads. Chrysaor was lying on the ground beside Joel.

Emily was stunned to see Agent B kneeling down beside the Muse, Terpsichore, and helping her to drink a cup of nectar. Other CRU agents worked among the ageing Olympians, helping to feed them.

'Dad, what happens now? We can't return to Olympus and we really can't take everyone to Earth, it would be too dangerous for them.'

Her father dropped his head. 'None of us can go anywhere, any more. We're all trapped here.'

Emily shook her head. 'No, Joel and I have our blue jewels. We can still open the Solar Stream.'

'I didn't want to tell you this until you were feeling better, but I doubt there will ever be a good time.'

Fear coursed through her. 'Tell me what?'

'Chiron insists the Solar Stream must never be opened again.'

'Why?'

'He believes the debris field is still in there, waiting to be released.'

'But I destroyed the arch,' Emily cried. 'It

can't come to Xanadu.'

'Yes,' he agreed. 'But the Solar Stream is massive. It's like a giant, powerful river. The direct route to Xanadu that Jupiter and his brothers created was just an off-shoot of that river. Chiron believes the debris field will continue to scatter and travel the length of the whole Solar Stream waiting for a place to finally come to shore. If we open it, there is a strong chance it will come through. Or even if it doesn't, anyone who tries to travel within it risks being hurt or even killed by the debris.'

Emily frowned. 'What about Earth? What happens if the CRU uses their blue jewel again? Will Earth be destroyed?'

'Let's not even go there,' her father said. 'I just pray for the sake of the planet they don't.'

Emily lay back down. 'I really messed up, didn't I? If I hadn't destroyed the arch on Olympus, we could have left here.'

'No one blames you. You did what you thought was best. You couldn't let the CRU find Xanadu, everyone understands that. Unfortunately, none of us realized what would happen once the arch was destroyed.'

Emily leaned forward and kissed Pegasus's soft muzzle. 'At least we destroyed the rock and stopped it from doing any more damage to you. We'll find a way to live here. Just as long as everyone is all right, that's all that matters.'

Her father sat back on his heels. 'I'm so sorry, Em. But you didn't destroy the rock. The Titan weapon is still in the Solar Stream. Even now, it's ageing everyone.'

Emily's eyes shot straight to her father. 'No! That's not possible. It was destroyed with Olympus.'

He shook his head. 'No, it wasn't. Look at Pegasus. He's still ageing.'

Emily stared at Pegasus and noticed the fallen feathers scattered around him. The pearling in his eyes was thicker than before.

'You mean this was all for nothing?' Emily cried. 'Going back to Earth and losing control of my powers – it was all for nothing! The CRU have finally won. The Olympians are dying and we're trapped on this jungle world with no way back to Earth.'

'Stop it, Emily.'

'But, Dad, I've ruined everything.'

'I said, stop,' her father said firmly. 'You tried your best. The Olympians were doomed the moment that box was opened. You had no control over that.'

Pegasus nickered in agreement and pressed his face to her.

'I should have been able to stop it!' Emily cried. 'I'm the Flame of Olympus, the last Xan! What's the point of all these powers if I can't protect the Olympians?' She climbed to her feet. 'I won't lose you, Pegasus! Not now and not ever. There has to be something I can do. I have Riza's powers. I'll use them all up if I have to, but I won't let you die! Do you hear me, Pegasus, you won't die!'

Emily ran into the temple. There had to be an answer locked somewhere deep within the thick stone walls. Some way to save them. It couldn't end like this.

'Why, Riza?' she shouted through the long, empty corridors. 'Why give me all these powers and not let me save them. It's not fair!'

Emily collapsed to the stone floor. Pegasus was dying. Paelen was dying. Diana and Apollo were both dying.

But it was the thought of losing her beloved Pegasus that cut the deepest. Life on Xanadu without him would be unbearable. She'd believed she had lost him once, back at Area 51, and that had nearly destroyed her. But at least, she'd thought it had been fast and painless. This was so much worse. Pegasus was in pain. He tried his best to hide it, but she could feel it from him.

'Please, Riza,' she begged, 'help him. I'll do anything you say. I'll let you take over my body, just save Pegasus.'

Riza stirred and Emily could feel her sympathy. *'I am so sorry, child. I love Pegasus too, but we cannot save him. Not even the Xan could stop time from running its course. Were he wounded, we could heal him. But this is age. It is natural. When the Xan lived, we existed outside of the boundaries of time. But still, we could not interfere with it, even if the Titans used it as a weapon. Pegasus will continue to grow old and then he will die.'*

'No!' Emily cried. 'I can't lose him. I just can't . . .'

It was the helplessness that hurt the most – to be so powerful, and yet so powerless.

'Em,' Joel called softly through the darkness.

He arrived at her side and pulled her into his arms. 'Vulcan just died. He and Stella were talking and he just collapsed and died.'

'I'm so sorry, Joel,' Emily said, holding him tighter.

'After everything we've fought for . . .' Joel's voice broke.

They clung to each other as they grieved over the losses they'd suffered and the impending loss of those they loved most. 'Paelen is like my brother,' Joel whispered. 'I lost my family in that car crash years ago, I can't lose him too.'

'There has to be a way,' Emily said. 'It can't end like this, it just can't.'

'But what can we do?'

'I don't know. But we have to try.' She pulled away from Joel and looked around. 'The Xan were the most powerful beings in the universe. Surely there is something they can show us.'

'*There is nothing to find here,*' Riza said.

'That's not good enough, Riza!' Emily climbed to her feet and reached for Joel's hand. 'If they have to die, it won't be without a fight. Help me, Joel. We'll tear this place apart if we have to. We must find a way to save them.'

Every day brought with it another loss. Emily, Pegasus, Joel and Paelen stood together at Chiron's funeral pyre. The ancient centaur had died peacefully in the night. No one said a word. There was nothing to be said. Each Olympian knew a pyre waited for them. It was only a matter of time.

Venus and Mars had passed two days before. At the loss of his mother, Cupid was inconsolable. The following day, the winged Olympian slipped silently into the dense jungle and hadn't been seen since.

After Chiron's funeral, Emily and Pegasus walked

away from the camp. The stallion's head hung low and he moved slower. Emily had discovered that when she touched him the pain was eased – even though the ageing process would not slow.

'I miss flying with you, Pegs,' she said sadly as she stroked his warm neck. 'Xanadu is so beautiful and yet we've seen nothing.'

Pegasus dropped a wing to invite Emily on to his back.

'No, I'm too heavy for you now.'

Sadness filled the stallion's eyes as he accepted that he was now too old and weak to carry her. 'Wait Pegs, I've got an idea. Let me carry you for once.'

Emily put her arms around his neck and focused her powers. They lifted off the ground and rose higher in the brilliant blue sky. 'I've been way too scared to try this,' she admitted. 'But Joel always said I could do it. Fly with me, Pegasus!'

Pegasus opened his wings and let the gentle winds of Xanadu blow through his remaining feathers. Emily supported him and moved them over the lush green jungle.

'It's just us, Pegs, for ever,' she said, trying to keep the tremble out of her voice.

Beside her, Pegasus whinnied in joy and raised his

head proudly in the air. He flapped his wings, knowing they weren't what were keeping him up. To Emily, he had never looked more beautiful.

Later that day, they returned to camp to hear that Diana had fallen down the temple stairs and broken several bones.

'Em, please help her,' her father said desperately. He was kneeling beside Diana's cot and holding her hand.

Emily saw his fear – the same she'd seen when her mother had become seriously ill. She suddenly realized just how much her father cared for the Olympian. It was much more than friendship.

'Please,' Apollo begged from the other side of his sister.

Diana's eyes were clenched shut in pain. Her face was pale and drawn and, for the first time since they'd met, she looked helpless.

'I'm here,' Emily said. She touched Diana and her powers began to work immediately as they knitted the broken bones back together and healed the internal injuries. After a few minutes, Diana sighed peacefully and fell into a deep, restful sleep.

'Thanks, Em,' her father said in relief.

'Yes, thank you,' Apollo added. 'I do not know what I would do without my sister.'

Apollo looked frail and delicate compared to the strong and powerful Olympian he had been just a few days ago. Emily's eyes returned to his twin sister. She realized neither of them had much time left.

'I've got to do something, Pegs,' Emily said as they walked away from the painful sight. 'I can't just stand by watching you all fade away.'

'*There is nothing to be done,*' Riza called.

'I don't believe you,' Emily shouted angrily to the empty air. 'You were the Xan! There has to be something.'

'*Come,*' Riza offered. '*It is time I showed you who we were. Learn, child. Learn the powers of the Xan and our limits.*'

Emily insisted on finding Joel first. 'Riza wants to show us something. Would you come with Pegs and me?' she asked when she found him.

'Sure,' Joel said. 'Do you think it will help Paelen and the others?'

Emily shook her head. 'Riza says there is nothing to be done. She's going to show us why.'

They walked together into the large temple. Emily spotted Agent B and two of his men in the entrance area and shot a black look in their direction. 'I really should have killed them at the museum.'

Pegasus nickered softly and nudged her.

'You don't mean that,' Joel agreed. 'Besides, we need their help with the others.'

'CRU agents helping Olympians? I would laugh if it wasn't so sad.'

Joel paused. 'Em, don't let anger change you. We're all going to be stuck here for a very long time. You're going to have to learn to get along with them.'

'Maybe,' Emily said bitterly. She looked up at Pegasus and stroked his face. 'But not until all the Olympians are gone. I just can't forgive what they did, Joel. Even if the weapon was going to kill everyone eventually, the CRU sped it up by sending it to Olympus.'

'You sound like me,' Joel said, 'before you and Pegasus came into my life. I was angry all the time too.'

'That was different.'

'Was it?' Joel asked.

They walked the rest of the way in silence as Riza directed them deeper into the temple. Emily's powers carried Pegasus down the steep steps and further along the twisting corridors than they had ever been before.

They eventually stopped at a solid wall. '*We hid our*

own origins in here,' Riza said aloud. '*This was our knowledge, not meant for others to see or learn.*'

Emily reached out her hand and touched a raised stone on the wall. 'Open.'

Dust and small pebbles rained down as a very tall, very thick door that hadn't been touched in thousands of years, groaned and slowly slid open.

'Wow!' Joel said as he walked into the room.

It looked nothing like the rest of the old stone temple. This room was massive, with shiny, silver metal walls. Bright lights shone from above and what looked like a huge computer console sat in the centre of the room.

'*This is Arious.*'

'Arious is a computer?' Joel asked.

'*She is more than a simple computer,*' Riza said. '*We gathered our collective knowledge here. This was our living archive. When we returned from a journey, we would insert ourselves into Arious and deposit what we learned. Then all the Xan would come and share the experience.*'

'So it became a single collective knowledge?' Joel asked.

'*That is correct.*'

'Were the Xan a tall people?' Joel asked as he looked up at the high ceiling and large deposit area.

'Everything here is so big and high.'

'*We were,*' Riza answered. '*We were mostly human in appearance, but much larger than you or the Olympians.*'

'Even larger than the giants?' Emily asked.

'*Not quite as large as the giants,*' Riza answered. '*Are you ready to learn?*'

'I am,' Emily agreed.

Emily moved forward into the receiver area. She looked back at Joel as Riza spoke. '*You and Pegasus must stay back. Emily will tell you what she learns, but you must not receive the knowledge directly.*'

Joel did as he was told and took several steps back to wait with Pegasus.

'*Emily, step forward and place your two hands on those raised platforms. The knowledge transfer will begin immediately.*'

Emily felt Riza retreat into her mind. She knew it would have to be her choice to receive the knowledge of the Xan. What was she about to learn? This moment would answer all the questions Emily had about herself. But now, as she stood on the threshold, she wasn't sure she really wanted to know.

Emily looked back at Pegasus. The ageing stallion was leaning heavily against the wall. 'For you, Pegs.'

She reached up and placed her hands on the two

receivers. At first, nothing happened. Then her eyes opened wider and Emily finally saw the Xan.

Their beauty stole her breath away. They were very tall and elegantly thin with extra-long, fine arms. They wore light, silken tunics that clung loosely to their tall frames. Though they were bald, their smooth faces were almost too lovely to behold and were filled with a kind of peaceful tranquility that Emily had never known before, yet somehow yearned to possess.

Their almond-shaped eyes held no colour and were like brightly shining pearls that contained the knowledge of the ages. In fact, everything about the Xan reminded Emily of living pearls. Their skin was smooth and held the iridescence of mother-of-pearl that changed colour as it caught the light.

The Xan didn't so much walk as appear to float in a kind of calm slow-motion. As they moved before her eyes, it was difficult to tell the men from the women. They were all magnificent.

The image changed and it was as though Emily *was* a Xan. Standing among them, she could feel how they felt. Experience the love and peace they held for all life. How the powers coursed through their fine bodies, enabling them to do anything. Manipulating all matter was easy. Time became inconsequential. Travel between worlds, simple. Enlarging Xanadu to make room for more species? It was a piece of cake!

Emily finally understood what it meant to be Xan.

But as the moments passed, things sped up. A sudden and sharp pain shot through Emily's head. The information was coming too quick to understand. Images of the past fired at her like rockets. Millions of worlds flashed before her eyes as she watched countless millennia pass by. It was like the most intense 3-D movie being shown in super-fast forward. The visions burned her eyes and cut through her like a knife. She thought her head was going to explode.

Emily started to scream.

'Em!' Joel cried.

'*No, Joel!*' Riza shouted as he ran to Emily. '*Do not touch us . . .*'

It was too late. Joel reached out to Emily. The sudden connection disrupted the flow as the information was now being shared between the two. Their joint cries of agony echoed throughout the temple as they both received the full, collective knowledge of the Xan.

21

Three days passed and Joel remained in a coma. When Emily awoke she had found Joel unconscious beside her. Pegasus had tried to wake him, but without success.

'Riza, what happened?' Emily had called. But there was no answer. If Riza was still with her, she would not speak or let her presence be known.

Paelen hadn't left Joel's side since Emily used her powers to carry Joel and Pegasus out of the temple. Brue was behind him, whining softly, and Stella would sit with them, watching Joel closely. Fear never left her eyes.

Emily made every attempt to use her healing powers to reach him. But nothing worked. He wouldn't wake up.

In her fear for Joel, Emily had been careless and left the door to Arious open. It hadn't taken long for Agent B and his men to find it. But when one of the CRU agents tried to acquire the knowledge, his mind had been shattered by the computer and he died shortly after.

The agent's death terrified Emily. Was the same thing going to happen to Joel? He too had received the knowledge of the ancients.

The Olympians continued to age and die around them. Emily no longer attended the pyre ceremonies. She felt too helpless. Since acquiring the knowledge of the Xan, she had learned that Riza was correct. For all their great powers, there was nothing the Xan could have done to halt the ageing process in the Olympians.

They were all doomed.

But Emily had gained something. The knowledge of how to control her powers. Those few moments within Arious had imparted to her a sudden understanding of how powerful she now was. But Emily would gladly have traded all her powers to save Joel and the Olympians.

Each day that passed saw Pegasus grow weaker. Chrysaor was now too old to walk more than a few metres. He settled at Joel's feet and had no intention of moving again.

By the start of the second week, Emily was dozing beside Joel when Mike jumped to his feet and barked excitedly. He leaped up on to Joel's chest and started to lick his face.

Startled awake, Emily shooed the dog away. It was then she noticed Joel's breathing had changed. As she watched his eyelids started to flutter.

'Joel!' Emily's cries reached her father and the CRU agents. 'He's waking up! Dad, Paelen, look, Joel is waking!'

Agent B knelt down beside him.

'Get away from him!' Emily snapped.

'Like it or not, Emily, I have medical training. We need every able-bodied human here if we are all to survive this. If I can help Joel, you won't stop me.'

'Let him check Joel over,' her father said, pulling Emily back.

Emily's heart pounded as Joel struggled back to consciousness.

'That's it,' Agent B said. 'Nice and easy, Joel, don't try too much at once.'

Joel's eyes fluttered open. 'Emily,' was his first, mumbled word.

'I'm here!' Emily cried. She leaned forward and kissed his cheek. 'Right here!'

He frowned and looked around. 'What – what happened? My head is killing me . . .'

Emily didn't know whether to laugh or cry. With so much sadness in the camp, so much loss, this was the first bit of joy in ages. 'You nuked yourself, you idiot!' she laughed. 'You touched me while I was in Arious. It zapped both of us.'

'Yes, you silly fool,' Paelen yelled. 'What were you trying to do? Kill yourself so you would not have to care for me? That is a poor way to get out of a bit of work.'

Joel suddenly sat up. 'The Xan!' he cried. 'I saw the Xan!'

'Calm down,' Agent B ordered. 'Lay back and rest. You've been in a deep coma and we don't know what damage has been done to you.'

'But I saw the Xan.' His eyes passed over everyone in the group. 'It was amazing. I saw everything . . .' Joel paused and frowned. 'But wait, I can't remember it all.'

Agent B said, 'We think the knowledge was too much for a human mind to take in. It's likely you have forgotten what you saw to protect yourself. You were fortunate to survive. One of my men wasn't so lucky.'

Joel frowned at the agent. 'That information wasn't meant for the CRU.'

'It wasn't meant for any human,' Agent B corrected.

191

'I can't remember it all either,' Emily said. 'It's been coming back to me in bits and pieces. I guess when you touched me, some information went to me and some went to you. All I do know is that Riza is gone.'

'Gone? Where?'

Emily shrugged. 'I don't know. But when I woke up, she wasn't there. I've tried calling to her, but she won't answer. I had hoped to recover her memories as well, but they weren't there. Arious just collects the big stuff, not details of personal life.'

Joel looked hopeful. 'Well, did we at least find a way to help everyone?'

Emily's eyes trailed over to Pegasus. Her voice became a whisper. 'No, Joel, there's nothing we can do.'

Joel closed his eyes, crushed by the information. 'So we just sit here and wait for everyone to die?'

No one answered. There was no need to.

'I just wish we had never found that stupid box,' Stella said. 'None of this would have happened. You would have all been on Olympus and I would be back with my parents.' Her angry eyes landed on Agent B. 'I don't care where you would have been!'

'It wasn't you,' Emily's father told her, 'or even the CRU who caused this. It was the Titans. If they hadn't created that weapon in the first place, there was no way it could have been found and used against the Olympians.'

Paelen shook his head. 'It is sad that we cannot go back and stop them.'

Everyone fell silent.

'Wait!' Emily rose and wandered away from the group, muttering softly. 'It will work! I can do it, I know I can. It will be dangerous. But I have the power . . .'

'Do what?' her father asked.

Emily's eyes flashed with excitement. She dashed back to Joel's side. 'Joel, we can do it!' she cried. 'I know how to stop the weapon! Why didn't I think of this before?'

Joel sat up. 'Em, what are you talking about?'

Emily started to jump up and down. 'I know how to save Pegasus and Paelen. We can save them all!'

'How?' her father demanded.

Emily ran to her father bursting with excitement. 'Arious showed me what to do. I have the power to send us back in time. We will go to ancient Greece and destroy that weapon before it can do any harm!'

22

'What?' her father cried.

'Yes!' Emily turned to Joel. 'The moment you are feeling better, I'll send us back to Cape Sounio. We'll destroy the weapon before it can be found. Then none of this will happen and everyone will live!'

Agent B shook his head. 'Time-travel is not possible. If it were, the CRU would have discovered it by now.'

Emily faced the CRU agent. 'No matter how big and powerful you think the CRU are, they could never be as powerful as the Xan. You can't do it, Agent B. But I can. And I've got proof.'

'What proof?' he demanded.

Emily looked at Stella. 'Tell them about the pots in the museum, the ones with Joel and me on them. You said they were from the past.'

'She's right!' Stella cried. She told the group about the two amphorae at the Acropolis Museum. 'They were from thousands of years ago. They even had Mike on them.'

Everyone looked at the dog beside Emily, excitedly wagging his tail.

'That proves we went back in time. We were there.'

Once again Agent B shook his head. 'It still won't work. Even if those pots prove you did go back in time, you obviously failed. The weapon still existed and Olympus was still destroyed. Us being trapped here proves that.'

'I don't know what happened,' Emily said. 'None of us do. But I've got to try – and you aren't going to stop me.'

'Agent B's right, Em,' her father said. 'Time-travel is impossible.'

'No it's not! Dad, the pots prove it. Now we know what's at stake, we'll be extra-careful.'

'OK,' her father surrendered, 'let's say it *is* possible. But it's too dangerous. We need you here, Em. You know this world. We don't.'

Emily shook her head. 'What about Diana? Dad, I know how you feel about her. I've seen you together.'

'Emily,' her father said quietly.

'It's OK,' she said. 'After Mom died, you were lonely. We both were. I know she would have loved

195

Diana and wouldn't want you to be alone. Neither do I. But if I don't try, Diana will die, just like Mom.'

'This isn't like fighting the CRU. Em, you're talking about time-travel. What if something goes wrong and you can't come back?'

'I know it will be dangerous,' Emily agreed. 'Until I entered Arious, I would never have considered it. But I've changed. The memories aren't all there yet, but they're coming. I know what powers I have and how to use them. I can do this.'

Emily paused and reached for his hands. 'Dad, it won't be Emily Jacobs going back there. It will be me – the new and improved Emily. I promise I will always be your little girl, but like it or not, I am also a fully powered Xan!'

The next day they were ready to go and the team was set.

Agent B was furious when Emily said he was not welcome. He claimed the mission was doomed to fail without him. But Emily refused and made it clear that she neither liked nor trusted the CRU agent.

Throwing up his arms in fury, Agent B stormed off into the jungle.

As everyone prepared to leave, Emily approached

her father. 'I guess this is it.'

There was fear in his eyes, but she knew he wouldn't try to stop her. He had opened up about his feelings for Diana and this was her only chance to survive.

'Promise me,' he said, 'promise me you'll be careful. Don't take any unnecessary risks. Just destroy that weapon and get right back here.'

'We will,' Emily promised.

She looked at her group of travellers. Joel was standing beside Paelen, who was seated on one of Brue's shoulders. Stella was in her wheelchair beside Pegasus. Mike, as always, was at Emily's side. 'Are we ready?'

Joel approached. 'It's up to you now, Em. What do you want us to do?'

'We all need to be connected.' Emily put one arm around Pegasus's neck and held Joel's hand with the other. Mike was lying on Emily's feet, panting softly. Soon everyone in the group was touching one another so that they were standing in one big circle.

'OK. Here we go.'

Emily took a deep breath and closed her eyes. Delving into the knowledge she had acquired from Arious, she focused her powers and commanded them to take them deep into the past; back to Earth, to the Temple of Poseidon at Cape Sounio.

As her powers surged, Emily felt the strangest sensations – almost like she was melting. She opened her eyes and could see everyone with her.

The world around them blurred. It became as though they were standing in the middle of a powerful waterfall. It didn't feel like they were moving at all. Instead, everything outside their circle was moving. Emily could no longer discern any clear shapes behind her friends. Loud whooshing sounds started to rise as they moved faster through time and space.

Suddenly something slammed violently into Emily's back. She was knocked forward and broke her physical connection with Joel and Pegasus. In that instant, the calm journey changed. It took all of her concentration just to keep everyone together. She could feel their terror and hear their screams as they somersaulted through time.

23

The journey ended as abruptly as it started. They came to a sudden stop on a very hard, smooth marble surface.

Emily was the first to open her eyes.

Pegasus was on the ground beside her, unconscious. His wings were open as though he'd been trying to fly. Emily crawled to him and stroked his neck and could feel his steady breathing.

Mike was awake and growled at a group of men staring at them. They were shirtless and wearing loin cloths. Their chests were bathed in sweat and covered with a film of marble dust. Crude cutting tools were in their hands as they stared and muttered quietly to themselves.

Several pillars rose high above them, looking fresh and new, while others were still in the process of being built. The entire area looked under construction. Overhead, the sun was shining brightly and Emily could taste sea-salt on her lips and hear the sea crashing around her from the bottom of the cliffs that surrounded them on three sides.

They were at Cape Sounio, that much was clear.

But the timing was all wrong. They were supposed to arrive long after the temple had been built and turned to ruins. Not during its construction. Emily shook her head, trying to figure out how she had got it so wrong.

Pegasus started to stir. He neighed softly and sat up.

'Take it easy, Pegs,' Emily whispered as she stroked him. 'Nice and slow. We're here. We're at Cape Sounio.'

Emily looked at Joel, who was waking. As she crawled over to him, her eyes landed on an unwelcome sight.

Agent B was sitting up and rubbing his head. He looked around in wonder. 'My God, it worked!' The CRU agent jumped to his feet and ran off the edge of the temple floor and down to the rocky ground. He approached the cliff edge and raised his hands in the air triumphantly. 'We're back on Earth!'

'What's he doing here?' Joel demanded as he wobbled unsteadily to his feet.

Emily shook her head. 'I don't know.' The others were just starting to stir. 'Check on Paelen and Stella.'

200

Emily stormed over to the CRU agent. 'How did you get here?'

Agent B grinned. 'The same way you did, I suspect. Considering you were the one who brought us here.'

'I didn't bring *you*!'

'True,' Agent B agreed. 'I hitched a ride at the last minute.'

'It was you!' Emily accused. 'You were the one who hit me in the back just as we were leaving. You broke my concentration. We could have all been killed!'

'It was a risk worth taking,' the agent defended. 'Though you did recover quite well.'

'Recover well?' Emily raged. 'Are you insane? Look around you. We're here at the wrong time. We were supposed to arrive after the temple was built, not before. Why did you do it? Do you really want this to fail?'

The agent shook his head. 'Just the opposite. I desperately need this mission to succeed, but it won't if I'm not here. I have experience and training in war situations.'

'What war? We've arrived here after the war. All I have to do is destroy the weapon and it's over. We didn't need you for that!'

'You can't be sure what you might encounter,'

Agent B said. 'You need me, you just won't admit it. Why won't you accept my help?'

Emily shook her head. 'How can you expect me to trust you after everything you've done?'

'Desperation is a powerful motivator,' Agent B said, brushing marble dust off his black jeans. 'If we destroy that weapon, it will be like hitting a reset button. I will be back in London, working at the CRU. You will be back on Olympus and none of this will have ever happened. We need never meet again.'

'That will happen anyway, with or without your help.'

'You can't be sure of that,' the CRU agent argued. 'Not with Pegasus distracting you.'

Emily gazed back at the temple. Pegasus was struggling to gain his feet on the smooth marble surface. She raised her hand and used her powers to lift him up. The stallion turned to her and nickered softly.

'See what I mean,' Agent B said. 'He's a distraction.'

Emily faced the agent and her expression darkened. 'Pegasus will never be a distraction. But you are! You make one move against us and I swear it will be the last thing you ever do. Let's just get this over and done with.'

'Agreed,' Agent B said.

They walked back to the temple together. Stella was attempting to speak with some of the locals.

'What's he doing here?' Joel demanded.

Emily explained and Joel was ready to kill Agent B. 'I guess there's nothing we can do about it now. But you try one more trick like that . . .' Joel warned.

'I know,' Agent B said, 'you'll kill me. Emily has already made that threat perfectly clear.'

Pegasus neighed softly.

Some of the construction workers were approaching him cautiously. Emily moved to the stallion's side and, when they set their eyes on her, they bowed their heads respectfully and smiled.

'I hardly believe this.' Stella returned with more of the men. 'They are very familiar with Zeus and all the gods. They have been visited by them. They truly believe in the gods and have accepted their presence on Earth. Our appearance here does not frighten them at all. They look at winged Pegasus as if they have known him always. Brue does not bother them!'

'Of course they accept us,' Agent B said. 'These people knew the Olympians were real. It's us in the modern age who stopped believing.'

'But what did they say?' Emily asked impatiently. 'Has Jupiter been here recently? Did they bury the weapon?'

'It is not good news,' Stella said. 'Zeus has never been here. These people hoped that if they built the temple to Poseidon, he would come and protect them from the Titans and their sea monsters.'

'The war is still on?' Joel cried.

Stella nodded. 'Their language is different to mine. Very ancient. But from what I can understand, a large village not far from here was destroyed by the Shadow Titans a few days ago. Everyone is scared. They fear the Olympians have abandoned them.'

'So the weapon is not here?'

'I do not think so.'

'That's not good enough,' Emily said. 'We have to be certain. Show me where you found the box.'

Stella directed Joel to where her parents pulled the golden box out of the rock. They were followed by the large group of construction workers.

'It was there,' she pointed.

'Everyone, stand back,' Emily warned.

Emily used her powers to crack open the ground where the golden box was found. She lifted huge chunks of solid rock and broke them up in the air until they were only dust.

'It's not here!' Emily repaired and replaced the rocks back in the ground. She shot an accusing eye at

Agent B. 'We're too early! If it hadn't been for you, we would have arrived at the right time and I could have destroyed that weapon by now.'

'How was I supposed to know I would throw you off?' Agent B defended.

Emily was stopped from saying more by a horrendous roar. It was coming from the sea.

Pegasus tried to rear and opened his wings.

The construction workers were the first to react. They threw down their tools and ran away from the temple. Mike started to growl and bark as he charged the edge of the cliff.

'Mike, come back!' Emily ordered. But the dog refused to obey. She used her powers to lift him from the cliff edge just as a huge tentacle crested the top and slammed down where Mike had been standing.

'What the . . . ?' Joel gasped.

'It is a sea serpent,' Paelen cried. 'Everybody run!' He started to kick at Brue's thick neck. 'Brue, you must move! It will devour us all!'

More of the huge sea-monster appeared as it crawled over the cliff edge and its hideousness was revealed. It had many heads, each with a mouth full of sharp teeth that snapped and snarled at them. Its slimy, grey body looked like a giant squid with at least eight long tentacles that flipped and flew in the air, reaching for them.

'It's the Hydra,' Joel shouted as he pushed Stella's wheelchair.

'That's not the Hydra,' Stella corrected. 'It's a sea-serpent!'

'It doesn't matter what it's called,' Agent B yelled. 'We'll be just as dead!'

As they ran, more sea-monsters crested the far side of the cliff, blocking their escape.

'We're surrounded,' Joel yelled.

Faced on three sides by the huge, ferocious monsters, the group huddled together. Joel caught hold of a long pole from the construction site.

Emily raised her hands and the Flame flashed.

Behind her, Paelen cried out as Brue dropped him to the ground. She rose up on her many legs. Suddenly the large, gentle creature threw back her two purple heads and howled in fury. Large deadly teeth filled her mouths and her eyes blazed red.

The Mother of the Jungle gave one last look at Paelen before charging the closest sea-serpent. As the serpent lunged forward to bite, one of Brue's heads flashed to the side and caught hold of one the serpent's necks, tearing its hideous head away from the body.

On the ground, Paelen helped Stella over to a pile of

uncut marble. They hid behind it while Paelen called instructions to the group. 'Do not just stand there, Emily, fire!'

Beside her, Agent B picked up a pole and was jamming it at one of the mouths of the nearest monster. But the heads were quicker and avoided the pole.

Sea-serpents were everywhere. Emily didn't have time to think. Only react. She shot flames at the nearest, but they had little effect beyond irritating the creature further.

Emily concentrated harder and turned the raging flames into a laser-like beam. The creature attacking her rose up on its tentacles and prepared to lunge. She directed the laser beam and severed all the heads at once. In its dying rage, the sea-serpent collapsed against the newly built columns of the temple and knocked them all down.

There was no time to celebrate. No sooner had Emily killed one creature than another rose from the sea to attack.

'Emily, behind you!' Stella warned.

Emily turned in time to see sharp teeth plunging towards her. Reacting instantly, she cut the head off with her Flame and jumped to the side to avoid it as it hit the ground. She turned her powers on the body of the creature and it collapsed in a dead heap.

Pegasus was doing his best to fight, but the ageing stallion was no match for the giant sea-serpent. Tentacles caught hold of one of the stallion's wings and hoisted him off the ground as sharp teeth bit deep into one of his rear legs.

Agent B charged and stabbed the neck of the monster holding Pegasus's wing. The creature howled and dropped the stallion. Pegasus hit the ground a few metres from Emily and cried out in pain.

Seeing him hurt drove Emily to rage. But this time, knowing what was at stake, she focused her fury. The intensity of the Flame increased as she spun in a tight circle and fired everything she had at the attacking monsters. The air was filled with acrid smoke as their bodies burned. Howls and roars rose higher as all the sea-serpents were cut down.

Stella was still hiding with Paelen behind the pile of marble. She only emerged after all the serpents were dead. She wheeled herself towards Emily but stopped short.

'Look!' she screamed, pointing at the cliff.

More creatures were crawling over the top.

'Em, stop them!' Joel cried.

Emily changed her tactics. She raised her hands and

used her powers to lift the creatures off the ground. Suspended high above the sea, they screamed and writhed as one. Emily used this opportunity to let loose a single blast of Flame that incinerated them all. A shower of ash was all that was left to drift back down into the sea.

Standing poised and ready for a third wave of sea-serpents, Emily waited. But when none came, she ran over to Pegasus. Blood was flowing from the stallion's nose but much worse than that, his back leg looked as if it had nearly been bitten off – there was blood everywhere.

'It's all right, Pegs.' Emily's trembling hands reached out to heal the wounded stallion. 'Just rest, it's over. They're all gone.'

Pegasus whined and laid his head down. His sides heaved as he panted heavily. Once healed, he calmed and rested.

Agent B knelt down beside her. 'How is he?'

'He'll be fine.' Emily sat back on her heels and looked at the agent with new eyes. He was covered in serpent's blood from the fight, and hadn't been afraid to take on the ferocious monsters. 'Thank you for saving Pegasus.'

He nodded. 'I told you, Emily. We're in this

together. If we are to survive, we must trust each other.'

Behind them Paelen cried, 'Stop, please!' Brue had returned to him and started to lick him all over. 'Please, Brue, I am unhurt, I do not need another bath!' He turned to Emily, 'Help me, before she drowns me!'

Emily rose shakily to her feet and walked over to the large Mother of the Jungle. Her heads and purple fur were covered in serpent's blood. 'He is fine, Brue. You protected Paelen perfectly.'

Joel came up to her side. 'Did you see what she became? She was just as ferocious as those monsters. I had no idea she could do that.'

'Time on Xanadu has tamed her,' Emily said, recalling what she'd received from Arious. 'On her old world, she was a deadly predator. I just hope we get her back to Xanadu before she reverts fully to her previous self.'

'I'm just glad she's on our side.'

Emily agreed, but then noticed his metal arm. It had a deep gouge and large tooth marks running along it. 'Joel, your arm!'

'I know.' Joel tried to fold back the metal over the exposed mechanisms. He flexed the arm and wiggled its fingers. Inside, they could see the pulleys and hydraulics working. 'Well, it may not be pretty, but at least it still works. A sea-serpent got hold of me and its teeth cut through the silver like it was butter. It would have killed me if Brue hadn't attacked it.'

Joel lifted Paelen back on to Brue's neck. Emily was still shaking as she sat beside Pegasus. Mike lay down beside her and put his head in her lap.

'What were those things?' Joel asked.

Pegasus sat up and neighed.

'He believes they belong to the Titans,' Paelen translated.

'The Titans?' Joel asked.

'Pegasus is right,' Paelen said. 'I am ashamed to say I could not fight. But Stella and I observed. All those serpents were trying to get at you, Emily. Everyone else was just in their way.'

'Why me?'

'Because you are the Flame of Olympus. Just as Olympians are drawn to you, the Titans are too. But their intentions are not as friendly. They will seek to control you. If that fails, they will try to destroy you.'

'Everyone wants to control me!' Emily stood and her eyes fell on Agent B. 'First it's you with the CRU and now the Titans. If this is true, we've got to go. It's too dangerous to stay a moment longer. I'll use my powers to send us further ahead in time. We'll come

211

back here after the war.'

'That works for me,' Joel said. 'If those serpents were with the Titans, I don't want to see what else they've got. Especially the Shadow Titans.'

'I agree,' Agent B said. 'We must leave here now.'

Pegasus remained on the ground. He nudged Emily's legs and invited her to sit again before trying to tell them something.

Paelen dropped his head. 'No, Pegasus, please. You must be mistaken.'

'What is it?' Emily asked.

'Pegasus says we must remain here. He believes it is our destiny to stay and fight. The pottery from the museum proves it. Today's battle was depicted on the amphora you saw.'

Emily recalled the pot. A girl dressed as an Olympian was firing flames at monsters. Then she looked over at Joel's torn-open arm, and Agent B, and finally to Mike lying beside her. His face was covered in blood from the monsters he'd fought. They were all depicted on the amphora.

'I know what we saw at the museum, Pegs. But it's too dangerous for us to stay. We're not prepared to take on the Titans. That was never the plan.'

'Pegasus is a very old Olympian,' Paelen said. 'He

existed long before many of us. He knows a lot of the history of the Titanomachy.'

'The what?' Emily asked.

'The war with the Titans,' Agent B explained.

'Yes,' Paelen agreed. 'Pegasus says his father spoke very little of the war. None of the Olympians who lived through it liked to talk about it. It was a dark time for us. But Neptune did once tell him of a power, more ancient than the Titans, who joined the battle at a critical moment. It tipped the balance of power and helped the Olympians defeat the Titans.'

Emily looked at the stallion. 'Pegs, what are you saying? That it was us?'

The stallion nodded and neighed.

Paelen continued. 'He says when you first mentioned travelling back in time, he considered the possibility that it was you. But then we planned to arrive after the war and he reconsidered. Now that we are here and have just defeated the Titan's serpents, Pegasus believes it is our destiny to stay. You, Emily, the last Xan, are the ancient power that helps the Olympians defeat the Titans.'

24

After the battle, the villagers invited them to join in a feast of celebration. Emily tried to turn down the offer, but the locals insisted. This was the first battle they had witnessed where the Titans had lost and it was a joyous occasion.

A large banquet was prepared with an endless supply of luxurious delicacies. Loud, cheerful music was played by local musicians and everyone danced. Emily sat beside Pegasus, eating olives and watching Stella chat with a boy from the village. She was showing him how her wheelchair worked. The boy didn't seem to understand much of what she was saying, but he smiled anyway.

Out on the dance floor Joel looked as if he was having a brilliant time. He'd covered his silver arm to hide the damage, but as he danced, the cover came free. But his pretty dance partner didn't react with shock or fear. Stella was right. These ancient people accepted their differences and welcomed them into their village much quicker than the people of their own time would have.

During the course of the evening, Emily had been invited to dance by several boys, but she wasn't in the mood. Her eyes kept darting around, waiting for the next attack. Agent B was doing the same. He was attempting to chat with the locals, but Emily could see that his wary eyes never stopped moving.

At the end of the celebrations they were invited to stay at the houses of the village leaders. As they walked back together, loud warning cries filled the air.

'What's all the shouting about?' Joel asked.

'I think the Titans have found us!' Emily cried. 'Look!'

The stars had been blotted out by a dark, moving cloud. As it got closer, they could see it wasn't a cloud at all. The sky was filled with flying warriors. They made no sound, but the sheer number of them was overwhelming.

Screaming filled the air as frightened villagers took up whatever weapons they had. The sound of clashing metal mixed with their cries as sword met sword.

'They're attacking the village!' Stella cried.

As more winged fighters arrived, Brue reverted back to her vicious self.

'Not again!' Paelen cried as Brue dropped him to the ground. Sharp, deadly teeth filled her two mouths and long sharp claws extended on her many feet. Her lips pulled back as both heads snarled in rage.

The ferocious Mother of the Jungle knocked Stella from her wheelchair and rose protectively above her and Paelen, roaring with deafening sounds they had never heard her make before.

'Emily look, Ninja Turtles!' Joel yelled.

Behind them, the narrow village streets were filled with monstrous-looking warriors. They weren't overly tall, but they were stocky and wore dark green helmets and armour. Joel was right. They did look like Ninja Turtles. But these were no pizza-loving movie heroes. They carried swords and were attacking anyone in their way.

'We've led them here,' Agent B said. 'Emily, get your Flame ready, this is going to be nasty.'

'We're surrounded!' Stella cried.

Pegasus shrieked and pawed the ground.

'We cannot fight them all. We must flee!' Paelen shouted.

Emily called fire from her hands and shot her laser-flame at the nearest attacking ninjas. As the laser touched their green armour, pieces fell away and they collapsed to the ground.

'Turn around, Emily,' Agent B cried.

Just ahead, the winged warriors were landing and they were able to get a closer look. These were blackbird-like things. They were tall, with leathery black armour and dark wings on their backs. Their heads were covered in helmets with beaks and black feathers.

'Joel,' Agent B called, 'get Stella, Paelen and Brue out of here. Emily and I will try to hold them back. Use that jewel of yours. Find Jupiter. Tell him what's happening.'

'I'm not leaving you!' Joel cried.

'Joel, go!' Emily shouted. 'You don't have any weapons. Tell Jupiter about the Titan weapon. Go now, while I try to stop them!'

The turtle warriors were now charging their way.

'Go!' Emily ordered.

Joel pulled the jewel from his tunic and commanded it to take them to Olympus. 'Follow behind us!' he cried.

Pausing only to get Stella back in her chair, Joel ran into the Solar Stream followed closely by the roaring Brue, who was carrying Paelen in one of her large mouths.

Agent B stood behind Emily. 'Just keep firing,' he yelled. 'No matter what, don't stop. We can't let them get hold of you.'

As Emily cut down fighters, it seemed that more and more were appearing from nowhere. 'There are too many,' she cried. 'I can't stop them all.'

Agent B screamed. Emily turned and saw that two turtles had caught hold of the CRU agent and were pulling his arms in opposite directions.

'Agent B!' she cried.

'Go!' the CRU agent howled. 'Forget me, just go!'

Pegasus reared and kicked one of the warriors attacking Agent B. The creature's helmet was knocked off – but Emily was shocked to see that there was no head inside. The turtle was hollow. But even without its head, it was still holding on to Agent B and pulling his arm in a gruesome tug-of-war with the other turtle.

Mike was at the warrior's feet, biting into the thick leather armour and growling viciously as he tore pieces away from it. Emily fired at the headless turtle and cut off the arms holding Agent B. Then she burned the arms off the second turtle. Agent B collapsed to the ground, moaning in pain.

Emily looked around desperately. They were surrounded. It was only a matter of moments before the winged warriors reached them. Even with all her powers, she didn't think she could get them all before she was cut down.

There was no time to pull the jewel from her pocket. Instead Emily closed her eyes and created a protection shield around her and Agent B. Concentrating as hard as she could, she cried, 'Olympus!'

The journey lasted the quickest blink of an eye. They were now in Olympus. But this was not the Olympus that she knew. Emily looked around at the devastation and was reminded of her first visit there after the Nirads had attacked and conquered it.

Somehow, this was much worse.

Fires burned and choking smoke filled the air. What few structures there were lay in ruins as marble pillars and collapsed walls littered the ground. There were no statues, no gardens and no art. This was truly a war zone.

Emily knelt down beside Agent B. He was groaning in pain. His arms, twisted at odd angles, looked badly dislocated and broken. She reached out to heal him, but her powers didn't work.

'While you were on Xanadu, did you eat any ambrosia?' she asked urgently.

The agent's eyes were clenched shut with the pain. 'No!'

'Why not?'

'Ambrosia makes humans immortal. I don't want to live for ever!' he cried through gritted teeth.

Emily reached into her pocket and pulled out her food pouch. She quickly ordered ambrosia cakes soaked in nectar. 'Here, eat this!'

'No!'

Emily looked around at the devastated landscape. A battle had recently been fought here which meant the fighters could still be in the area. 'I can't heal you if you haven't eaten ambrosia. Now you will open your mouth and eat this or I will force it into you. You know I can do it.'

'I don't want to live for ever!' he cried in agony.

'You won't. When you want to die, I'll kill you. But right now, you are going to eat!'

With her powers, Emily pulled the wounded CRU agent up to a sitting position. 'Open your mouth, Agent B,' she ordered. 'Don't make me do it for you.'

Emily force-fed the CRU agent the whole ambrosia cake. 'Chew and swallow!'

He collapsed back on to the ground and Emily held his hand while the ambrosia coursed through his system. After a few minutes, she could feel her powers starting to heal his broken arms.

Agent B moaned as he healed. Before long, he could move his arms. He sat up and looked at Emily with fury in his eyes.

'That was wrong, Emily, and you know it! You forced me to eat it against my will.'

'Just like the CRU is planning to force me to become their ultimate weapon?'

'That's different!'

'No it's not!' Emily fired back. 'You don't want to live for ever, fine. But do you want to die right now? You talk about Pegasus being a distraction. You with two broken arms are a bigger distraction. I did what I had to do. We can fight about it later. Right now, we're exposed. I think we should find somewhere to hide.'

Emily helped him up as they made their way to a collapsed building. Safely inside the broken structure, Agent B sat down for the last bit of his recovery. 'Any ideas where we are?' he asked.

Emily gazed around. 'Usually the Solar Stream delivers us near Jupiter's palace, but this doesn't look anything like the palace area.'

'This is a war, Emily. Nothing looks like it should on a battlefield.'

The sound of roaring filled the air. Flames shot across the darkened landscape. Emily and Agent B peered through the debris and saw three huge dragons tearing across the area, setting fire to anything that moved.

'Dragons?' Emily cried. 'The myths didn't mention anything about dragons, or those things attacking us at the village!'

'What myths have you been reading?' Agent B said, now fully recovered. 'Of course there were dragons! Did you expect Jupiter and Saturn to be throwing snowballs at each other? This is a war of epic proportions. It covered the cosmos and destroyed worlds!'

'How am I supposed to help with that?' Emily suddenly realized the depth of trouble they were in. Everything they had faced until now, from the Nirads to the Gorgons, and even the CRU, had been child's play compared to this.

'I don't know,' Agent B said. 'Our first job is to find Jupiter and see what he has to say.'

In the distance the three rampaging dragons stopped. They lifted their heads and seemed to be sniffing the air. Suddenly their heads snapped in the direction of where they were hiding. Smoke seeped from the

222

dragons' nostrils as their eyes sought their location.

'Uh-oh,' Agent B said. 'I think we're in big trouble.'

As if called by a silent whistle, the dragons started charging. The closer they got, the bigger they seemed to grow. Before long, Emily felt like she was facing down three very large and very angry ten-storey buildings.

'Why are all the monsters here so big?' Emily cried.

'I really don't know,' Agent B answered. 'I just hope you're feeling strong!'

Standing behind her, Pegasus nickered and nudged her gently in the back. He was telling her she could do it. She just hoped his faith in her was justified.

'Stay here with Pegs,' Emily ordered as she crawled out of the debris. 'If this fails, find Jupiter and tell him to hide the Titan weapon somewhere else.'

Mike started to snarl and bark. He darted out of their hiding place and charged the tall, scaly foot of the nearest dragon.

'That is either the bravest dog I've ever seen,' Agent B called, 'or the dumbest!'

'Mike!' Emily shouted, running after the dog. 'Get back here!'

Now that she was out in the open, the three dragons focused on Emily. She could feel their swelling hatred.

Roars shook the area as they inhaled deeply and shot burning plumes of fire directly at her.

Emily crouched and felt the flames lick her. On the ground around her the rocks melted and turned to pools of molten glass. Broken marble pillars were charred black and crumbled under the intense heat. But for Emily there were no burning sensations. In fact, she felt nothing at all.

Bathed in the dragons' flames, Emily rose slowly to her feet. The more they spat at her, the stronger she felt. 'Do you want to play with fire?' she shouted. 'Try this!'

Emily raised both her hands. A single brilliant blaze of laser-light filled the night sky as she shot all she had at the dragons. There was no time for the monsters to react or even scream. In an instant, they were turned to ash.

'Emily!' Agent B ran out from their cover. 'Are you all right?' He caught hold of her and checked her all over. 'Their flames didn't even singe your tunic! How is this possible?'

Emily shrugged. 'I don't know, but it doesn't matter right now. Where's Mike?'

The sound of barking broke the silence. They heard Mike yelp and squeal before turning silent. 'Mike!'

Emily cried. 'Mike, where are you?'

The sound of many feet walking on rubble filled the air. Several giants led by a centaur emerged from under cover. Emily spotted Mike in the arms of one of the giants – his mouth was being muffled by the enormous hand.

Emily immediately recognized the centaur. 'Chiron!'

The centaur was younger than when Emily had known him. His man's upper torso was strong and muscular, while his horse's body was lean and steamlined. The centaur's chestnut-coloured hair was long and wavy.

Emily tried to embrace him, but Chiron reared on his horse legs and pointed his loaded bow at her.

'Chiron, it's me! Emily!'

Chiron's face and upper body were bathed in dirt and sweat and he had deep weeping burns on his rear flanks. His expression was dark and threatening as he spoke unfamiliar words. He flicked his bow, ordering them to raise their hands.

Doing as ordered, Emily saw that most of the giants were covered in burn marks. She didn't recognize any of them, but it was evident they had all been fighting the dragons.

Pegasus stepped forward and made a long series of

sounds. Chiron spoke back to the stallion and lowered his bow, but his suspicious eyes never left Emily.

'Pegs, please tell him who we are!'

'No, Pegasus, don't!' Agent B ordered. 'They can't know who we really are or where we're from. If we don't tread very carefully, we could change history and alter the future as we know it. We should have as little exposure to the Olympians as possible.'

'But he's hurt. They all are.' Emily took a cautious step towards the centaur. 'Will you at least tell him that I can heal him? He's covered in burns. Please tell him to take my hand.'

Pegasus nickered and nodded towards Emily.

Chiron frowned, but moved closer. He held out his left hand, while still clutching his loaded bow with the other.

'It's all right,' Emily said softly, 'we're friends. You just don't know it yet.'

Emily took the centaur's hand. Chiron bucked at her touch and turned to look back at the wounds on his flanks. In moments, the deep burns faded and healed completely. The centaur lifted a rear hoof and flexed his leg. There was no pain.

Chiron nodded at Emily and Pegasus and turned to speak to his giants. The tall men responded by surrounding the group and raising their clubs and weapons. Chiron turned and started to lead them forward.

'What's happening?' Emily asked.

Agent B looked around. 'I think we've just been captured by the Olympians.'

25

For half the night, Chiron led them over rough terrain and rubble. Emily was careful to keep her hand on Pegasus as they moved. The stallion was growing increasingly fatigued and was starting to stumble over the debris. When that happened Emily used her powers to lift him off the ground and carry him.

As a dull and moody dawn arrived, they encountered more tired Olympians. Most Emily had never seen or met before. There were winged Olympians, snake-like Olympians and many other war-weary and defeated creatures. Yet as she passed, they all stood and looked at her curiously. Those who could move started to follow.

'Pegs, look,' Emily said. 'They don't know me, but they must feel that I'm the Flame. They are drawn to me.'

'That could be a good thing, or a bad thing,' Agent B said tightly.

A giant shoved the CRU agent in the back and

grunted a few harsh words. 'More likely a bad thing,' he finished.

Chiron held up his hand and they stopped. They were standing before the ruins of a building. Emily thought it could have been Jupiter's palace, but it seemed to be in the wrong area.

Standing high above the entrance were three winged women. There were living snakes woven in their hair and their faces had a pale green pallor. They snarled and threatened anyone who came near the ruins.

Emily gazed up at the angry women and was reminded of the Gorgons. 'Who are they?'

Agent B shrugged. 'I'd say by the looks of them, they're the Furies.'

'The what?'

'The three Furies,' Agent B explained. 'They were known as the avengers of crime and levied cruel punishments on those who broke the law.'

'I've never heard of them.'

Agent B shook his head. 'Honestly, Emily. If we somehow survive this, I am going to get you some books on mythology. For all your time with the Olympians, you know almost nothing of them!'

'How do you know so much?'

'Once the Olympians became known to the CRU,

we were all ordered to study the mythology to familiarize ourselves with what we were up against.'

The first Fury flew down to the group and challenged Chiron.

While they argued, Emily lowered Pegasus to the ground. 'How are you doing, Pegs?' she asked softly as she stroked his muzzle. 'Are you OK?'

Pegasus neighed softly.

'He's exhausted,' Agent B said, 'and he hasn't eaten in hours. None of us have.'

Emily pulled out her food pouch and waved her hand over the top to produce a large supply of ambrosia cakes for the stallion. 'Go on and eat, Pegs.' She handed an ambrosia cake to Agent B. 'You might as well also. Since you've already been exposed to it, there's no point going hungry.'

A familiar voice called strange words from behind the giants. When they parted, Emily was stunned to see a young man walking between their legs. He was no more than eighteen or nineteen with dark, wavy hair, smooth clear skin and bright eyes. He was well-built, with a strong, muscled chest. In his hand he carried a tall trident. But it was his eyes that Emily recognized first — they were as sparkly grey-blue as a stormy ocean.

'Neptune,' Emily called, 'is that you?'

Pegasus nickered excitedly as recognition struck him. Painfully, he climbed to his feet as his old wings fluttered and shed feathers on the ground. There was no mistaking his joy at seeing his father alive again.

But the feelings were not returned. Neptune wore a dark, threatening expression. He pointed his trident at Emily and spoke the language of the Olympians. Though Emily couldn't understand his words, the message was clear. He had no clue who they were.

Pegasus whinnied and stepped forward, but Neptune wouldn't listen. He flicked the end of his trident. Pegasus was lifted off the ground and tossed several metres away. The ageing stallion crashed down into a broken pile of marble pillars, landing on his wings. He cried out in deep pain.

'Pegasus!' Emily turned on Neptune. 'He is your son, you idiot!' She shouted in a tone that she would never have dared use with the Neptune from her time. Emily fired a quick blast of power that tossed Neptune backwards violently. He struck a giant and knocked the legs out from under him. They both fell to the ground in a confused heap.

'Emily, no!' Agent B cried. 'Don't kill him or Pegasus will never exist!'

'I'm not going to kill him,' Emily shouted, 'but no one hurts Pegasus, not even his father!'

Neptune rose and pointed his trident at Emily. It was well known that the weapon could shoot a lethal blast of water that was powerful enough to cut an opponent in half. Emily realized Neptune wasn't playing or waiting for explanations.

As the first blast of water shot towards her, Emily raised her hands and easily deflected the water away. It struck the giants around her and knocked them to the ground.

Emily reached forward with her powers and hoisted Neptune off the ground. 'Stop it!' she shouted at him. 'We're here to help you!'

But Neptune wasn't giving up. Once again, he turned his trident on Emily. But Emily was faster. Her powers wrenched the trident from his hands. The weapon shot down to Agent B.

'Hold this while Neptune and I have a little chat!'

Emily rose in the air and met Neptune high above the heads of the giants.

'Emily, no!' Agent B shouted. 'You could change the future!'

'Would you trust me, please?' she cried.

Suddenly, from the pile of rubble, Pegasus screamed.

A teenager stood before him with his hands pressed tightly on the stallion's head.

'No!' Emily yelled. 'Leave him alone!'

Emily dropped Neptune and flew directly over to the boy who was hurting Pegasus. She tackled him away from the suffering stallion. They tumbled together and fell into a deep, open pit of rubble.

Before they struck the bottom, the boy put his arms around Emily and hugged her tightly. He spun them both around so that it was only him who took the impact of hitting the floor of the pit. 'Emily, it is me,' he cried, 'Jupiter!'

Emily lay on top of the boy. His dark eyes were bright and filled with mischief and he had a devastating, sculpted smile that revealed deep dimples in each cheek. There was no mistaking that he was very handsome, but she could see no traces of the Olympian leader in his face.

'Jupiter?' Emily frowned. 'Is it really you?'

'How many other Jupiters do you know?' he teased. 'Of course it is me.'

'And you speak English?'

Jupiter rose and offered his hand to help her up. His grin broadened. 'I do now. My nephew, Pegasus, just taught me.'

Emily couldn't understand what was happening. 'How?'

'When I touched him,' Jupiter explained, 'I saw who he was and where he came from. You have certainly come a long way. I am deeply grateful for your help. Pegasus is correct. We must stop my father's weapon before it destroys us all.'

Emily was almost too stunned to speak. 'You – you know everything?'

'Yes,' he grinned. Then his teasing eyes sparkled. 'I also know everything about you.'

'Such as?'

'Well, let me see,' he said lightly. 'You started your life as a human and then became known as the Flame of Olympus. But the truth is you are the last Xan, an ancient race of myth and legend. It is you who will help us end this brutal war with the Titans. Am I correct?'

Emily was still too shocked to move. The joy at seeing Jupiter alive again was too much. She had hoped to find him here in the past, but never expected him to look like he did. The sparkle in his young, teasing eyes was making her heart flutter and the way he spoke reminded her so much of Paelen.

Jupiter put his arm around her waist and grinned as

he levitated them both out of the pit to where Neptune was standing, once again holding his trident on Agent B and Pegasus. Jupiter released her and ran over to his brother. He placed his hands on Neptune's head.

As Jupiter transferred the information, Neptune staggered. When he recovered, he knelt down before Emily. The blue in his eyes softened to the colour of a calm, warm sea – the colour she knew and loved.

'Please forgive me. I did not know.'

'It's not me you should apologize to!' Emily dashed over to where Pegasus lay. Agent B was with him and struggling to help him to rise.

'I've got you now, Pegs,' Emily said gently as she lifted him out of the rubble and healed his damaged wings. 'This is happening to you too often. I wish everyone would just leave you alone.'

'Pegasus, my son,' Neptune cried, 'please forgive me. I sincerely believed you were Titans here to destroy us.' He put his arms around Pegasus's neck and embraced him tightly.

'You told him!' Agent B accused. 'Are you insane? No one should know their own future, especially the Olympians!'

Emily shook her head. 'It wasn't me, it was Jupiter. When he touched Pegasus, he read his mind. Now he knows everything about us and learned our language. He's just showed it all to Neptune.'

'Jupiter? Where is he?'

'Here,' Jupiter said. He approached Agent B and offered his hand. 'After what Pegasus has shown me, I am surprised that a CRU agent would wish to help. But my nephew has faith in you.'

'You're Jupiter?' Agent B said incredulously. 'How? You're just a kid.'

'A kid? I am much more than just a kid. I am Jupiter!'

'I don't understand any of this,' Agent B said. 'How could you learn our language so quickly?'

'We are Olympian,' Jupiter said, as if that explained everything.

Emily watched Jupiter speaking with the CRU agent and was painfully conflicted. She had known him for ages. Her Jupiter – old Jupiter. He was powerful, but more like a sweet, elderly grandfather. But this Jupiter was an even more powerful young man of Joel's age. Cupid, who was considered the most beautiful Olympian, had nothing on him. Despite the grime of battle, Jupiter's skin was smooth and golden. His eyes were sparkling and his muscled body stronger than Joel's.

Pegasus nudged Emily and nickered softly.

Emily could see the stallion was laughing at her sudden reaction to young Jupiter. 'Stop it, Pegs.' She blushed.

Jupiter stroked Pegasus's face and grinned at Emily. 'What have I missed?'

Emily blushed again and shook her head. 'Nothing important. But we do need to talk. Can we go somewhere quiet?'

Jupiter nodded and motioned to Neptune. 'Call Pluto, Juno, Vesta and Ceres; they must hear this too. Then we can make our plans.' He returned to Emily and took her hand. 'Come, there is not much left of the palace, but there is still a council chamber where we can speak privately.'

Before they entered the damaged palace, Jupiter paused to address his people and gave a short speech. When he finished, he called one of the giants forward and gave him instructions. The others bowed to Jupiter and returned to their duties and the Furies took their position at the entrance again.

'You didn't tell them everything, did you?' Agent B asked.

Jupiter tilted his head to the side. 'I am young, Agent B, not stupid,' he said. 'You are correct. No one should know their own future. It is best if no one other than the first Olympians know who you really are. I just sent the giants to alert my people. Your friends are out there somewhere in the middle of this battle. They must be found and delivered here unharmed.'

When Vesta arrived, with Juno and Ceres, Emily's heart thrilled to see her teacher so young and alive. She ached to throw her arms around her, but Vesta looked at Emily with deep suspicion. It was only after Jupiter shared his knowledge that the three women warmed to her and spoke English.

'You are the last Xan,' Vesta said in shock, 'and you are part of the Flame that arrived in Olympus a short while ago. It burned across our sky in a brilliant ball of light and crashed to the ground in a large crater.'

'Riza is already here?' Emily cried. She looked around at the rag-tag team of fighters and through a hole in the palace wall to the barren, burned lands outside. 'But I thought the Flame gave you all more powers. It helped you win the war. You once told me the Flame was the source of your powers.'

'It is true we have become much more powerful since it arrived,' Jupiter explained. 'But so have the Titans. They seek to steal the Flame from us and take it to Titus. This is the battle we fight and the cause of the war. If the Titans succeed in controlling it, they will enslave us and all the worlds around us.'

'But Saturn is your father,' Emily said. 'Can't you talk to him and get him to stop?'

Neptune shook his head. 'Our father is insane. He was once told that his children would overthrow him. He is so desperate to keep control that he had us imprisoned in Tartarus until Jupiter managed to escape and set us free.'

Agent B shook his head. 'The myths said that he ate all of you. But when Jupiter was born, your mother, Rhea, fed Saturn a rock instead of the baby. Jupiter was raised on Crete and finally freed his brothers and sisters by making Saturn throw them up.'

Jupiter started to laugh. It was soft and deep and made Emily flush.

'Do you always believe everything you read?' He laughed. 'That story is madness. We were all born on Titus, a sister world to Olympus. Our father did not eat us. Nor did he disgorge us. What he did was imprison us until I was able to escape. I went back and freed my brothers and sisters. It is true that we have spent a great deal of time on Earth. But then we came to live permanently in Olympus. We hoped to remain here free from Titus and our father.'

'But when that Flame arrived, everything changed,' Neptune continued. 'Our father and some of his brothers attacked us, trying to take it for themselves. To end the war, we have considered extinguishing it.'

Pegasus whinnied loudly as Emily cried, 'No, you can't do that!'

Emily caught hold of Vesta's hands. 'If you extinguish the Flame, everything in the future will change. I would not be here and I will never know Pegasus.'

'I do not understand,' Vesta said. 'I was confused by what Jupiter has shown me.'

'It's very simple,' Emily began. 'Not long from now, you will take the heart of that Flame and hide it in a girl on Earth. It will live within her, unknown, for her whole life. Then when she dies, it will pass to another girl, and then another, for countless generations, until the time comes when I will be born with the heart of the Flame. I will live in a place called New York City and it is there that Pegasus will find me. He will take me to Olympus to enter the Temple of the Flame and it will be brought forth in me.'

'But there is no temple built to the Flame,' Vesta said. 'It burns deep in a crater in the ground.'

'If Emily says there is a temple built to the Flame –

and as I have seen it in my nephew's mind – it must be made so,' Jupiter insisted. 'If we win the war, we will build the Temple of the Flame.'

Agent B looked at Emily in confusion. 'I never knew that was how you came to have all these powers.'

'No one in the CRU knows,' Emily said. 'It was my destiny.'

'And now that destiny is in grave danger,' Agent B said. He looked at the Olympians. 'Listen to me, all of you. It is critically important that you follow through on what you have learned from Pegasus. If anyone deviates from what was meant to happen, it will change the future. That could be devastating for Earth as well as Olympus.'

'Of course,' Vesta said. 'We will act on what we have learned.'

Emily approached Jupiter. 'Have your people heard anything of Joel and Paelen yet? They've been out there alone with no weapons for too long.'

'I have seen who they are in my nephew's mind. Joel is resourceful. I am sure they are fine. But I will order more giants to look for them.'

When Pluto arrived, he was as young and attractive as his brothers. As the Big Three stood before Emily, she smiled to herself – they looked more like a boy band than the leaders of Olympus.

Pluto took the news of their arrival with his usual calm. It was decided that one more Olympian should be invited in on the secret. Chiron was called to the meeting and introduced properly to Emily. The centaur bowed deeply and apologized for his rudeness earlier and thanked Emily for healing his wounds.

'So what can we do to help find Saturn's weapon?' Emily asked. 'If we don't destroy it now, there is no future for any of us.'

'Of course,' Jupiter said. 'I am sickened to think that our father could create such a thing. Could he really hate us so much?'

'Father is insane,' Vesta said. 'Nothing he does surprises me any more.'

'But where would he build it?' Agent B asked. 'Can we go there and stop him?'

Jupiter shook his head. 'If this weapon is as powerful as that, he will keep it well hidden and protected while it is being developed. It could be anywhere: Titus, Tartarus or any of a hundred worlds. We will send out our spies, but it will take time.'

Emily found herself mesmerized by the way Jupiter combed his fingers through his thick, dark hair. As he flexed his arm muscles, Emily's heart pounded until she had to look away.

'As it is,' Jupiter continued, 'Saturn has used his new powers from the Flame to create an army of monsters and a fearsome race of fighters, the Shadow Titans. They are unlike anything we have ever encountered before. They have swarmed over parts of Earth and Olympus in a bid to defeat us and take the Flame.'

'I think we might have just met them,' Agent B said. 'On Earth in Greece. Some look like large blackbirds and some look like giant turtles.'

'That is them,' Jupiter said. 'Though there are two more types out there as well.'

'But you can beat them, right?' Emily asked. She looked at Pluto. 'Can't you just wave your hand in the air and kill them?'

'You cannot kill that which is not alive,' Pluto said. 'Believe me, I have tried.'

'What do you mean? I'm sure I killed a few.'

'No, Emily, you destroyed them,' Jupiter corrected. 'The Shadow Titans are not living beings. That leathery armour of theirs is nothing more than an empty shell. They have eyes, but no body. They do not speak and do not feel pain. A Shadow Titan will

243

not surrender when surrounded. They fight until there is nothing left to fight with.'

Agent B rubbed his newly healed arms. 'So I have learned.'

Pluto continued. 'The Shadow Titans are aptly named. They are merely the walking shadows of four original warriors: Aronder, the Minotaur; Mertik, the Turtle Warrior; Dythram, the Blackbird Warrior; and finally, Quinux, the Dragon Warrior. It sounds as though you have met the Blackbird and Turtle Shadows only.'

'The Minotaur is fighting with the Titans?' Emily cried. 'How is that possible? He lived peacefully in Olympus until the disaster struck. He could be mean-tempered, but he wasn't evil or bad.'

'None of them are evil,' Jupiter said. 'The Four Warriors are prisoners, just as we once were. As long as they exist, Saturn can create a limitless supply of Shadow Titans who answer only to him. In time their numbers will swell to overthrow us. With or without father's weapon, if we do not stop the Shadow Titans, we will be defeated.'

'Then it would seem logical to either free or destroy the originals before that happens,' Agent B said.

'True,' Jupiter agreed. 'But they are kept locked

away. We do not know where, though we have spies out searching for them.'

'What about the Hundred-handers?' Agent B asked.

Emily frowned. 'The what?'

The CRU agent looked at her in exasperation. 'Really, Emily, you must read those myths!'

'What about them?' Chiron asked impatiently. The centaur was pacing the chamber with his arms crossed over his chest. His hooves clopped noisily on the floor and he appeared greatly agitated.

'I read all about the Titanomachy,' Agent B said. 'It was written that the Hundred-handers helped you defeat the Titans.'

'That is madness,' Juno cried. 'Saturn keeps them imprisoned deep in Tartarus. We could not free them when we escaped. They are trapped there for ever.'

'Well, you'd better try again,' Agent B said, 'because all the ancient myths say the same thing. They help you win the war.'

Jupiter stood before Emily, and peered at Agent B. 'Are you certain you can trust this man? I may not know everything about the CRU, only what Pegasus has shown me. But from what I saw, my instincts say I should not believe him.'

'Normally I'd feel the same,' Emily agreed, 'but Agent B wants to go home as much as I do. The only way that can happen is if we destroy that weapon and win the war. So if he says the Hundred-handers can help, I believe him.'

Chiron continued pacing the floor. 'If this is so, how do we do it? How do we get into Tartarus to rescue them with all the Shadow Titans guarding the prison?'

'By destroying the Shadow Titans first,' Joel called as he entered the chamber. He was followed by Paelen on Brue and Stella being pushed by a satyr. The goat-boy nodded at Jupiter and the others respectfully and left the chamber.

'Joel!' Emily ran and hugged him tightly. 'Are you all right?'

Nike, the Winged Victory, was standing beside Joel. She was tall and elegant as she spoke softly to Jupiter in their language.

Jupiter approached. 'Yes, Nike, thank you,' he answered in English. 'These are the ones. You have done well.'

Paelen reached a wizened hand to Emily. His face was filled with relief at seeing her. 'How did you get away from the village? There were so many of those things coming at us. They are here in Olympus too.

We tried to fight them, but they are too strong. I might have defeated them if I could only have stretched myself out again.'

Emily smiled at her old friend. 'I'm sure you would have, Paelen. But those things are the Shadow Titans. We nearly didn't get away from them. A couple of Turtle Shadows caught hold of Agent B and thought he was a wishbone. They broke both his arms.'

'I'm fine,' Agent B said gruffly. 'But what happened in Greece was just a preview. It seems Saturn has a limitless supply of them.'

'Finding that weapon and stopping the Shadow Titans must be our first priority before we attempt to free the Hundred-handers from Tartarus,' Jupiter said. 'We must make our plans.'

'Who are you?' Joel demanded. He looked around the room. 'Where's Jupiter? We really need to speak with him.'

'Joel, this *is* Jupiter,' Emily said as she introduced the Olympians.

The shock on Joel's face was mirrored by Paelen and Stella. 'But you're all so young!'

'So we have been told,' Jupiter said. 'But that does not alter the situation.' He looked Joel up and down and pushed against his chest. 'You look strong enough for a human, but can you fight? Have you been trained?'

Joel shrugged. 'Not really.'

Jupiter turned to Agent B, Emily and then Stella. 'What about you? Have any of you been trained in warfare?'

Agent B raised his hand, but Stella shook her head.

Emily said, 'Until now, I've just been using my powers.'

'Powers are good,' Pluto said. 'But they are not enough. Not against the Titans. You will need more.'

'You have done well.' Jupiter addressed Emily and her friends after days of intense weapon's training. 'Better than we could have hoped. Now it is time for you to join your regiments.'

'Regiments?' Emily repeated. 'No, we've got to find that weapon. The whole future depends on it. We've got to go with the spies to try to find it.'

'I agree,' Agent B said. 'These kids aren't equipped to deal with war. We came back here for the weapon, that's all. Winning the war is down to you and the Hundred-handers.'

Jupiter looked at his brothers. Pluto nudged him. 'Go on, Jupe, tell them.'

'We are losing the war,' Jupiter said flatly. 'Each day

sees more Olympians wounded or captured and taken away while the number of Shadow Titans and monsters grows. Our spies have said there are no signs of the weapon being developed.'

'We believe,' Chiron added, 'that Saturn does not feel the need to create the weapon because we are being defeated without it.'

'You can't lose the war,' Joel said. 'The myths said you won! You are the Big Three, you have amazing powers. All Olympians do. You can't lose.'

'The myths were wrong,' Jupiter said sadly. 'Unless we can find a way to turn the tide, it is only a matter of time before we are forced to surrender.'

'Surrender?' Joel cried. 'You can't!'

'Can you offer another solution?' Neptune asked.

Jupiter reached for Emily's hands. 'There is only one way to change our fate. We need you to fight with us, Emily. You are Xan. You have the power to defeat the Shadow Titans with the wave of your hand. From what I have learned from Pegasus, you cannot be hurt and you have the power to heal.'

Emily heard the words and her blood ran cold. Jupiter was saying the exact same thing that Agent B had said to her. That she was the ultimate weapon.

'Jupiter, please,' Emily begged. 'Don't ask me to do

this. I am not a weapon.'

Jupiter shook his head. 'I did not call you a weapon. But you are Xan. You can turn the tide. If we can show Saturn that you are with us, he may stop this insane war.'

'Saturn can't know that Emily is Xan,' Agent B said. 'No one can know who she is.'

Chiron joined Jupiter. 'He will not know you are Xan, but unless you join us on the battlefield, we will lose this war without that weapon ever being created. When that happens, there will be no future for any of us.'

26

Emily needed time to collect her thoughts – there was so much to think about. But after a full day of weighing it up, she was no closer to any answers.

'Riza, where are you?' she called softly. 'I need you to tell me what to do.'

But deep in her mind, there was only silence. Could it be that Riza was gone for ever? Emily had grown used to Riza being with her. Now she felt empty and alone.

She looked at Pegasus. Without the weapon around, his ageing had stopped. But he was still very old and in pain. 'What am I supposed to do, Pegs?' she asked. 'If I join the war, I'll become the weapon Agent B said I was. But if I don't, the Olympians will lose.'

Pegasus nudged her and licked her hand. She already knew what he wanted her to do. He'd told them that an ancient power had joined the battle and helped them win. If that was true, it meant she was that ancient power, and must join the war.

'Emily, are you all right?' Agent B approached and sat down on a broken pillar beside her.

'Not really,' Emily said without looking up.

He reached for her hand and Emily looked up in surprise as he squeezed it gently. 'I can't imagine what you're going through right now, so I'm not going to tell you what to do. Ultimately, the decision is yours. But know this. If you decide to join the fight, Joel and I will be right beside you. This isn't what any of us wanted, but in all honesty, fighting beside the Olympians may be the only way for us to go home.'

'So I become the ultimate weapon after all,' Emily said miserably.

Agent B shook his head. 'I am so sorry I called you that. It was wrong of me. That night in the museum seems a lifetime ago, doesn't it?'

Emily nodded.

He caught her chin and lifted it to face him. 'Listen to me, Emily. You are not a weapon. I know that. So do you. And if you decide to join the battle, it will be as a skilled soldier, just like the rest of us, and not a weapon.'

'And if I don't join the war?'

'Then we'll take whatever comes. We could go back to Xanadu and live out the rest of our lives there.'

'With no more Olympus and no Earth?'

The CRU agent shrugged. 'It's a tough choice, but it is your choice. None of us will tell you what to do.'

Emily looked at the agent. 'Why are you being so nice?'

He shrugged again. 'I guess I'm finally seeing life through your eyes, well away from the CRU.'

'What do you see?'

Agent B stood. 'Someone who will make the right decision.'

War was ugly.

There were no other words to describe it. It was so much worse than Emily could have ever imagined. Days and nights blended together in a kind of frenzied exhaustion that no amount of rest could relieve.

Emily, Pegasus, Joel and Agent B were kept together and served with Chiron. Paelen, Brue and Stella were sent to work with Vulcan in his forge, making weapons.

Spending all day fighting beside the best Olympian warriors, Emily learned all she could about the Shadow Titans. Using her powers, she managed to capture two Turtle Shadows and one Minotaur Shadow. But they weren't prisoners for long. The creatures tore themselves apart, breaking out of their bonds. The Olympians learned nothing from the experience other than that the Shadow Titans were mindless creations designed solely to kill.

When they'd first arrived in Olympus, Emily had found an empty notebook in some building rubble. It was a beautifully bound book with a fine, engraved gold cover and clean white parchment pages. She had never kept a journal before, but with the war raging all around her, she wanted to start one.

Each day she recorded everything she experienced, including the losses the Olympians were suffering. She noted down the names of the fighters she'd known who had died before she could heal them or who had been captured by the Titans. It broke her heart the day she had to write down Vesta and Juno's names. Though they weren't necessarily dead, they joined the long list of the missing.

After another long day, they returned to their shelter to rest and eat. Pegasus was lying down behind Emily, devouring a large supply of ambrosia cakes mixed with chocolate ice-cream. At her feet, Mike was contentedly eating the meal that Emily had prepared for him.

While they ate, Emily scribbled notes in her journal. When she finished writing, she shuffled through the pages. There were no dates that she could record, as Olympians did not keep track of time, but she had named each day in numerical order, starting with their arrival to the present.

'We've been here one hundred and fifteen days,' she announced.

'Wow,' Joel said. 'No wonder I'm tired. After all that time, it feels like we're no further ahead.'

'I know,' Emily agreed, 'but Chiron says we're making advances. The Shadow Titans are being driven out of Olympus.'

Joel nodded. 'I had hoped we could have attacked Titus before now. If we could capture Saturn, we could end this before the weapon is created.'

'They've tried. But Jupiter says Saturn's gone into hiding. They can't find him.'

Agent B arrived looking as tired as they felt. His CRU clothes were gone. He now dressed as an Olympian and had built up his body with all the training and fighting.

Emily and Joel's feelings towards the CRU agent had changed. Agent B had proven himself time and time again with the Olympians. He kept up morale with a supply of ridiculous jokes, lifting their spirits at the end of a gruelling day's battling. Neither she nor

Joel had ever expected the CRU agent to have a sense of humour.

His sensitive side also emerged; each night, after Joel had gone to bed, he would stay up with Emily while she and Pegasus walked through the camp, healing all the wounded. He said little, but would always offer his quiet support.

As he sat down wearily at their table, Emily pulled out her food pouch. 'What would you like to eat?'

The agent shook his head. 'Nothing, thanks. I'm too tired.'

'You've got to eat,' Joel said. 'You're the one always bugging me to do it.'

Agent B hid his head down in his hands. 'It's called, "Do as I say and not as I do", Joel,' he muttered. 'I'm older than you, I can boss you around.'

'And I can force you to eat, remember?' Emily teased. 'Now, what would you like?'

Agent B lifted his head and leaned in to her. 'Are you threatening me, young lady?'

Emily looked down at Mike. 'Do you think I'm threatening him?'

The dog barked and wagged his tail.

Emily grinned at the CRU agent. 'He says I am. So you'd better eat.'

Agent B finally surrendered and asked for a plate of ambrosia cakes and a cup of strong black coffee. After all their time there, he had come to enjoy Olympian food, but still hated nectar.

'We'll be moving out again tonight,' he told them. 'There are reports of a huge wave of Shadow Titans and dragons arriving on Olympus. They're heading this way.'

It had soon become apparent that Emily was the magnet that was drawing the most dangerous Titan warriors to them.

She had now become the bait.

As long as the Titans focused their most powerful warriors on capturing Emily, Jupiter and his fighters could command battles in other parts of Olympus. Pluto and Neptune with their fighters were separately engaging the Titans on Earth, while Minerva and her team of Harpies concentrated on getting spies to Titus to learn if they were starting to develop the weapon.

'Have you heard anything from Paelen?' Joel asked Agent B. 'Is he OK?'

Agent B nodded. 'We had a message this afternoon. They are all safe, but on the move. Right now Stella is working closely with Vulcan on a fire-sword based on Emily's powers. All her idea. They are hoping to have a prototype ready soon. If it works, all our warriors will have a much better chance against the Shadow Titans.'

Relief washed over Emily. She hated being separated from them. But with Paelen's age and Stella's disability, they were safer and more useful away from the main fighting. The arrangement worked perfectly, as Stella had come up with several successful weapon designs that were already in use.

Emily knelt down to Pegasus. She stroked his face and patted his neck. 'You OK, Pegs?' she asked.

Pegasus nickered, but turned away, refusing to look at her.

'Pegs?' Emily said in concern. 'What's the matter?'

'Em, what's wrong?' Joel joined her by the stallion.

'I don't know.'

She grasped the stallion's muzzle and physically turned his head. When they looked into his eyes, they both gasped.

Agent B knelt down. 'What is it?'

'Look at his eyes,' Emily cried. 'They're solid white!'

'Pegasus, can you see?' Joel asked.

The stallion snorted and tried to turn away.

Agent B called a satyr away from his meal. 'Talk to Pegasus, ask him what's wrong.'

Like all the fighters on the battlefield, the satyr now

spoke English. Jupiter insisted it become the Olympian language of war. It was new and none of the Titans could understand it.

'Tell us, Pegasus, what is wrong?' the satyr asked.

Pegasus neighed softly. He turned his head to Emily and invited a stroke.

'Well?' she demanded. 'What did he say?'

The satyr dropped his head. 'He says the war is nearly over.'

'How does he know?' Agent B asked.

'Because Saturn has started to develop the weapon. Pegasus is ageing again.'

'Pegasus, no!' Emily now understood. Pegasus was blind.

How could she not have noticed? He had been moving slower. She'd had to stay close at his side to protect him from the attacking Shadow Titans.

Agent B rose. He caught the satyr's arm. 'Find Jupiter and his brothers. Tell them what has happened. Tell him we're out of time. We've got to make our move against Saturn now!'

27

Stella pushed her wheelchair closer to the workbench. Theo, a giant, was at her side, waiting for his instructions. He'd been assigned to stay with her as her personal assistant and was very attentive.

Vulcan was mixing metals in a deep cauldron to help with her new flame-sword design. 'This formula should be more stable. Those other metals melted too quickly. But if we get this right, your idea may just work.' He grinned at her. 'You do have a unique talent for this, Stella. Perhaps when the war is over, you will stay with me. We could do amazing things together.'

Stella's heart swelled with excitement. To be invited to stay and work with Vulcan was a dream come true. She knew him from the Greek myths as Hephaestus: the most talented craftsman and engineer in all mythology.

Vulcan didn't care if her hair was an uncombed mess or if her hands and fingernails were filthy from working in the forge. He didn't nag her to wash the soot off her face. He let her try new ideas and encouraged her to keep designing.

It had taken her some time to get used to him – just as it had taken time for him to get used to her and her wheelchair. Unlike the other Olympians, Vulcan was not known for his beauty. In fact, some would say he was grotesque. His face was scarred and pockmarked from the molten metals he worked with. He was hunched over and had artificial legs just like Joel's arm. His voice was gruff and his manner rude. Vulcan said what he thought. Good or bad.

'The mould is ready when you are,' Stella called to Vulcan as she wheeled her chair away from the bench. 'The central channel should be deep enough to allow the flame to keep burning while the weapon is in its sheath.'

'Very good,' Vulcan said. He lifted the cauldron of molten metal. 'This is ready to go.'

He carried it over to her workbench and poured the enriched liquid gold into the mould she had created. Until now, most of the Olympian's weapons had been pieces of metal pounded into shape. This was a new design and Stella was anxious for it to work.

Acrid smoke filled the forge as the metal met the

mould. When he finished pouring, Vulcan inspected the cooling weapon with a critical eye. 'There is no reason this should not work. Not if the mix is correct.'

The cooling mould was lowered into a tray of cold water. Steam shot up and covered them all in a damp film. 'That should temper it nicely,' Vulcan said. 'With a bit of luck, we should be able to test it tomorrow. But we need Emily here to charge it with her powers.'

'Have you heard from them?' Stella asked.

Vulcan wiped a grimy cloth across his sweaty brow. 'Chiron sent word today. They are moving. We have agreed to meet up so that Emily can enrich the weapon. We must tear down the forge and prepare to go later today.'

Stella hated moving. It was such a lot of effort to break down an entire forge and workshop. But with Shadow Titans still in Olympus, they couldn't remain in one place very long.

While they waited for the sword to cool, they started to pack up. But with the work only just beginning, shouts came from outside the workshop and a moment later Seren and Jasmine charged in. The twin centaurs were Stella's age and they had become firm friends.

'Shadow Titans have found us,' Seren cried.

'They have fiery dragons with them,' Jasmine added. 'We must go now!'

Paelen was seated on Brue at the back of the workshop. He and the large Mother of the Jungle spent every day there, despite the intense heat. Paelen was now almost completely deaf and could no longer walk on his own. At the excitement, he and Brue came forward. 'What is it?' he shouted. 'What is happening?'

'Dragons!' Vulcan yelled up to him. 'We must flee!'

'But the sword isn't ready. We can't leave it,' Stella cried.

'Take it with you,' the twin centaurs shouted together.

Stella reached for the sword, still in its mould, and laid it across her wheelchair's armrests. 'I've got it, let's go.'

Vulcan peered out of the workshop doors and cursed. 'There are Shadow Titans coming this way.' He pointed at the giant. 'Theo, leave everything else. Just get Stella and Paelen out of here. Meet us at the appointed place.'

The giant nodded, but as he reached for Stella roaring filled the area.

'The dragons are here!' the giant cried. 'It is too late to run!'

263

At the sound of the rampaging monsters, Brue growled. Over time she had proved to be a valuable member of their group as elements of the ferocious creature she had once been were now always present. Long sharp teeth protruded from her mouth. Her many legs had tearing claws on them and she could call up a fighting aggression at moments of danger. She was devoted to Paelen, but lethal to any Shadow Titans or monsters that came near.

Paelen had also been trained to use a sword and, together, seated on Brue's shoulder, they were a lethal team.

As Brue's two wild heads thrashed the air, snarling and biting, Paelen drew his weapon.

'Brue, Paelen, no!' Stella cried. 'Stay here!'

Paelen looked at Vulcan and raised his sword. It was almost too heavy for his withered arm to lift. 'We will slow them down,' he shouted. 'Get Stella and the sword away from here. Win the war!'

Before moving through the door, Paelen turned back to Stella and shot her a beaming, crooked grin. Suddenly he no longer looked like a weak, little old man. There was something in his eyes – something very young and wonderful. 'It was an honour to know you, Stella,' he shouted, bowing as best he could. He tossed her a small ring. 'Please give that to Emily. Tell her that I have loved her – always.'

And with that, the Mother of the Jungle ran into the open and straight at the nearest dragon.

'Stop!' Stella wheeled herself to the entrance of the forge. In the bright sunshine, Brue was tearing after the dragon. The monster was more than triple her size, but that didn't stop the fearsome Mother of the Jungle.

'Paelen, jump!' Stella warned. 'Get away from there!'

But Paelen was deaf to Stella's cries. He stabbed his sword deep into the dragon's lower leg. Brue's two heads attacked higher up, tearing huge chunks from the dragon and bringing the beast down.

The monster howled in pain. Its distress calls drew the other dragons away from the workshop. When they arrived at the fallen dragon, they drew in tremendous breaths.

'Paelen, get out of there!' Stella shrieked.

But it was too late. A deadly stream of flame shot from the dragons.

'Paelen!' Stella cried as grief tore through her. 'Paelen, no!'

She could not see her friend for all the flames. All she saw was fire and the outline of the wounded dragon also being incinerated in the attack.

Theo was standing behind her, watching. 'Paelen is dead,' he said, 'but he has given us time to escape. We must not waste it.' He lifted Stella in her wheelchair and carried her away from the forge. But as he ran, his movements caught the dragons' attention. They charged after him and struck Theo in the centre of his back with a force that knocked Stella from his grip.

Stella cradled the sword as she screamed and fell several metres to the ground. Her wheelchair took the brunt of the impact as its wheels buckled and frame shattered. Keeping hold of the prototype weapon, she started to drag herself away.

Behind her, Theo fought one of the dragons. The monster was taller, but the giant was stronger. He wrapped his hands around the creature's neck and squeezed. A terrible cracking sound filled the air as the bones snapped.

As the dead beast collapsed to the ground, the others attacked Theo. The giant was overwhelmed and driven down to the ground. He fell just a few metres from Stella. Above him, the dragons stood together and were inhaling deeply.

Theo threw himself over Stella, keeping her protected in the crook of his arm. Lying beneath him, she heard the roaring flames of the attacking dragons and then the giant's terrible, pain-filled screams. Theo was being burned up. But still he would not move and expose her to the dragon's fury.

Theo took it all so that she might live.

28

Emily fired a blast of flames at the legions of attacking Shadow Titans. They were instantly destroyed. But right behind them was another wave. This was the biggest assault yet. Joel was on one side of her while Agent B stood strong on the other. Their swords were drawn and they were cutting down anything that came near.

Pegasus was behind Emily. He was screaming and struggling to rise. Emily kept her protective powers around him. But Pegasus didn't like that. He wanted to join the fight.

Mike was running wild and attacking the Shadow Titans. For reasons none of them understood, the fearsome creatures ignored the dog, and so Mike was able to tear pieces of armour from countless Shadow Titans while Joel finished them off.

All across the battlefield, Olympians fought the Shadow Titans. Monsters that, in later myths, would be portrayed as enemies, fought side by side with Jupiter's forces. Giant crabs caught Shadow Warriors in their massive claws and cut them in half. They scurried across the battlefield, taking down many warriors.

The deadly Harpies, daughters of a Titan, filled the skies with their screeching battle cries. The terrifying winged fighters swooped down on the Shadow Titans. With their clawed feet, they tore them to pieces.

The Hydra was also fighting on the side of the Olympians. The many-headed serpent slithered through the battle, catching hold of the Shadow Titans and bashing them together until there was nothing left.

But still, the Olympians were losing.

Chiron charged breathlessly up to Emily. A deep gash ran across his sweat-covered chest. 'We are surrounded,' he gulped. 'There are too many and we are overwhelmed. Please, Emily, use your powers, get us away from here before they capture us all.'

Joel had a deep wound on his leg while Agent B had been struck across the back. Both were bleeding and looked on the verge of collapse.

Chiron was right. This battle was lost. Emily stood still and closed her eyes. She cast her powers out over the immense battlefield and caught hold of any ally that lived. Concentrating as hard as she could, she sent everyone to the meeting point.

One moment they were on a vicious battlefield surrounded by Shadow Titans, the next they were in a peaceful open meadow. Beautiful wildflowers covered the ground and a gentle, fragrant breeze filled the air.

This was a part of Olympus that had never seen the war. It was the Olympus Emily and Joel remembered. Not the devastated areas ravaged by war.

Emily healed Joel first and then Agent B. Then she made her way through the resting warriors, healing all she found who needed her. Before long, she was able to return and was sad to discover there was nothing she could do to ease Pegasus's suffering. The stallion's ageing was accelerating.

As Emily lay down beside him, Nike, the winged Victory, landed on the ground before her.

'We are so glad you have arrived,' Nike said. 'Please come, we need you. Stella has been badly wounded. Vulcan fears the human child is dying.'

'Please stay here with Agent B, Pegs. I promise I'll be right back.' She gave him a quick pat on the neck before lifting herself and Joel into the air to follow Nike.

Wounded Olympians were everywhere. But these

were not fighters. They were the workers that supported the war effort by preparing food, making clothing and manufacturing weapons to be used on the battlefield.

'What happened?' Joel asked. 'These people were supposed to stay safe and away from the fighting.'

'The Titans attacked Vulcan's forge,' Nike explained. 'We captured one of their spies. Under interrogation, he told us that Saturn knew of Stella's sword design. Fearing it might work, he sent monsters to kill her and destroy the sword before it could be tested.'

A pair of young centaurs ran up to Emily. They were both limping badly and had deep burns across their backs.

'Please hurry,' Seren begged.

'Stella is fading,' Jasmine finished. 'You must save her.'

They entered a tent filled with the worst wounded. Not far from the opening, Vulcan was being tended by his assistants. He was burned and had a deep head wound.

'Vulcan,' Joel cried. 'Em – you've got to help him.'

Emily approached Vulcan, but he waved her off. 'Not me, save Stella first.'

'Come,' the twins beckoned, 'she is this way.'

Emily and Joel walked among the wounded. At

the end, they approached a bed where Stella lay. She was deathly pale and barely breathing.

Emily immediately crouched at her side and touched her. 'What happened to her?'

'It was terrible,' Seren started. 'Vulcan's workshop was destroyed. Theo tried to get Stella away, but there were too many dragons. When they attacked him, he shielded her with his body, but then crushed her when he died.'

Stella's breathing returned to normal as Emily's powers began to work. Colour returned to her face.

'Hey, where's Paelen?' Joel looked around. 'I thought he'd be here with Stella.'

The twin centaurs lowered their heads. 'I am so sorry, Joel,' Jasmine started. 'Paelen and Brue were lost in the battle.'

'What do you mean, "lost"?' Emily gasped.

Seren told them of Paelen's bravery against the dragons.

'We tried to find his body after the fire, but there was nothing left,' Jasmine added. 'He and Brue were completely burned up.'

'Paelen died saving us,' Vulcan added gruffly, approaching Stella's bed. 'He drew the dragons away from the forge and gave us time to escape. He, Brue and Theo will be remembered always.'

'Are you sure?' Joel's voice broke. 'Maybe he got away.'

Vulcan patted him on the back. 'I am so sorry, there is no mistake. He was killed by the dragons.'

'Why?' Joel cried. 'Why did he do it?'

'Joel, listen to me,' Vulcan said. 'Paelen was very old and fragile. He no longer had the strength of an Olympian. With the Titan weapon being developed, his ageing increased. He knew he would not last much longer so he chose his own time to die. Paelen may have been a notorious thief who liked to steal my tools, but he died a brave hero.'

Emily collapsed to the floor. She couldn't speak and could barely breathe.

Joel fell beside her. 'It's my fault. I told him to stay here. I thought he and Stella would be safe away from the fighting.'

They clung to each other in disbelief.

How could this happen? They were a team. They were meant to be together always.

As night fell, a heavy silence filled the large encampment as they grieved over the many losses. No one spoke the words, but everyone feared that, even with Emily's help, the war was lost.

A small campfire burned and cast embers into the sky as Joel fed another chunk of wood into the flames. 'I really can't believe he's gone,' he muttered.

Emily was too grief-stricken to speak. She had a special bond with Paelen and the cut ran deeper than she thought possible. Pegasus was on the ground behind her and nudged her gently.

Agent B spoke softly. 'Listen to me,' he said. 'Yes, Paelen is gone. But if we win this war, if we destroy that damn weapon and hit the reset button, then when you go back to Xanadu, he will be there waiting for you. Just as young and strong and as much of a troublemaker as you remember him. Paelen's sacrifice will not be in vain.'

Too filled with the loss of Paelen and Brue to sleep, Emily, Joel and Agent B spent the whole night sitting together.

At dawn Vulcan returned to their small camp. Everyone was surprised to see Stella with him. She was in a new golden wheelchair with a blanket covering her legs. The wheelchair was unlike anything they'd ever seen before. Stella did not have to use her arms to move it. There was no battery pack or motor to get it to go, it just moved on its own.

'Stella,' Joel called, 'are you all right?'

Heaviness rested in her eyes. She looked like she hadn't slept either. She nodded and smiled sadly at Vulcan. 'Vulcan was up all night making this new chair for me. Her name is Maxine.'

'Your wheelchair has a name?' Joel asked.

Stella nodded. 'She's beautiful, isn't she? Maxine will take me anywhere I ask her to. I still don't know how he did it without his forge, but he did.'

Vulcan put his arm around Stella's shoulders. 'It is a special chair of wheels for a very special girl.' He focused on Emily. 'Up until now, Stella and Paelen would never tell me who they really were or where they came from. It was a secret they kept to themselves. But last night, Stella finally explained. She told me what happened to Olympus in the future, about Xanadu, who you all are and how you have come to destroy the Titan weapon. You have risked everything to be here for us.'

'We had no choice,' Emily said. 'Not if Olympus is to survive.'

Agent B agreed. 'This war must be won by the Olympians and that Titan weapon must be destroyed or there is no future for any of us.'

Vulcan nodded. 'And so it will be. Now that I know

what is at stake, I will do everything I can to see you all safely back home.'

Stella looked down at her hand. She pulled a ring off her finger and held it out to Emily. 'Paelen asked me to give this to you right before he . . .' her voice trailed off. She looked up at Emily. 'He told me to tell you he loved you. He always has.'

Emily took the ring. It was a blue sapphire set in a beautiful silver band. Paelen knew her favourite stone was sapphire. 'Where did he get it?'

Vulcan chuckled softly. 'He stole it from Minerva. I made it for her ages ago.'

Emily offered him the ring. 'Here, please give it back to her.'

Vulcan shook his head. 'No, you keep it. Paelen wanted you to have it. I am sure Minerva will understand.'

Emily put the ring on her finger. She always knew Paelen cared for her, but she never realized just how much. 'Oh Paelen . . .'

Stella nodded to Vulcan. 'I think you should show them.'

Vulcan produced a sword. It was elegant in design and made of gold. A deep channel ran down the centre of the blade.

'This is it,' he said softly. 'This is what Paelen died for. Stella's sword. Even in the heat of battle, she kept it with her and protected it. If this works, we may stand a chance against the Shadow Titans.'

'But the forge is gone,' Stella said. 'Even if it does work, we can't make any more.'

'We can build a new forge,' Vulcan said. 'I know the formula to this metal and we have your mould. If it works, we can start producing swords immediately.'

'We still need to test it,' Stella said.

'Indeed we do.' Vulcan approached Emily. 'I understand you are grieving. But we need your help.'

Emily stood, but without enthusiasm. She felt like something inside her had died with Paelen.

'Come on, Em,' Joel put his arm around her. 'Paelen wouldn't want us to be defeated by this. We've got to keep going.'

Emily nodded. 'I'll try. What do you need me to do?'

After some failed attempts, Emily found a way to use her powers to keep Stella's sword design burning. She discovered if she cut her finger and wiped a tiny amount of blood down the central channel, it would fuel the sword.

'OK, so it's burning,' Emily said softly. 'Now what?'

Vulcan grinned triumphantly. 'We use it to burn up the Shadow Titans.'

Joel shook his head. 'Fire doesn't destroy them. We've already tried. It's only Emily's Flame that can do it. So even though your sword is burning, it's still just fire.'

'This is not simply a fiery sword, Joel,' Vulcan said. 'It is very special. Tell me, what do you need to destroy a shadow?'

Joel frowned. 'I'm not sure.'

'To remove a shadow, you need light,' Agent B answered.

'Exactly,' Vulcan agreed. 'Not fire, but light. The Shadow Titans are created from the shadows of the original Four Warriors. Vesta tells us that Emily contains the power of the sun. You are the only one who has been able to destroy the Shadow Titans with ease because you use your sun's power. You use *light*.'

'We thought this sword could contain some of your sun power,' Stella explained. 'If it works, it should be able to destroy a Shadow Titan as easily as you do.'

Agent B took the burning sword from Vulcan's hand and inspected it closely. The flames along the shaft continued to burn brightly without destroying Emily's blood. 'You think this could win the war?'

'It could help,' Vulcan said.

Agent B swiped the sword in the air. No matter what he did or how he tried, the flames would not extinguish. 'All we need now is to capture a Shadow Titan to test it.'

'Already done,' Vulcan said. 'Stella and I wish to invite you to the test.'

29

As they walked to the test site, Joel pulled Emily aside and told the others to go on without them. He held up Emily's hand and looked at the ring Paelen had given her.

'I knew how Paelen felt about you. I've always known.'

Emily shook her head. 'Why didn't he ever say anything?'

'Because Paelen was my best friend,' Joel choked. 'He knew my feelings for you, so he said nothing.'

'Paelen knew?'

Joel nodded. 'He said we both came from the same world so we were meant to be together. He said he would have to be content just being your friend.'

'Oh, Paelen,' Emily whispered. 'I should have told him how I felt.'

'What do you mean, "how you felt"?' Joel's voice sounded strained.

'No, Joel, it's not like that. I wasn't in love with Paelen. I cared for him as a friend. It's you I . . .' she paused.

'What?'

Emily dropped her head. The war was taking so many people away from her. She couldn't let this moment pass without Joel knowing how she really felt. Finally she lifted her eyes. 'I love you, Joel.'

Joel pulled Emily close. 'I love you too.'

And he kissed her.

It was long and tender and filled with many promises.

When they arrived at the test site, they were surprised to see the Big Three. Emily heard that Venus had just returned from Tartarus to look for the Hundred-handers, but didn't know if she had found them or not.

'I was sorry to hear about Paelen.' Jupiter walked towards Emily. 'His was a great loss for all of us.'

Neptune nodded. 'I think when this war ends, we should build a statue to him and Brue. I believe he would like that.'

Emily swallowed and nodded. 'He would.'

Beside Emily, Pegasus nickered softly.

'Pegasus says he is ageing faster,' Neptune translated.

281

'Saturn must be nearing completion of the weapon.'

'We've got to destroy it before you all get older,' Joel cried.

'Have you not noticed?' Neptune said. 'We are already ageing.'

Jupiter gave Emily a wide grin that deepened his dimples. 'Yes, I am losing my youthful glow! Do I not look older to you? More mature?' He flexed his arms and puffed out his broad chest. 'I am not as handsome as before.'

Emily chuckled at what he was trying to do to cheer her up. There was something about him that so much reminded her of Paelen. A cheekiness that constantly surprised her. 'You look fine, Jupiter.'

'Stop it, Jupe,' Neptune said. 'Leave the poor girl alone.' He looked at the others. 'This is why we have gathered together here. The time has come to make our final move on Titus before Father launches that weapon on us.'

Vulcan held up the flame-sword. 'This is the weapon we spoke of. Emily worked out a way to light it. We are about to test it on the Shadow Titans you brought in.'

'This should be fun,' Jupiter said, rubbing his hands together. 'Bring them forward.'

A gigantic crab ambled sideways on multiple legs towards them. Two large nets were suspended high in the crab's front claws. Trapped inside the nets were Shadow Titans. The warriors were silent as they tried to fight and cut their way free.

'These represent the four types of warriors,' Jupiter said. 'Vulcan, test your sword.'

Inside the nearest net were a Minotaur Shadow and a Turtle Shadow. They were thrashing and struggling to get out. When they saw Vulcan approach, they tried to reach through the net to grab him.

'They're just like zombies,' Joel whispered to Emily. 'Not frightened for themselves. All they want to do is kill.'

'I hope this works.' Emily was standing with Pegasus and could feel him shivering as though he were cold. But it was a warm day. 'Are you OK, Pegs?'

The stallion nodded and leaned in closer to her. There was something about the way he moved that frightened her. She was reminded of old Chiron right before he . . . Emily stopped the thought. Paelen's loss was too fresh and painful. Instead she focused on the test.

With the flaming sword held high, Vulcan slashed at the net. The ropes gave way and the two Shadow

Titans crashed to the ground. The crowd gasped as the Shadow Warriors advanced on him.

With the skills of working with weapons all his life, Vulcan dodged the Shadow Titans' attacks. With a single, quick slash, he cut the Minotaur Shadow in half. The hollow armour collapsed to the ground in pieces and became still. With a second swipe, the Turtle Shadow followed the first.

The Olympians went wild. They clapped their hands and roared as Vulcan made quick work of the Blackbird and Dragon Shadows.

'Pegasus, it worked!' Emily cried as she threw her arms around his neck. 'I wish you could see. The Shadow Titans fell apart when Vulcan touched them with the sword.'

Pegasus whinnied and nodded his head.

Vulcan waved the flame-sword in the air triumphantly. He called Stella forward and ensured that everyone knew it was her design that defeated the Shadow Titans. While Stella's name was being chanted by the crowd, Vulcan called to his workers. 'Build me a forge, we have weapons to make!'

Vulcan's new forge burned night and day as the workshop produced flame-swords. Stella worked closely with Vulcan, supervising the construction of more moulds. Soon they were being produced in their thousands.

Emily charged each blade with a small amount of her blood. As soon as a sword was finished and lit, it was given to an Olympian and they were sent back out on to the battlefield.

While the main battle continued, Jupiter and his war chamber gathered together, and requested that Emily, Pegasus, Joel and Agent B join them. First to speak were Venus and Minerva as they gave their full reports on what they had learned on their spy missions.

The good news was they had found where the Hundred-handers were being held on Tartarus. It would be difficult and dangerous to free them, but not impossible. Thousands of Shadow Titans guarded the prison, but with the new flame-swords, and enough fighters, they stood a chance of breaking in.

An unexpected bonus was that they had discovered the Four Warriors were also in Tartarus. They were kept locked in the deep underground prison. It was from this location that Shadow Titans emerged in a steady stream of fighters.

Then the bad news came in the report from Minerva. She stood before the group.

'In the short time we were on Titus, we could not find where the weapon is being created. But we all felt its awful effects. It stripped us of our powers and made us all gravely ill. We could not remain there long without risking our lives. Even now I feel weak and aged from the short exposure to it.'

'What about the Titans?' Agent B asked. 'Aren't they affected by their own weapon?'

Minerva shook her head. 'We do not know. We could not find one living Titan there – though there were thousands of Shadow Titans. Whoever, or whatever, is working on that weapon is either immune to its effects or they are the living-dead.'

Minerva finished by warning that an assault on Titus would be nothing less than a suicide mission for those who went. She sat down, looking drawn and exhausted. Her short visit to Titus had taken a heavy toll and she and her team needed time to recover.

Jupiter faced his war council. The youthful smile left his face and Emily saw a hint of the man he was becoming.

'We have no choice but to go back to Titus. That weapon must be captured before it is completed. The only way we can hope to achieve this is with the help of the Hundred-handers. We will gather our best fighters and go to Tartarus to free them. From there, we will journey to Titus to take on the Shadow Titans. While our fighters and the Hundred-handers engage the Shadow Titans, a select group of us will move on the weapon and secure it.'

30

While they prepared for the first assault on Tartarus, Vulcan began working to create the golden box that would house the weapon. Having seen the box for herself in the future, Stella volunteered to help with its design and construction.

Emily delighted in watching the young Jupiter, Neptune and Pluto train. They were showing many more powers than she knew they had and mixed using them with the flame-swords. They could fly, levitate things and move impossibly fast. They were stronger than she ever imagined. She finally understood why they were called the Big Three.

But as each day came and went, Emily's concern for Pegasus grew.

The stallion was growing weaker. His natural glow faded and then stopped completely. He no longer ate solid food. The most Emily could get into him was soft chocolate ice-cream mixed with nectar.

'Come on, Pegs, eat,' Emily said softly as she held ambrosia cakes before the stallion's mouth. But Pegasus turned away.

Pegasus never stopped shivering. He was constantly cold and Emily made sure he was always draped in several blankets. All his feathers had fallen out and the hair covering his body was now baby-fine.

The only relief from training and worry for Pegasus came when Stella would visit their camp to show off a crazy new addition to her super wheelchair, Maxine. It could now fly and also carried several hidden weapons, including the silver dagger with the marble handle and green jewel. Stella and Vulcan had made it together and Stella laughed, knowing it was the same dagger her parents would find in the future. Best of all, the wheelchair also included a place for her very own flame-sword.

Two nights before they were to leave for Tartarus, Neptune entered Emily's small camp and asked to speak with her and Pegasus privately. Instead of moving the resting stallion, Joel and Agent B excused themselves.

Neptune took a seat before the fire. He stroked Pegasus's side and wouldn't meet Emily's eyes. 'We need to talk,' he started heavily. 'It is about Pegasus.'

His manner and tone caused a flutter of fear in Emily's stomach. 'What about him?'

Neptune sighed heavily. 'Pegasus knows it is time for him to go.'

Emily's hand shot up to her mouth. 'No . . .'

'Yes, Emily,' Neptune said. 'He has remained alive for as long as he can – perhaps longer than he should have, because he could not bear to leave you. But now he is old and so very tired. Pegasus knows the battle you are facing. You will need all your wits about you and must not be worried about him.'

Emily was shaking her head. 'No, please. Pegs, I can fight fine with you beside me. I always have. We're a team. I need you . . .'

'Look at him, Emily,' Neptune said. 'Look and really see him. See how he is suffering.'

Emily gazed at her beloved Pegasus. He was blind and painfully thin. He had no teeth and he was always cold. The stallion was in terrible pain. She knew it. But the thought of letting him go was unbearable.

'Please, Pegs,' she whispered desperately.

Neptune lowered himself to the ground beside her. Pegasus's head was lying in Emily's lap and she could feel him struggle for each breath.

'It is time for Pegasus to rest. He has earned it.'

'I can't let him go.'

'You must,' Neptune said. 'Emily, your love for him is keeping him here. But it is not fair on either of you. You must release him.'

'How can I lose him?'

'You will not lose him, not really,' Neptune said. 'Once you destroy that weapon, everything will go back to the way it once was. He will be waiting for you on Xanadu. Just like Paelen and Brue. He will be there, Emily. Just as young and powerful as you remember him. When you go back there, the two of you can finally visit all the continents you wanted to see.

'That is the Pegasus you know,' Neptune continued. 'Not this suffering, blind old stallion. Let him go, Emily. Let your love for Pegasus free him.'

With shaking hands Emily stroked Pegasus's head. She couldn't bear it. This was Pegasus. Her Pegasus. 'I can't . . .' she whispered.

Pegasus raised his head from her lap weakly. He nickered softly and licked her hand.

'He is begging your forgiveness for leaving you, but he must go.'

Deep sobs poured from Emily. She used her embroidered handkerchief to collect her tears before they could fall and hurt the dying stallion.

'Oh, Pegasus . . .'

Emily kissed him on his closed eyes. 'I don't want you to hurt any more. Go to sleep, Pegs,' she spoke softly. 'Just know that I love you. I have always loved you and I always will. Go now and be free.'

Emily collapsed over Pegasus as grief overwhelmed her. Beneath her, she could feel his laboured breathing even out. Moment by moment it was becoming more shallow. With a final soft sigh, it ended.

'Pegasus!' Emily howled.

Neptune was beside her, murmuring softly. But Emily couldn't hear him. She couldn't feel Mike beside her whining and putting his paw on her. She couldn't see anything or do anything but howl over her loss. This wasn't like when he disappeared at Area 51. This time, there was no mistake. His head rested in her lap, silent and still.

Joel heard her cries. He crouched beside her. His hand rested on the stallion's featherless wing. 'Pegasus?'

'He's gone, Joel,' Emily whispered.

Joel didn't try to hide his tears. Pegasus had meant almost as much to him as he did to Emily. Losing Paelen and Pegasus in such a short time was unbearable.

Agent B knelt down on the ground behind Emily.

292

He rocked her gently in his arms. 'Let it out, Emily,' he soothed softly as she broke down. 'Just let it all out.'

31

'Pegasus is dead...'

Emily wanted to write more in her journal, but failed. Each time she tried, tears threatened to fall and she had to stop.

Suddenly she was cast back to the dark days, right after her mother had died. Back when the world made no sense and all she knew was pain. She couldn't eat, couldn't sleep and couldn't do much of anything.

Neptune had told her that Pegasus wasn't really gone. If they found and destroyed the weapon, he would be waiting for her on Xanadu. But there were no guarantees that they would find it. Minerva had made that clear in her report.

Knowing she might see him again in the future couldn't stop her grief in the present.

Emily used her powers to light Pegasus's funeral pyre. Joel stood beside her holding her hand. Agent B stood on the other side of Emily. He remained silent and unmoving during the short ceremony, standing with his arm wrapped around her shoulders.

Most of the people in the large camp knew of the old winged stallion that had lived with Emily and was her constant companion. Only a select few knew who he really was and how much he meant to the Olympians. It was those few who attended the pyre.

Stella, Seren and Jasmine stood back with Vulcan. When the fire burned down to embers, Vulcan came forward and scooped up some of the ashes. Saying nothing, he and his three assistants slipped away quietly and returned to their forge.

After a long and sleepless night, Emily rose and walked away from the camp. She needed time alone. Mike, however, never obeyed when Emily told him to stay. So, like it or not, the dog remained close at her side.

The large camp was still set up in the beautiful meadow. There had been no signs of Shadow Titans, despite them remaining there for some time. Emily had learned to 'feel' when the Shadow Titans were near and knew they were safe for the moment.

She and Mike wandered along a beautiful, trickling steam. The sun was shining brightly overhead. Around them, birds sang beautifully in the tress and the huge, car-sized butterflies she had always loved in Olympus fluttered from one oversized flower to another.

The day was perfect. But for Emily it meant nothing. She felt lost and alone without Pegasus at her side.

'*I am so sorry, Emily. I know how much you and Pegasus meant to each other.*'

'Riza!' Emily cried, shocked at her sudden return after so long. 'Where have you been?'

'*Where I have always been, child. Deep within you.*'

'But why haven't you said anything? I've called for you, but you've been silent. We've been through so much. I really needed your help.'

'*You don't need my help, Emily, not really. You did fine before I became known to you. You have done fine until now.*'

'But what happened? Where did you go?'

'*I never left. But when you received the knowledge of the Xan and Joel touched us, the information was too great and it was killing him. I did all I could to protect him, but it weakened me greatly.*'

'You saved his life?'

'*How could I not?*' Riza asked. '*He is our Joel. But after that, I was too weak to speak to you. Too weak to warn you away from your actions.*'

'What actions?' Emily asked. 'You mean coming back here?'

'*Yes,*' Riza said. '*It was very dangerous to try. You are playing with time, Emily. Not even the Xan would attempt that. There is no telling what damage could be done to the future with your presence here in the past.*'

'It couldn't be worse than what already happened to Olympus and possibly Earth. It was a risk I had to take.'

'*I know,*' Riza said. '*I also know that you are young and need to make your own mistakes. So I have remained silent to let you do what you must. But when Pegasus died, part of you died with him. You must bring that part back if you are to succeed in this.*'

'You know what we are planning?'

'*Yes,*' Riza said. '*And I have come to realize that you were correct. I believe you were destined to be part of this war. But that does not remove the danger you pose to the future if you are not very careful. You must go to Tartarus to free the Hundred-handers. Then you will go to Titus to destroy that weapon. But heed my warning, Emily. Within you is the power to kill the strongest of Titans. That must never happen. You may destroy all the Shadow Titans you encounter. But if you kill a full Titan, you will alter the future.*'

'I'll be careful,' Emily said softly. She sat down in the tall grass. Mike sat beside her, panting happily. He put his paw on her arm, asking to be petted. Emily stroked the dog's warm fur and pressed her face to him. 'I just need a bit of time before we go.'

'*Time is the one commodity you do not have,*' Riza warned. '*You already know this, but your grief over Pegasus is blinding you to it. The weapon is nearly complete. The Titans will use it against the Olympians the moment it is ready. Everyone here will die if you do not stop it now. There will be no future to protect.*'

Riza's words cut through Emily's grief like a knife. They were in grave danger and she was wasting precious time. Jupiter had said she should take all the time she needed to recover. But that was something they couldn't spare.

Emily stood, now resolved. 'Please tell me, Riza. If this works and if I destroy the weapon, will it reset time? At first, I was certain this was the right thing to do. But now I don't know. Can you tell me: if I destroy that weapon, will Pegasus and Paelen be waiting for us on Xanadu like nothing ever happened?'

'*Yes, child,*' Riza confirmed, '*if you succeed, time will go back to the way it was before the golden box was opened. All you have lost will be restored – including Pegasus and*

Paelen. But know this. There will be a price to pay.'

Emily's heart leaped. 'To get Pegasus and Paelen back, I'll pay anything!'

Emily returned to camp a changed person. Grief had been replaced by solid determination. Nothing was going to stop her from getting back to Pegasus.

She found Joel and Agent B and told them of Riza's return. 'We must go now,' she insisted. 'The sooner we finish this, the sooner we can get back to Xanadu.'

They found the Big Three talking with Venus and Minerva, working out the finer details of the next move in the war.

Emily's renewed energy was infectious and spread like wildfire. Jupiter called forward the large war camp and suspended himself high in the air so that his voice could be heard by all the Olympians gathered together.

'My people,' he shouted, 'now is the time to make our move. The Shadow Titans are increasing their numbers on Earth. We will journey back to Delphi and engage the Titans fully. We will show them once and for all that we will not tolerate their assaults on Olympus or Earth. They will experience the power of our new flame-swords. They will feel our strength and determination. It is time for Saturn to stand down.

Pack your weapons and prepare for battle. We leave at sunset!'

The crowds roared and cried Jupiter's name.

Emily and Joel looked at each other. 'Delphi – isn't that in Greece?' asked Joel.

Agent B was watching the crowd. 'Something is very wrong here.' He shook his head.

'How do you know?' Joel asked.

'I can feel it,' he said darkly. 'Maybe Neptune can enlighten us.'

They made their way through the dense crowd until they reached Neptune, who was locked in deep conversation with Chiron.

'Neptune, what's Jupiter talking about?' Emily asked softly. 'We need to go to Tartarus, not Delphi.'

The two Olympians looked around to be certain no one was within listening distance. 'We have been suspicious for some time,' Neptune whispered, 'but now we are certain. There are Titan spies living among us in this camp.'

'How can you be sure?' Agent B asked. 'Has anyone been interrogated?'

Chiron shook his head. 'No. That would give light to our suspicions. But as a fighter yourself, you must realize we have been left untouched far too long. Emily draws the Titans and their Shadow Titans everywhere she goes. And yet, after all this time here, we have not been disturbed once.'

Agent B nodded. 'I was considering the same thing. Saturn knows of the danger Emily poses to him and his people. He also knows about the flame-swords. He'll be playing for time while they finish the weapon.'

'Precisely,' Neptune agreed. 'So we are all heading to Earth. While most of our fighters engage the Shadow Titans at Delphi, some of us will slip quietly away and head to Tartarus and then Titus. This war will be won with stealth, not open battles.'

'Good plan,' Agent B agreed. He turned to Emily and Joel. 'This is it. One way or another, our fate will be determined tonight.'

32

In record time the camp was struck and everyone prepared to leave. Even those who had never fought before had been trained and outfitted with weapons. Only the very young would be exempt from fighting. This was to be the final battle in the war. Its outcome would determine everyone's future.

As the sun set, Vulcan, Stella and the twin centaurs found Emily, Joel and Agent B. Stella had a large grin on her face.

'Here it is,' she said proudly. She leaned over and pointed to a covered box suspended from her seat. 'It's the golden box, just as I remembered it. Maxine is going to carry it for us.'

Emily and Joel knelt down and pulled the cover from the box. Emily traced her fingers along the imprint of the Big Three. 'It's really beautiful.'

Agent B joined them. 'I told you it was a piece of art.'

'You were right,' Emily agreed, 'but I can't wait to bury it in the ground.'

'Amen to that!' Joel said.

When they stood, Vulcan handed out several small packages. 'I myself do not believe in luck. However, I hope these bring us all the best of it.'

Emily opened her gift. Inside was a small, silver Pegasus charm on a braided chain. The stallion was in flight and looked as young and powerful as he always had.

'I made these from the ashes of Pegasus,' Vulcan explained, 'so that he might be with us in this final battle.'

Emily was too touched to speak. Joel had always cared a great deal for Vulcan, but she never knew just how quietly thoughtful he really was. She threw her arms around the grimy Olympian and hugged him tightly.

'I'll never take it off!' she cried. 'Now we can't lose. Pegasus will protect us!'

Joel also gratefully received his pendant. He helped Emily put hers on before fastening his own.

Emily watched in surprise as Agent B also put on his pendant. When he caught her watching him he shrugged. 'It can't hurt.'

Emily raised her hand in the air. 'To Team Pegasus!'
The others cheered. 'Team Pegasus,' they cried.

'Now, if you are ready to go,' Vulcan said, becoming serious, 'we have been asked to join Jupiter. He wants us all to stay close together.'

'We're ready,' Emily said. 'Let's finish this.'

The Olympians arrived on Earth in their thousands. At Delphi, the locals greeted their arrival with relief and gratitude. The Titans had been killing everyone they caught and destroying village after village.

Emily and Joel looked around in wonder. They were halfway up a high mountain, surrounded by other, even taller, tree-covered mountains. Delphi looked nothing like Athens or even Cape Sounio. It was hard to imagine they were even in Greece. It looked more like the mountain ranges in West Virginia or the Carolinas.

'I haven't been here since the accident that crippled me,' Stella said. 'It looks so different. There are no ruins.'

'What ruins?' Seren asked.

Stella pointed to a large marble temple further down the mountainside. Its tall pillars climbed high into the sky and it had solid sides and a marble roof. It looked very much like an Olympian building. 'The ruins were there.'

'How?' Jasmine asked. 'This place is new. The humans have only just completed it.'

'It's a long story,' Stella said, 'but one day, there will be ruins here.'

'What is that temple?' Emily asked.

'That's the Temple of Apollo at Delphi,' Stella explained. 'It is in there that the Oracle sat to foretell the future. It was said she could channel Apollo and speak to all the gods.'

'Who is Apollo?' Jasmine asked.

Emily started to explain about Jupiter's son, but Agent B stopped her. 'That's enough, Emily. Remember, what you say can affect the future. It's best not to say more.'

'Sorry,' Emily said to the twins, 'he's right, I shouldn't say any more.'

A shouted warning came from further down the mountain. There were thousands of Shadow Titans converging on them. The sky above was filled with the dark-winged Blackbird Shadows and, mixed amongst them, were monsters of all shapes and sizes. Some walked, while others crawled, slithered or flew.

Agent B cursed. 'Neptune was right. There were

spies in the camp. The Titans have been waiting for us. It's a trap.'

'This is perfect.' Jupiter sounded unfazed as he turned to Emily. 'You, my brothers and I will engage the flying Shadows. We will destroy as many as possible while our other fighters take up their positions in the mountains. The Titans must believe we are making our final stand here.'

Vulcan and Chiron approached Joel and Agent B. 'Everything is set. We are just waiting for our armour to arrive. We have sent several crabs to collect it all. We will leave the moment it gets here.'

Higher on the mountain, Emily stood shoulder to shoulder with the Big Three. Jupiter was on her right. When he caught her looking at him, he winked and grinned, rubbing his hands together excitedly. 'This is going to be good!'

On her other side, Neptune and Pluto weren't quite as enthusiastic as Jupiter, but their excitement showed as they gathered their powers together to take on the Shadow Titans.

Emily grasped her new Pegasus pendant, brought it to her lips and kissed it for luck. 'For you, Pegs!'

'Now!' Jupiter shouted.

With the most powerful Olympians at her side,

Emily unleashed the Flame and fired great blasts of fire beams into the sky, which instantly vapourized every Shadow Titan they touched.

Beside her, Jupiter shot lightning and thunder bolts at flying snakes, dragons and Shadow Titans as they swooped down towards them.

Neptune and Pluto directed their powers at the creatures climbing up the sides of the mountain, taking out large groups of monsters with every blast.

Further below, the battle intensified as Olympian went up against Titan. Giant crabs fought dragons. The Hydra took on a flying snake and made quick work of it. The Furies and Harpies caught hold of Titan monsters and carried them away. Even the smallest satyrs raised their flame-swords against the Shadow Titans.

'Emily, look!' Joel cried.

On the neighbouring mountain, the most terrifying monster Emily had ever seen was cresting the top. No creature from any horror movie could compare to the 'thing' that was coming for them.

Its overwhelming hugeness made the tall mountain look like a tiny hill. It was shaped like a twisted octopus with at least twenty tentacles that flashed and flew in the air around it. The creature had an undulating bulbous body that moved like a half-filled water balloon. Its wet, slimy, mottled brown skin left a trail of smouldering acid behind it. There were no eyes that Emily could see. But the monstrosity had vision, as it tore up huge trees and tossed them at the gathered Olympians.

'What is that?' Agent B cried.

Jupiter turned and sucked in his breath. 'It is the Copac-ra!'

'No, you must be wrong,' Neptune argued. 'It is locked deep in Tartarus. Not even the Titans will approach it.'

'And yet, there it is,' Pluto said.

'How could Father get it here?' Jupiter asked. 'No one can command the Copac-ra.'

'It doesn't look like anyone is,' Emily cried. Above them the Copac-ra caught hold of a flying Shadow Titan and pulled it to its moving body. A hole opened and the Shadow Titan disappeared into a grotesque mouth. Another tentacle caught hold of a screaming human fighter who suffered the same fate.

'It's eating everyone it catches,' Joel cried. 'It doesn't matter what side they're on.'

Emily raised her hands in the air and prepared to fire at the monster.

'*No, Emily, you must not!*' Riza cried. '*The Copac-ra*

is the last of its kind. It must be protected. In the future it will live peacefully on Xanadu.'

'That's the future!' Emily cried. 'Right now, that thing is about to eat all of us.'

'Use your powers, child,' Riza called. *'Send it to Xanadu. Set it free.'*

'How?' Emily said.

'Trust me,' Riza said softly. *'You know what to do. Just focus on sending it to Xanadu. I will do the rest.'*

Lifting her hands again, Emily summoned all her powers. 'Xanadu,' she called. 'Go to Xanadu!'

Emily felt Riza working with her and guiding her powers to send the Copac-ra to Xanadu. The air around the monster sparkled and the creature vanished.

'Father is sending everything at us,' Jupiter cried. He looked around at the monsters and Shadow Titans swarming the mountains around them. The Olympians and humans were badly outnumbered. 'This war will not be easily won.'

'We need the Hundred-handers,' Chiron called. 'Keep the Shadow Titans occupied while we collect the last of our armour.'

Emily and the Big Three focused their efforts on stopping as many Shadow Titans as possible while, lower down the mountain, the Olympians engaged the

Shadow Titans in hand-to-hand combat. The glow of flame-swords rose from the mountainside as they used their weapons against the Shadow Titans.

As the long day progressed, Emily feared they would never beat the relentless Shadow Titans. They never tired. But the Olympians and humans did. Despite their best efforts, on sheer numbers alone, the Shadow Titans were gaining ground against them.

Chiron appeared behind Jupiter, wearing part of a Dragon Shadow's armour. If the situation had been less desperate, Emily would have laughed. The front half of the centaur looked just like a Dragon Shadow Titan. But when he turned, his back end was still that of a chestnut horse.

Behind him, Joel was dressed as a Minotaur Shadow. His whole body was covered in armour with only his head exposed. He held a Minotaur helmet in his hand. Even in these critical moments, Emily allowed herself a moment to appreciate how attractive Joel looked in the armour.

Agent B was shockingly convincing as a Blackbird Shadow. The wings of the warrior hung limp at the back, but he had learned to mimic their walk. Minerva and Venus were also suited up and looked frighteningly like the Turtle Shadows.

Venus was lightly binding Seren and Jasmine's hands to give credibility to their presence on Tartarus. The plan was to deliver the twin centaurs and Stella to the prison as 'prisoners'.

'We have your armour ready,' Chiron told the Big Three.

Emily continued to fire her powers at the masses of Shadow Titans. As she stopped to take a breath, she turned to Chiron. 'How did you get the armour?'

'Each suit is made up of several Shadow Titans destroyed by the flame-swords,' Chiron explained. 'Joel has chosen a Turtle Shadow for you.'

The Big Three took over from Emily as she put on the Turtle armour. Before Minerva secured her breastplate into position, Agent B pulled Emily aside. In his armour-covered hand was a small leather-bound book.

'Would you hold this for me?' he asked, handing her the book. 'Put it with your own journal. I've been keeping one too. If anything should happen to me—'

'Nothing is going to happen to you,' Emily insisted, feeling very uncomfortable at the turn in conversation.

'I hope not,' he continued, 'but if anything should, I want you to have this. Then if you succeed in destroying that weapon and hitting the reset button, I'm asking you, as a friend, find me in London – my address is in the front of the book. Find me and please, get me away from the CRU.'

He tilted his head to the side and smiled. 'You know me now. You know I'll fight you. Get me to Olympus or Xanadu, it doesn't matter which. Show me this journal. Force me to read it –' he grinned again '– as only you can. I have written secret messages to myself that only I would understand. I have warned myself to leave the CRU.'

'Why are you doing this?' Emily asked.

'Really, you don't know?' he asked incredulously. 'After all this time here, I have come to care a great deal about you, Joel and all these crazy Olympians. He said. 'I can no longer be part of any agency that seeks to destroy them and exploit you. Once the other "me" reads this journal, I'm hoping he will help you bring down the CRU. I know things, Emily. Things that can expose the Central Research Unit for what it really is.'

Emily could see the sincerity in his intense blue eyes. She accepted the journal and slipped it in her tunic pocket beside her own. 'I promise,' she said finally. 'Whatever happens, I will find you and make you read this.'

'Thank you,' Agent B said. He pulled on the Blackbird helmet. 'Now finish getting suited up. We leave the moment you're ready.'

Once they were all in the leather armour of the Shadow Titans, Emily and the Big Three combined their powers together. They all held hands and gathered close as Jupiter, Neptune and Pluto closed their eyes.

'Tartarus' they shouted.

33

Emily wondered if she would ever get used to visiting new worlds. It was one thing to read science fiction books or see other worlds in movies, but nothing could prepare her for the strange places she'd been.

The sky above was dark and stormy, just like the Nirad world. But unlike the dry arid air of the Nirad world, on Tartarus vicious winds tore through the seams of her armour. It was cold, wet and miserable. The ground was rough and muddy. Nothing grew here and, as she gazed around, she could see no trace of wildlife.

'What a wretched place,' Agent B called through his helmet.

'It is a prison world,' Jupiter explained. 'Nothing lives here but the unfortunates imprisoned far below us.'

Because of the Blackbird helmet covering his head, Emily couldn't see Jupiter's face. But she could hear the anguish in his voice. This had been the place of his childhood, where Saturn had imprisoned him and his siblings until they escaped.

Jupiter and his brothers were dressed as Blackbird Titans like Agent B, but strangely, it was easy to tell them apart by their walk and movements.

'This way,' Jupiter called as he led them forward. 'From this moment on, we do not speak, no matter what we see or hear. Understood?'

Everyone nodded.

Each move they made had been carefully planned long before they arrived on Tartarus. Emily, Joel and Agent B followed directly behind the Big Three as they led the way to the entrance of the prison.

The area was teeming with Shadow Titans. As they moved slowly past the thousands of Shadow Titans, Emily's Flame itched to be freed against them. But their disguises were working. They were not stopped and walked freely among them.

At the prison entrance, Shadow Titans shoved and carried captured Olympian prisoners. A good number of the Olympians Emily knew personally. Jupiter and his brothers knew them all. It took strength for Emily not to call out and try to help them. Not one of them paused or broke their disguise as they watched some of their people being abused by the Shadow Titans.

The heavy main doors to the prison were open, causing a choking stink to rise from below. The Olympians began their descent down the endless stairs cut into the rocky walls. Acrid smoke from the burning torches clogged the dank, stagnant air.

Emily looked back up the stairs behind her and watched Vulcan in his Minotaur armour carrying Stella, while Minerva carried Maxine.

Seren and Jasmine's faces were filled with fear as the centaurs concentrated on not slipping on the wet steps. Their fear wasn't an act. The prison on Tartarus was terrifying.

They descended deeper into the bowels of the prison; down past the levels containing the Olympian prisoners. They passed real Shadow Titans delivering prisoners to the cells. The warriors didn't give them a second glance. Emily was worried that Chiron's exposed body would give them away. But the centaur had been right. The Shadow Titans did not notice the difference. They were simply drones following orders, with no free thought or independent movement.

They managed to make it deeper than they imagined possible. Venus took the lead and led them to where

316

she and her team had found the Hundred-handers. No words were spoken; she just gave a quick nod that directed them.

They left the stairwell and travelled down a dark, damp corridor that looked like it had seen very little traffic. At the end, they encountered another set of narrow steps.

In her bulky Turtle armour, Emily's shoulders touched the walls on either side of her. Up ahead, Jupiter and his brothers had to turn sideways to walk down the stone steps. If the Hundred-handers were as big as it was suggested, how did they get down there? And more importantly, how would they get out?

Jupiter had said the Olympians' powers did not work within the walls of the prison. Here, they were as vulnerable as humans. With no Shadow Titans around, Emily gave a little push of her powers and felt herself lifting off the floor.

'Yes!' she cheered softly. The Olympians' powers may have been neutralized in Tartarus, but hers weren't. She was still a powerful Xan.

At the very bottom of the stairs, they stepped into several metres of foul-smelling, slimy water that soaked through the armour on their feet. Emily found it very slippery and it took all of her will not to cry out in disgust. She looked over at Joel and could see, by the careful way he was putting his feet down, he felt the same.

'Paelen would have had something funny to say about this,' she whispered softly to Joel.

'Shh!' Agent B hushed.

Joel shrugged at her and then nodded.

After following Venus through a narrow passage, the walls opened up. They entered a deep and impossibly large cavern that was dimly lit from a roof far above their heads.

The deeper they walked into the cavern, the more their senses were assaulted by the worst stink Emily had ever encountered in her life. It smelled like rotting vegetables mixed with old sweaty gym socks and just enough scent of skunk to make a person violently ill. It was worse than the worst of the grey Nirads and nearly made Emily gag in her helmet.

Looking around, she could tell the others were feeling the same. Seren and Jasmine were pinching their noses while Stella held her hand over her nose and mouth.

With every step, the smell got worse. Just when Emily didn't think she could take any more, they came across three massive prison cells along the walls of the cavern. The steel bars in the front of the filthy, wet cells rose up to at least five levels.

They approached the first cell. Jupiter and his two brothers removed their helmets and leaned closer to the bars. They started to speak softly in Olympian.

In the dim light, she could not see who they were talking to. But then she heard heavy shuffling as something big moved closer to the bars. Emily nearly screamed when she saw her first Hundred-hander. She had been warned by Stella and Agent B about what the myths said they looked like. But nothing could have prepared her for the creature she now beheld.

It was huge. From its sturdy shoulders sprang a hundred long arms with thick hands and fingers. At least fifty heads extended from its neck and Emily watched in astonishment as they all spoke together as the Hundred-hander talked with Jupiter and his brothers. The sound reminded Emily of music concerts she'd been to when the crowds sang in unison with the singer.

'This is Briareos.' Jupiter turned to Emily. 'He is the strongest of the Hundred-handers and has agreed to help us if we free all his brothers from here.'

'I thought there were only three Hundred-handers?'

'There are,' Jupiter agreed. He pointed to another

319

cell. 'There is Cottus and, in the final cell, Gyges. But they have other brothers down here. The Cyclopes.'

'Are you going to free them all?'

Jupiter shook his head. 'Not me, Emily, but you. Our powers will not work within this dark place of misery and our strength is not enough to open the doors. But you are unaffected by Tartarus. Will you open these cell doors?'

'Of course,' Emily agreed.

Everyone took a step back as Emily removed her helmet and stood alone before the immense door. She reached out with her powers and commanded all the cell doors on their level to open.

Moments later, the air was filled with the horrendous sounds of the creaking and groaning metal hinges that had not been opened in thousands of years.

When the prison door swung open, Briareos and his two brothers charged out of their cells and ran to each other in a noisy reunion.

'So much for a stealthy escape,' Agent B said. 'I am sure they can hear those three on the surface.'

'Perhaps,' Vulcan agreed, 'but it will take more than all the Shadow Titans in Tartarus to contain them again. The Titans had to trick them into their cells long ago. The Hundred-handers will not be fooled again.

They are free and will remain so.'

The sounds of other calls filled the noisy chamber as Cyclopes charged in and greeted their brothers.

Joel came up beside Emily. His eyes were as big as saucers. 'Are they cool or what?'

Emily nodded. 'They sure are.' Then she turned away, fighting a wave of nausea. 'But they sure could use a bath!'

As the massively huge Hundred-handers greeted all the Olympians, the sound of organized marching filled the air.

'I think we've got company,' Agent B said.

Jupiter donned his helmet. 'All right everyone, just as we planned it. Minerva, take your team and head up. Free as many Olympians as you can on the way. Then take Cottus, Gyges and the Cyclopes back to Earth and arm them with flame-swords. We must let the Titans see we have the Hundred-handers on our side.'

To Venus he said, 'You and Briareos stay with us. We will free the Four Warriors and then head straight to Titus for the weapon.'

Shadow Titans had begun to pour into the cavern. They drew their weapons and charged forward blindly.

The pent-up fury from their long imprisonment

exploded as the Hundred-handers and Cyclopes attacked the Shadow Titans. Despite being badly outnumbered by the Shadow Titans, the large fighters made easy work of them.

'Whoa!' Joel watched mesmerized. 'Now I get it. Look at them go!'

'Draw your flame-swords, let us move!' Jupiter shouted.

Standing up front with Jupiter, Neptune and Pluto, Emily joined the fight and charged forward through the swarming Shadow Titans. She shot blast upon blast at the attacking warriors. Briareos took up the rear and waved half of his hundred hands at his departing brothers, while he used the other half to keep tearing Shadow Titans apart.

With the light of her powers guiding the way, Emily spotted the entrance the Shadow Titans were using to enter the cavern – it was huge, large enough to fit Briareos and his brothers.

Shadow Titan reinforcements were arriving every second and the fighting intensified. But the combined efforts of the Olympians, Hundred-handers, Cyclopes and Emily cut a path through the warriors.

With Minerva leading her fighters in one direction, Venus led Jupiter's group in another. There seemed to be an unending supply of Shadow Titans as each step they took was blocked by more warriors. They fought their way to the stairs that would lead them up and out of the prison. Emily stole a glance behind her and watched Joel and Agent B fighting shoulder to shoulder.

Further back, Vulcan had put Stella in Maxine as he wielded a flame-sword in each hand. Stella used her own weapons against the attackers. Even the very girly centaur twins looked fearsome as they shouted and fought their way through the Shadow Titans.

They emerged from the stairwell and Venus led them into a long corridor. But the Shadow Titans did not follow.

'Where are they going?' Joel asked, pulling off his helmet. His face was bathed in sweat. 'Why aren't they following us?'

'I do not know,' Neptune said. 'But I think we should be on our guard. Something feels very wrong here.'

Jupiter stopped the group. 'Venus, how far?'

Venus removed her Turtle helmet. 'Not far at all. They are just down at the end.'

Emily peered down the silent, dark corridor. 'This feels like a trap.'

'I agree,' Jupiter said, 'but we do not have much

choice. We will not succeed if they keep creating more Shadow Titans. They must be stopped.'

He studied the large group with him. 'Chiron, will you, Stella and the twins wait here? Briareos will stay with you for support. Do what you can to keep others from coming after us. We will find the Four Warriors and free them.'

The remaining fighters followed Venus towards the door at the end of the corridor. It was made of thick bronze and appeared heavily secured. As they drew closer, they could hear moaning coming from behind it.

'That is Aronder,' Jupiter said. 'I recognize his voice. He is suffering.'

'They all are,' Venus added.

Jupiter inspected the door. He called his brothers forward. 'Together, we push on three.'

As they pushed against the bronze door, Emily raised her hands, ready to fire at anyone on the other side. But behind the open door was a sight more horrible than anything she could imagine. Even after the horrors she'd witnessed first-hand on the battlefield, she was unprepared for the sight of the original Four Warriors.

Suspended from the ceiling was the Minotaur. Thick chains cut into his bleeding wrists and wrapped around his feet to keep him in place. His sturdy man's body was covered in deep burns, and soft moans came from his bull's mouth.

Beside him was the Blackbird Warrior. But in the flesh, he didn't look like a warrior at all – just a very large blackbird. Like the Minotaur, he was suspended in the air by thick chains that pierced through his large black wings, while floor chains wrapped around his clawed feet. His head was lowered and his long black beak hung open as a soft, pain-filled mew issued forth. The feathers on the bird's back were singed off.

The Turtle and Dragon Warriors also looked vulnerable and writhed in pain. These were large, intelligent animals and nothing like the deadly Shadow Titans that were created from them.

No more than a metre in front of each of the Four Warriors was a hole in the floor. Emily approached the nearest hole and discovered it was a chute. But she couldn't see where it led.

'My God,' Agent B said, pulling off his helmet. 'What is happening here?'

At their approach, the Four Warriors lifted their heads and spoke words Emily couldn't understand. She didn't need to. It was obvious they were begging for help.

Vulcan pointed to a large, round, slowly turning cut crystal behind the warriors. Attached to the back of the crystal was a thick and powerful magnifying glass. Imprinted on the surface of the glass was the outline of the four armoured Shadow Titans. 'Look here. This is how they are casting them. First the light strikes the magnifying glass with the designs of the armour. It passes through the crystal and hits the Four Warriors. The shadows they cast create the Shadow Titans!'

'How is that possible?' Joel said. 'It's just a glass crystal.'

As they watched, the crystal turned again.

'Shield your eyes!' Vulcan warned.

With little time to spare, everyone put their hands up to their eyes. Even so, they could still see a searing white light and feel a great temperature rise in the room. As it intensified, the Four Warriors cried out in agony.

The light faded, the temperature dropped and the crystal continued to move around on its slow turntable. Lying on the floor before each of the Four Warriors was a newly created Shadow Titan. The hollow, armoured creatures rose to their feet. Without a backward glance at their creators, they took a step forward and disappeared down the chutes.

Jupiter ran up to the Minotaur. 'Help me,' he called to the others. 'Their suffering must end now!'

Emily was already moving. She burned through the chains binding the Four Warriors to the ceiling. When they were free, the others were waiting to receive them.

'Mind the crystal,' Pluto warned. 'It will be turning against us soon.'

'Oh no, it will not!' Vulcan cried. He approached the large round crystal and magnifying glass, hoisted it off the turntable and cast it aside. It struck the stone floor and shattered into thousands of harmless pieces.

Behind where the crystal sat, they saw the light source. It was a very small fire no bigger than a fist. No fuel fed the flame. It was simply burning on a small marble plinth.

'*That is part of me!*' Riza called in alarm. '*I can feel it. That Flame-shard landed here and has been the cause of their suffering. I am the reason for this terrible war.*'

'No, Riza,' Emily said. 'It was the Titans. They found the fragments of Flame and figured out how to do this.'

'So that is why the Shadow Titans are drawn to you,' Agent B reasoned after Emily explained what Riza had said. 'You carry the Flame within you – the source of their creation. We must extinguish it before they can do it again.'

'*Do not let them extinguish the Flame,*' Riza called in alarm. '*Pull it into you. Perhaps this Flame-shard will contain my lost memories. I ache to be made whole again and not remain in fragments scattered throughout the universe.*'

Emily approached the Flame and held out her hand. She didn't need to do anything; the Flame leaped from the plinth into her outstretched hand.

'Em!' Joel screamed.

But Emily was smiling. 'Joel, it's OK. It feels strange, but really wonderful. Like a piece I've been missing has suddenly been found.' She could feel Riza's joy. But it was tinged with sadness. The Flame-shard did not contain her lost memories.

With the Flame secured deep within her, Emily turned her attention to the Four Warriors lying on the floor, moaning softly. One by one, she reached out and let her healing powers work on their burns.

'How did the Titans figure out how to do that?' Joel asked.

'I have no idea,' Jupiter responded. 'But it is truly a twisted mind that could conceive of such a hideous plan. Saturn's malevolence knows no limits.

This was nothing less than pure torture.'

When Emily finished healing the Four Warriors, she stood. 'At least we've stopped it.'

'YOU HAVE STOPPED NOTHING!' a bodiless voice boomed.

A blinding flash filled the room as the Solar Stream opened. Huge figures burst from the light. Before anyone could react, a large net was tossed over Emily and Mike, and then Joel. They were dragged back into the Solar Stream and disappeared.

34

Stella heard shouts from within the chamber where the Four Warriors were held. Before Chiron and Briareos had a chance to charge down the corridor, Jupiter burst from the chamber.

'Titans have captured Emily and Joel! They used the Solar Stream to get in and out. They are gone.'

Chiron cursed. 'How? Our powers do not work down here. Nor do the Titans. How could they do it?'

'I do not know,' Jupiter mused. 'Perhaps they have more of the Flame.'

'This will not stop us!' Neptune cried. 'There is too much at stake.'

'But we've got to go after them!' Stella cried. 'We can't let Saturn hurt Emily or Joel.'

Jupiter cast his helmet aside violently, his face a portrait of fury. 'Father has gone too far. He must be stopped!'

Agent B put a reassuring hand on Stella's shoulder.

'Saturn can't hurt Emily.' He paused and rubbed his chin. Though she does have one very big weakness. Joel. He is still human and very vulnerable. They might try to use Emily's emotions against her and threaten to hurt him if she does not cooperate.'

'How do you know this?' Jupiter asked.

'Because that's exactly what the CRU planned to do.'

Jupiter started pacing the corridor. He pounded the wall with a fist and chipped pieces of stone. 'We cannot go after her,' he finally said.

'What!' Stella cried. 'We have to.'

Neptune looked at his younger brother and nodded. 'Jupe is correct. Saturn wants us to abandon our attempts to get the weapon from Titus. If we waste precious time going after Emily, they will complete the weapon and launch it against us.'

'But it's Emily and Joel!' Stella cried.

Agent B nodded his head. 'They're right, Stella. This is just a manoeuvre to distract us from the main mission.'

'But they'll hurt them.'

'I do not think so,' Jupiter said. 'At least not right away. Father has had his spies watching us for some time. He knows Emily has great powers, but I doubt he knows who she really is. Saturn would never knowingly try something like this against a Xan. In taking Emily, he has bitten off far more than even he can chew.'

'We should actually pity him,' Agent B said. 'I have seen first-hand what happens when Emily loses her temper.'

Jupiter retrieved his helmet. 'This could play in our favour. While Emily occupies Saturn, we must move on Titus. Let us make for the surface and get out of here.'

They had to fight their way out of the prison. On the surface, they were met with more Shadow Titans. The now healed Four Warriors stood with Jupiter.

Briareos was a wonder to watch as he took on hundreds of Shadow Titans at once. Not one of the warriors ever made it anywhere near Stella or the centaurs. With the Hundred-hander at their side, they were beating back the Shadow Titans until it was clear enough for the Big Three to combine their powers and transport everyone from Tartarus back to Delphi on Earth.

The place they returned to looked nothing like the Delphi they had left. The ground was littered with Shadow Titan armour and dead monsters. There was still fighting, but it was in the distance. Stella looked over to the mountain across from the temple. The two Hundred-handers were standing tall above the trees and stomping and tearing their way through the forces of the Shadow Titans.

In just a short time after their arrival back on Earth, with the renewed Olympian forces, the Cyclopes and the Hundred-handers, the battle was turning. Though the Shadow Titans were not surrendering, they were taking heavy losses. It was only a matter of time before they were all destroyed.

'Our success here will mean nothing if the Titans launch their weapon,' Jupiter said. 'We have no time to waste. We must leave now for Titus.'

Everyone volunteered to go on the mission to Titus. But the Big Three were very selective about who should go with them.

Agent B and Stella would bring the golden box, accompanied by Vulcan, Briareos and the Four Warriors.

Once again, the Big Three united their powers. Standing closely together, they lifted their heads and shouted, 'Titus!'

35

It was dark and silent as Emily and Mike emerged from the Solar Stream. No sooner had the Solar Stream opened, than Emily and the dog were cast out and it closed firmly behind them. Whoever or whatever had taken them from Tartarus had moved faster than she imagined possible. She hadn't had time to get a good look at her attacker, let alone fight back. All she'd seen was something large in black.

Nor had she been able to see Joel. Fear clutched her heart that he had been taken somewhere else.

'Joel!' Emily shouted. 'Joel, are you there?'

Only Mike's whines could be heard from beside her.

Emily knelt down and patted the dog. She raised her other hand and summoned the Flame. But no matter how large the Flame grew, nothing drove back the oppressive darkness. Beneath her was a cold stone floor, but she could not see or feel walls. There was no wind, no sound. Just blackness.

'It's OK, boy,' she assured Mike. 'We'll get out of here.'

Emily rose and fired a blast of laser-light. She followed the glow as it travelled through the darkness until it faded away in the distance. Somehow, the place felt limitless. Her next attempt was to lift her and Mike up to try and fly out. That didn't work either. There seemed no end to the darkness.

'Let me out of here!' Emily howled. She fired an even more powerful blast into the darkness. It did nothing. She spun in the air, firing blasts of Flame in all directions.

'*Emily, stop,*' Riza called softly. '*Do not speak aloud to me; they are listening. Just settle down on the ground and hear me.*'

Emily stopped firing and landed on the dark floor.

'*Sit, child, and listen. You are in a very special prison called an Energy Void. I cannot remember the details of where or when, but someone dear to me was once trapped in such a place. They learned the more powers they used, the larger and stronger the trap became. It is like a black hole. Energy goes in but never leaves.*'

'But—' Emily started.

'*Shh . . .*' Riza said. '*Do not let them hear you speaking. Just listen. There is only one way out of an Energy Void.*

But this may prove impossible for someone like you.'

Emily wanted to ask how. Hearing her thoughts, Riza continued.

'Emily, you feel things very deeply. But here in this prison, your emotions are your greatest enemy. Like your powers, emotions feed the trap. Your fear for Joel strengthens the walls. Your suffering over Pegasus and Paelen secures the roof. Worry for the Olympians keeps the locks solidly in place. All these thoughts contain you here. The Titans do not need to do a thing to defeat you. You are defeating yourself.'

'How do I fight them?' Emily thought.

'This is where escape will be difficult. You must renounce your emotions and lock your powers deep within yourself. Think only of those things that give you a sense of quiet. Mentally go to a place of peace, where your emotions are at their calmest.'

Riza was right. In this dark and frightening place, finding a way to peace and calm would be impossible while the war raged on without her.

'Then the Titans have already won.'

'EMILY.' It was the grim voice she heard in Tartarus. Mike started to growl and then bark.

'Who are you?' Emily demanded.

'Some call me Cronus. You know me as Saturn.'

'Let me out of here!' Emily shouted. She stood up and tried to find the source of the voice.

Up ahead, the tiniest spark of light seemed to pulse and then grow into the shape of a man. But it wasn't solid – more like a fuzzy image from a poorly received television station. The image was large and imposing. But the face was familiar. She could see glimpses of the older Jupiter, Neptune and Pluto.

Mike charged Saturn but ran right through the image. Finally he returned to Emily's side, growling softly.

'I will not release you until you tell me who you are and where you come from.'

Emily frowned. 'How can you speak my language?'

'A secret language cannot remain secret if one has good spies,' Saturn said casually. 'And I have the best.'

'They're not that good if they don't know who I am.'

'Perhaps not,' Saturn agreed. 'So, who are you? Why are you here?'

'I'm here to help the Olympians,' Emily said. 'But I shouldn't have to. They're your children. Why are you trying to kill them?'

'Yes, they are my children!' Saturn spat as his face twisted in fury. 'Yet they show me no loyalty. They seek to overthrow me and would see me imprisoned in Tartarus.'

'Isn't that where you locked them up?'

'You do not know what you are talking about,' Saturn said dismissively. 'I will defeat them just as easily as I have defeated you.'

'You haven't defeated me,' Emily said. 'You just think you have, but you are wrong.'

The image shimmered and sparkled. Emily knew he was growing angry.

'Do not try my patience, child,' Saturn warned. 'I know how much you care for the human boy. I will not hesitate to hurt him.'

'I'm warning you, Saturn,' Emily challenged, 'the Gorgons once threatened those I love. I melted one of them and the other turned to ash. If you hurt Joel, I swear I'll do the same to you!'

'Threats from a child!' Saturn laughed.

It was hard for Emily to hate him with a face so much like Jupiter's. 'No, Saturn,' she said calmly. 'A promise from a Xan!'

'*Emily, no,*' Riza hushed. '*You must not tell him any more.*'

'Xan?' For an instant, Saturn's image flickered. Then he burst into harsh laughter. 'There are no Xan. They

338

were myths created by our elders to frighten us.'

'Oh really?' Emily continued. 'And I suppose that Flame you used to make the Shadow Titans was created by you rubbing two sticks together.'

'It came from a dying star that crashed on Titus,' Saturn said, 'nothing more than that.'

'It came from me!' Emily shouted. The Flame flashed in her hand brightly. 'Does this look familiar?'

Emily could feel Riza's distress and hear her warnings. But she and Riza were different people from two very different worlds. Riza was from Xanadu, a world of calm and peace. Emily was born and raised on the tough streets of New York City. No one threatened her friends and got away with it. Even if they happened to be the leader of the Titans.

'You are lying,' Saturn insisted. 'I do not know who you are or where you come from, but you are no Xan – they are just a myth.'

'Are you willing to risk it?' Emily demanded. 'I don't want to hurt you, so I am giving you a choice. Return Joel to me. Release us and end this wretched war.'

'Or?' Saturn said.

'Or I can lose my temper and things will get very ugly very quickly.'

Saturn hesitated, but only for an instant. His image

became solid. 'If you are truly Xan, your powers will keep you trapped here for ever. I will give you the boy as a gift to show you I can be generous. But I will not release you or end this war. My treacherous children will be punished for their defiance. I will launch my weapon against them and be done with it. Then we will discuss how you are to serve me.'

The image of Saturn vanished.

'Serve you?' Emily cried furiously. 'Never!' She fired blast upon blast into the darkness, trying to break out of the void.

'*Emily, stop!*' Riza cried. '*You are only fortifying the walls of your prison. Control your temper now before it is too late!*'

Emily's temper flared as she thought back to Riza, 'I know you said I shouldn't destroy a Titan. But I swear, if Saturn launches that weapon against the Olympians, it will be the very last thing he does!'

36

'Everything is dead.' Stella looked around Titus.

The moment they arrived on Titus, Stella noticed how much it looked like Olympus from the brief glimpse she had seen of it from the future. The air felt the same and, just like Olympus, there were magnificent marble buildings and structures.

'It's just like Olympus after the CRU sent the weapon there.'

The trees around them were dry and withered. The grass was brown and no birds, animals or insects could be heard.

'This is what Olympus looked like after our attack?' Agent B said in quiet shock.

Stella nodded. 'It was so beautiful and yet so dead.'

'Olympus and Titus were magnificent twin worlds,' Jupiter said sadly. 'In creating that weapon, Saturn has destroyed this world just to defeat us.'

There was something in his voice that caught Stella's

341

attention. Jupiter didn't sound right. He didn't look right either. He was starting to hunch over. She looked around at the other Olympians – they too were looking ill.

'What's wrong?' Agent B removed his Blackbird helmet and checked on Jupiter.

'We are near the weapon,' Jupiter gasped. 'Minerva warned us, but I did not believe it would affect me as quickly as it has. We must find it before it kills us.'

The Minotaur snorted and pounded the ground. The Turtle Warrior pulled himself inside his shell and squealed in pain while the Blackbird Warrior cawed and Dragon Warrior roared. Even Briareos was having violent reactions to the proximity of the weapon.

Stella wheeled her chair over to Vulcan and touched his arm lightly. 'Can you feel in which direction the pain is coming from?'

'Everywhere,' he groaned.

'Be more specific,' Agent B ordered sharply. 'We can't stop the weapon if we can't find it!'

Vulcan balled his hands into fists. He stood upright and removed his helmet. His face was pinched in terrible pain. He turned in a slow circle and pointed at a beautiful pillared building rising in the distance.

'It is from in there, Saturn's palace.'

'Of course it would be,' Agent B moaned. 'Look. That's where all the Shadow Titans are posted.' He checked the sky around him. 'At least I can't see any flying Shadows. They're probably on Earth for the final battle.' The CRU agent drew his flame-sword. 'I hope you Olympians can pull yourselves together because Stella and I can't fight them all alone.'

Pluto was doubled over in pain. 'I have no powers with that weapon exposed,' he said through gritted teeth. 'But at least I can still wield a sword.'

'So can I,' agreed Jupiter, drawing his own weapon. 'We must move now before that thing finishes us.'

Stella pulled out her own flame-sword from its sheath mounted on her wheelchair. 'Maxine, I need your help,' she said to her chair. 'Please take me to Saturn's palace. We must get to the weapon.'

Beneath her, her chair reacted to the request. The wheels started to turn as the chair moved forward.

Long before they reached the palace, the Shadow Titans became aware of their presence on Titus. They charged along the cobbled roads and attacked the Olympians with all the ferocity they possessed.

Once again, Briareos proved his worth. Even under the sickening effects of the weapon, he was a powerful fighter. He cut a clear path through the masses of Shadow Titans.

But the Big Three were weakening. Moment by moment, they slowed down and struggled for breath.

Jupiter was struck in the back by an unseen Shadow Titan's sword. The armour he wore protected him, but he was still knocked to the ground. Agent B fought his way over to the fallen Olympian and used his flame-sword to destroy a warrior. He helped Jupiter climb painfully to his feet.

'We cannot win like this,' Jupiter panted, holding on to the agent's arm for support. 'The weapon's power is too great. It will kill us long before we reach the palace.'

'You and Stella are our only hope. I beg you, get to the palace and secure the weapon in the golden box. With it covered, our strength may return. Go now, before it is too late.'

Stella commanded Maxine to take her up in the air. 'Agent B, Maxine can carry us!'

'You're sure this thing can lift us both?'

Maxine swooped down as Agent B leaped in the air and caught hold of one of her wheels.

'Yes she can!' Stella cheered as Maxine carried them

above the fighting, towards the palace. 'She can do anything!'

Agent B used his free hand to slay as many Shadow Titans as he could with his flame-sword.

Behind them, the battle raged on. Briareos loomed high above the attacking warriors. But the huge Hundred-hander was slowing. Even from this distance, they could see the pain etched on his filthy face.

'If he goes down, they all go,' Agent B warned. 'Hurry up, Maxine, we must stop that weapon!'

As they approached the tall palace, Stella noticed movement on the roof. 'Someone's up there.'

'That's the highest point in the area. It's a perfect launch pad for the weapon.'

Stella asked Maxine for more speed and to land on the roof. With his flame-sword held high, Agent B jumped away from Maxine just as the wheelchair touched down on the smooth marble surface.

They stopped several metres short of a figure who might once have been a man. It was too shrivelled up to tell what it was now. In its arms it struggled to carry a large stone. The very same stone Stella had witnessed falling out of the golden box so very long ago.

'That's it, that's the weapon!' she cried.

'Is this what you are looking for, human?' the

shrivelled creature asked. 'You are too late. In moments I will be dead and you will witness Saturn's greatest triumph. The moment we reach Olympus, I will detonate it. The weapon's powers will grow and spread across the cosmos, destroying every living Olympian there is. This victory is worth my suffering.' The creature held up a blue stone that looked similar to the one Joel and Emily had.

'No!' Agent B cried. He raised his sword and charged.

Six Shadow Titans burst on to the palace roof and ran at the CRU agent.

'Stella, do something. Stop him!' Agent B cried as he took on all the attacking Shadow Titans.

There was no time to think. The old man held up the jewel.

Stella dropped her flame-sword and drew out her small silver dagger. Vulcan had taught her how to throw it with deadly accuracy. But that was practice. This was the real thing.

'Olympus!' the old man cried.

Stella grasped the dagger by the blade and held her breath.

The Solar Stream opened in front of the old man and he started to move.

Stella used all her strength to throw the dagger.

It struck the hideous creature squarely in the chest. He dropped the stone and staggered sideways, falling away from the open Solar Stream.

'The stone, Stella,' Agent B shouted. 'Get it in the box.'

'Maxine, move,' Stella cried. 'Get me to that stone.'

Stella threw herself from her wheelchair and struggled to free the large golden box from beneath her seat. 'Release the box.'

The wheelchair tipped itself back until the box came away from the restraining brackets. It hit the slippery marble roof and slid further away.

Stella cursed and tried to roll the stone over to the golden box. But as she moved and felt its weight, she knew she could never lift it into the box.

'Maxine, push it closer to me!'

The wheelchair did as she commanded and pushed the golden box to where the stone lay. Stella raised herself up as high as she could and lifted the heavy gold lid.

'Agent B,' she yelled, 'the stone is too heavy for me, I can't lift it into the box.'

There were only three Shadow Titans left fighting Agent B. Around them lay the scattered remnants of the other fighters. His flame-sword flashed in the air as he cut down a fourth Shadow Titan. With only two remaining Turtle Warriors left, Agent B dashed back to Stella.

'Get ready with the lid!' He dropped his sword and hoisted the heavy stone into the air. Just as he was about to place it in the box, the two Turtle Warriors charged forward and pierced through Agent B's armour with their swords.

The CRU agent gasped in agony. Stella saw the blood-covered blades sticking out the front of his armour. The Turtles pulled their weapons free and stabbed again.

'Get the lid,' Agent B gulped. As he fell over, he used the last of his fading strength to drop the stone into the golden box. Struggling with its weight, Stella managed to close the lid on the weapon.

Agent B fell back on the palace roof and became still.

Stella struggled up on to the box. Without a weapon, she stared defiantly into the covered faces of the advancing Shadow Titans.

37

'Saturn,' Emily shouted, 'where are you, you liar!'

Emily wasn't sure how long she had been in the Energy Void. But certainly it was long enough for Saturn to bring Joel to her if he'd really intended to.

She paced, furious at her imprisonment. What was happening outside? Were the others all right? Had they made it to Titus to get the weapon?

With Mike close at her side, Emily continued to shoot out blasts of power, hoping to find a weakness. But every time she did, Riza said she was making her prison stronger.

'*If you really want to get out of here,*' Riza warned, '*you must find calm. Stop using any of your powers. Deny your anger and your grief. Bring peace to yourself. That is the only way to defeat an Energy Void.*'

Emily had heard the same thing time and time again, but wondered how she was supposed to put her emotions aside when everything was at stake. Finally she sat down and extinguished the Flame in her hand. Sitting in the darkness, she focused on calming her breathing.

'*Very good,*' Riza said. '*Now, go somewhere in your mind. Go to where you are most peaceful. Imagine yourself there and nowhere else.*'

Emily closed her eyes. Mike laid his head in her lap as she softly stroked the length of his warm body. She imagined that Mike was Pegasus. They were walking together on their private silver beach. It was night and the stars were reflected like diamonds in the water. The air was warm and fragrant and the only sounds she could hear were the stallion's hooves in the water.

A sense of calm washed over Emily. There was nothing else. Just Pegasus and her. No war, no violence and no loss – just the still waters, the stars and the winged stallion at her side.

Emily was at peace.

After a time, she lifted her head and felt a gentle breeze on her face. But as the moments passed, it changed. It wasn't as warm as it had been. In fact, it smelled musty and damp. She opened her eyes.

The silver beach was gone. Pegasus was gone. It was Mike's head on her lap, not the stallion's. Emily found herself sitting on a cold stone floor in a very deep pit.

'*You did it!*' Riza cried. '*Emily, you defeated the Energy Void despite your emotions. I am so sorry I doubted you.*'

Emily climbed, disoriented, to her feet. One moment she was with Pegasus on their silver beach, the next she was alone in a damp pit with Mike. The sound of dripping water was everywhere. Everything came back to her. She had been imprisoned in a limitless dark place. There was the war, the Titan weapon, and Joel.

Saturn had Joel!

'Yes, Riza,' Emily said angrily, 'I am emotional. But that doesn't mean I'm weak. It means despite all these powers, I still care. And right now, what I care about is finding Joel!'

High above her was a faint light. Using her powers she pushed and lifted off the ground. The urgent need to find Joel became overpowering. If Saturn had hurt him, there would be no stopping her.

At the top of the pit, Emily was greeted by several Shadow Titan guards. She dispatched them efficiently with her Flame efficiently. The door was next as she used her powers to tear it off its hinges.

'C'mon, Mike, let's find Joel!'

Out in the corridor, Emily was reminded of the prison at Tartarus. The thick stone walls were covered in a film of wet mould just like in the prison and the musty air smelled the same. She recalled the brief journey through the Solar Stream. It was too fast and too short.

'This is still Tartarus!'

Jupiter had told her the prison at Tartarus was massive. It went very deep underground and would offer the Titans protection from the effects of the weapon. How was she to find Joel?

She knelt down beside the dog and scratched behind his ears. 'I've been thinking like a human, when I have the powers of the Xan!'

Emily put her arms around the dog, closed her eyes and envisioned Joel's face. She focused on transporting to where Joel was. The next moment, she arrived in a dark cell.

'Joel?'

'Em?'

Mike barked excitedly. Relief washed over Emily when she saw Joel crouching down to greet the dog. He was filthy, but alive!

'Thank God!' Joel cried as he threw his arms around her. He lifted her off the floor and gave her the biggest hug and kiss she'd ever had. 'I've been worried sick! Where have you been?'

'Saturn locked me in something called an Energy Void.'

'You escaped an Energy Void?' A young man, just a bit older than Joel, climbed down from an upper bunk.

'Em, this is Prometheus,' Joel said.

Emily frowned at the attractive young man. 'As in Prometheus Oak?'

'Kinda,' Joel said. 'But this is the original. He's a Titan.'

Emily raised a flaming hand to Prometheus. 'Get away from us!'

'No Em,' Joel cried. 'He's cool. Prometheus has rebelled. Not all the Titans are on Saturn's side. Those that oppose him are locked down here with us.'

'What Saturn is doing is wrong,' Prometheus said. 'I could not stand by and let him destroy his own children with that foul weapon. After Olympus, Saturn plans to defeat Earth. I'm here because I challenged him.'

'Em, we've got to get out of here,' Joel said. 'But we can't break down the cell door. Not even my silver arm will work on it.'

Emily gave Prometheus one last wary look. 'You're sure we can trust him?'

'I promise,' Joel said. 'He's already helped me. The Shadow Titans wanted to kill me, but he managed to stop them. I owe Prometheus my life.'

'I'm sorry I doubted you,' she said. 'But this has been a really rotten week for me.'

'I understand,' Prometheus said. 'However it will get much worse if we do not stop Saturn. I have heard he has secured a volunteer to deliver the weapon to Olympus. He has already left here. The fool will surrender his life to Saturn's cause.'

'Not if we can stop him,' Emily said.

Emily raised her two hands. The bars tore away from the walls and the whole front crashed to the stone floor with a clang. Around them, other Olympian prisoners called to be freed. She stood still and summoned her powers. With a single thought, Emily commanded *open*! All the cell doors flew open and the prisoners were freed.

Moments later, Shadow Titans charged into the cell block and started attacking the escaping Olympians.

'*You will not escape here!*' boomed another voice.

Emily turned and saw Saturn in the flesh. He was much bigger than she expected as he and several other full Titans entered the cell block.

'Stay back, Saturn!' Emily called. 'I'm not in the Energy Void now. Your powers may not work down here, but mine do!'

'Impudent child, of course my powers still work here – greater than ever before. Do you really think you can challenge me?'

'I warned you,' Emily shot back, 'you may be a Titan, but I am Xan. Must I prove it?'

'*Emily, no,*' Riza warned. '*You must not kill a Titan. It will change the future.*'

'There are no Xan!' Saturn shouted as he lifted his hand.

Emily was struck with a blast that lifted her off the ground and smashed her against a cell wall. She had never encountered this kind of power before. It knocked the wind out of her and left her head spinning as she slumped to the floor.

'Em!' Joel cried.

'So easily defeated,' Saturn laughed as he and the other Titans advanced on her. 'Let me see how easily you die.'

Emily panted heavily as she slowly recovered. 'Stay back, Joel. Saturn is about to meet a very angry New Yorker!'

Prometheus pulled Joel and the dog further back. 'I do not know who your friend is, but she is about to die.'

'You don't know my Emily,' Joel cried. 'Go get

them, Em. Show them how we do things downtown.'

Emily rose unsteadily to her feet. She was still badly winded and knew she was in the fight of her life. Saturn had powers greater than she expected. He could hurt her. Perhaps even kill her.

She lifted her hand and the Flame rose high. 'This is your last warning, Saturn,' she panted as she staggered forward. 'End the war now!'

In answer, Saturn shot another blast of energy at Emily. Once again she was knocked violently off her feet and struck the floor painfully.

'Emily!' Joel cried.

Emily moaned and raised her hand to Joel. 'Stay back.'

Her nose and ears were bleeding and she felt like she'd just been hit by a freight train. Twice. Saturn really packed a punch.

But then again, so did she.

Emily sat up and unleashed the Flame. She shot a blast of power at Saturn that made the Titan cry out as he was knocked backwards down the length of the cell block.

She climbed to her feet just as the other Titans raised their hands. They combined their powers and fired everything they had at her. Emily thought Vesta had prepared her for anything. But her teacher had never imagined she would be taking on the Titan leaders.

It took all of Emily's concentration to keep from being ripped apart by the Titans' immense powers. But just as she felt herself slipping, Emily remembered something she'd learned about herself. She was not human any more. She was not Olympian. She was a Xan without a body – made up of pure energy. There was no need for energy to fight energy.

Emily calmed and dropped her defences. The Titans' full powers stuck her and knocked her back once again. But they could not destroy her. Emily realized she was just like the Energy Void. The more they threw at her, the stronger she became.

Across from her, the Titans' faces were showing the strain of their efforts. Saturn rose and let out a furious cry as he merged his powers with the others.

Sparks filled the air and the atmosphere was charged with energy. But Emily took it all in. She focused her own powers and fired back with a blast that filled the prison corridor with blinding white light.

The Titans closest to her cried out as they were instantly vapourized by the Flame. Saturn and the survivors were thrown back against the wall. They collapsed to the floor in a groaning, burned heap.

'*Oh Emily*,' Riza called sadly. '*What have you done?*'

'What I had to!' Emily shot back.

Behind her, Joel was on the floor, covered by Prometheus and two other Olympians. Prometheus's back was raw and bleeding from the burning heat that had filled the corridor. Olympians were scattered around the area, moaning softly from their wounds.

Emily ran to them and set about healing Prometheus and the other Olympians. She pulled them off each other and beneath them found Joel and Mike. 'Are you all right?'

Joel nodded. 'Thanks to Prometheus and these two.' He sat slowly up. His skin was bright pink with burns. But without Prometheus's protection, it would have been a lot worse. 'Wow, Em, you really did show them!'

Emily looked around. 'Where are the Shadow Titans?'

'You destroyed them,' Prometheus said.

'Prometheus, thank you so much for saving Joel,' Emily said. 'But now, will you help us save the Olympians?'

'Of course,' the Titan said. 'What can I do?'

'If we use my powers, will you direct us to Titus?'

* * *

They arrived in Titus in the middle of the battle. Jupiter and his team were fighting with all their strength against the thousands of swarming Shadow Titans.

'Where is Saturn keeping the weapon?' Joel asked Prometheus.

The tall Titan pointed to Saturn's palace. 'He developed it deep underground and then it was delivered there. That is where they were launching from. But we are too late.'

'How do you know?' Emily demanded.

'Because I am well,' said Prometheus sadly. 'So are the Olympians in their fight against the Shadow Warriors. If the weapon was still here, we would be very ill. It must have been sent to Olympus already. It will destroy everything there first before the powers reach here. It will soon kill all of us.'

'No!' Emily howled. She realized Prometheus was right. The Big Three looked young and strong as they took on the Shadow Titans. The Four Warriors were almost unstoppable as they used their flame-swords to dispatch all who came near. Briareos was destroying Shadows by the hundreds.

'We can't be too late!' Emily lifted them into the air and flew towards Saturn's palace. As they drew near, Emily saw Stella on the roof – and there was the golden box! But as she looked closer she saw that Stella was in grave danger – two Shadow Titans were coming at her, their weapons raised.

Emily fired a blast of Flame that instantly destroyed the two Shadow Titans.

'Is the weapon still here?' Joel demanded as they landed on the roof.

Stella nodded. 'It's in the box.' She slid off the sealed box and dragged herself over to Agent B. She struggled to remove his helmet. 'Help him!'

By the time the helmet came free, they could see that Agent B was already dead. Emily reached out and stroked the CRU agent's face. 'This isn't over between us, Agent B,' she said softly. 'I'll see you again very soon.' She leaned forward and pulled the Pegasus pendant from around his neck and kissed his forehead gently. 'I'll give this back to you then.'

'Agent B stopped fighting to put the weapon in the box,' Stella said sadly. 'He gave his life for the Olympians.'

'He really did change,' Joel said. 'When it came down to it, he took the side of the Olympians.'

Emily knelt before the golden box and felt its weight with the stone sealed inside. She grasped her pendant. 'It's over, Pegs, and we'll be home soon.'

'Over?' Prometheus said. 'Far from it. There are still many Shadow Titans to be destroyed. And although you wounded Saturn, you did not defeat him. He will rise again.'

Joel reached out a hand to Prometheus. 'Yes he will rise, but Jupiter and the Olympians will put him down. Saturn is destined to stay in Tartarus.'

'How can you know this?' Prometheus said.

Joel looked at Emily and Stella. 'Trust me. I know.'

They flew back to the battlefield where the last Shadow Titans had fallen.

Mike charged back to Emily, happily wagging his tail as he carried a Turtle's helmet.

Jupiter embraced Emily tightly. 'Thank the stars! We feared the worst. When Father took you, we did not know what would happen.' He lowered his head and gave a slight smile as his eyes twinkled. 'Can you forgive me for not coming after you?'

'There's nothing to forgive. You had to come for the weapon.' Emily pointed at the golden box. 'And there it is, locked safely in the box thanks to Stella and Agent B.'

'Where is Agent B?'

'He died protecting you,' Stella said softly.

'Then he shall be remembered for all time as a Hero

of Olympus.' Jupiter gave Emily a cheeky wink. 'I wonder what the CRU would think of that.'

'I think Agent B would be thrilled. The CRU? Not so much.'

Joel put his arm around Emily. 'Come on, Em, let's end this. I don't like having that thing hanging around. How about you destroy it and we can all go home.'

'Not yet, Joel,' Neptune said. 'There is still one more thing we must do.'

38

They arrived at the Temple of Poseidon at Cape Sounio. Neptune had been right. There was one more thing to do. The past had been changed and the Big Three were still young.

'We must be the same,' Neptune insisted, 'to avoid altering the future that you know.'

'Your age can't make that much difference,' Emily argued. 'Please just let me destroy the weapon.'

'No,' Jupiter said. 'We must be how you remember us.'

Emily hated the thought of exposing them to the weapon again. It was dangerous and pure torture. But their minds were set. It was only the Big Three who needed ageing so it was time for the other Olympians to say their farewells and go.

'Are you sure you cannot stay with me?' Vulcan asked Stella. 'I will be lost without you.'

Stella hugged the large Olympian. 'I wish I could.

But I need to go back to my family and my life. But I promise I'll never forget you and everything you've taught me!' she told him tearfully.

'Thank you for everything, Vulcan. I'll see you soon,' Emily promised.

'Soon for you perhaps,' Vulcan grumbled. 'It will be an eternity for me.'

'And me,' Chiron added. He bowed at the waist. 'You are all strong warriors and have earned your place among us.'

The war was far from over and the Olympians were needed elsewhere. Now with only the Big Three, Emily used her powers to open the hole in the ground where the box was to be buried.

Joel lifted out the gold box from Maxine and placed it on the ground before them. He undid the clasp and held the lid at the ready. 'OK, I'll hold it open until you look the way we remember and then I'll close it again.'

Jupiter looked at his brothers. 'We are ready.'

Joel opened the golden box and the Big Three collapsed to the ground, writhing in agony as the Titan weapon affected them.

It took all of Emily's willpower not to close it again as she watched the three young Olympians start to age.

As each second passed, their hair grew longer and went coarse and grey. Long beards appeared on their once-smooth faces. Their eyebrows grew bushy and long and deep wrinkles cut across their skin. Their strong chests shrank back and revealed the bodies of much older men.

'Now, Joel!' Emily cried when Jupiter looked as she remembered him.

Joel slammed the box shut.

The Big Three were barely conscious. Emily touched each of them, hoping her powers would at least ease their suffering. It worked. Before long, they sat up.

'This is how you knew us?' Pluto cried, looking at his brothers. 'We are old men!'

Emily nodded sadly, already missing the young men she had come to know and care for. 'But you are still very powerful.'

Jupiter tried to raise himself in the air. 'I cannot fly any more.'

Neptune tried. 'And I cannot transport myself! We are but mere shadows of our former selves. How are we to continue?'

'You will always be the Big Three,' Emily said. 'When you combine your powers, you are unbeatable. What you look like doesn't matter. You taught me that.'

'Then I was a fool,' Jupiter sighed, but then started to chuckle. 'Well, I guess there are some women who find older men more charming.'

'Indeed, brother,' Neptune agreed.

Needing to go back to the battle, Jupiter gave Emily a final, powerful hug. 'I cannot tell you how grateful we are that you came to us. I will miss you all more than you can imagine.' Suddenly the young twinkle returned to his eyes. 'Perhaps even more than I will miss my youth!'

'Please be careful,' Emily said, embracing each of them.

Before leaving, Joel reminded them not to acknowledge ever having known them from the past when they'll first meet during the Nirad conflict.

'I understand,' Jupiter said. 'The future and your memories of it must be protected. But that does not mean I will not be counting the days until I see you again.'

With one final nod, the Big Three used a Solar Stream jewel to return to the battle.

'Now what?' Stella said.

'Now we destroy that weapon!' Emily said. 'Joel, you open the box and I'll fire all I've got at it.'

'Wait!' Stella cried. She pulled out the silver dagger

she'd used on the Titan and handed it to Emily. 'My parents found this dagger beside the box. When they open it, I want this to be inside instead of the rock. It stopped the Titans from sending the weapon to Olympus. Vulcan helped me make it and I'll want it back to remind me of him.'

Emily grinned. 'Good idea.' She stood back as Mike sat down on the ground beside her.

Joel knelt down behind the box and reached for the lid again. 'On the count of three. One . . . two . . . three!'

Emily summoned the Flame just as Joel opened the lid. She shot all she had at the Titan weapon. The stone glowed brilliant red and then disappeared with a snap. But in the instant the weapon was gone, Joel and Stella vanished.

'Joel?' Emily cried. 'Joel, where are you?'

Panic gripped her as she looked around for Joel and Stella. Maxine was still there. On the ground where Joel had been standing, Emily found his clothes and Pegasus pendant. Stella's was sitting on the seat of her wheelchair.

'Joel!' Emily howled.

'*Calm yourself,*' Riza called.

'But Joel is gone!'

367

'Yes, he is,' Riza agreed. '*Do you not understand? This was Agent B's reset button. Things have returned to the way they were before the weapon was found. Many thousands of years from now, Stella's parents will open the gold box and find only the dagger you are about to place in it.*

'*Without the weapon, life on Olympus, Xanadu and Earth will continue as though this incident never happened. And without the weapon, there was no need for you to come back into the past.*

'*When you return to Xanadu, you will find Joel and the others will not remember anything. For them, there was no travelling into the past because you have changed that timeline. Only you and the Olympians remaining here will ever know what truly happened.*'

Emily was too confused to grasp what Riza meant. 'But if this was the reset button, why are Mike and I still here?'

Riza laughed lightly. '*I told you, child, we are Xan. We live outside the boundaries of time or space. We are not bound by its rules. Mike was touching you when you destroyed the weapon. You protected him. He exists outside the boundaries of time too.*'

'*Now, Pegasus is waiting. Take us home.*'

368

Epilogue

Emily and Mike arrived back on Xanadu at the very moment when Apollo had returned from Olympus to tell them that Jupiter was very ill and that they must go back to Olympus.

But now everything was different and, instead, Apollo announced that there was a feast planned to celebrate the discovery of Xanadu and that the Big Three were on their way.

Emily stood in stunned silence, unprepared for the reaction she received upon her return. Because there hadn't *been* a reaction, except for the shock of the dog's sudden appearance. As far as everyone was concerned, she had never left.

But Emily was knocked out of her stunned state as soon as she set eyes on Pegasus.

'Pegs!' she squealed and ran to the stallion. She joyfully threw her arms around his neck and hugged him tightly. He was young, strong and magnificent, just the way she remembered him. Emily swore they would never be parted again.

Emily was overcome with emotion when she saw Paelen too. She hugged him tightly and nearly squeezed the life out of him.

'I love you too, Paelen,' she laughed. Then she hit him for being such a foolish hero in getting himself killed by dragons.

Paelen looked at Emily as though she had lost her mind. He checked her forehead for a temperature and suggested she might need a long break.

'I'm not crazy, Paelen,' she cried happily. 'I'm just so glad that you're alive and young again!'

Emily's joy continued as she greeted each of the Olympians she had lost. Diana stood with Emily's father, looking just as youthful and beautiful as she remembered. Apollo was strong and sure. They were all there and they were all young.

Emily tried to explain everything that she had been through. But even with Mike at her side as proof and the Pegasus pendants, they still didn't believe her.

For Emily, it was hardest to see Joel again.

Riza had warned her that there would be a heavy price to pay when she returned. Emily just never imagined this would be it. No one believed her. Not even Joel.

Everything they had shared together in the past was lost. The kiss, finally admitting their feelings for each other – it was all gone. He didn't remember, because for him, it never happened.

The Big Three arrived at the camp accompanied by the Olympians who had served in the war; including the Hundred-handers, the Four Warriors and Prometheus.

Vulcan was with Seren and Jasmine and pushing Maxine. He charged up to Emily. 'I have waited long enough! You must go back to Earth and fetch my Stella back. The forge has not been the same since she left.'

Emily grinned at the gruff Olympian. 'I will, I promise.'

Vesta arrived and put her arms around Emily. 'How I have waited to talk to you about this. The time has been eternal!'

Everyone in the camp listened in stunned silence as Jupiter finally told the full story of the Titan war – including the arrival of a group of time-travellers, led by a certain young lady and powerful Xan – who saved them from defeat.

'I've been waiting an eternity to tell this tale.' Jupiter embraced Emily tightly. 'Now that we have caught up with each other, we can finally speak of our shared past and let the true history be known to everyone!' He presented her with two very old books. 'In the heat of the last battle on Titus, you left these behind.'

Emily's eyes flew open. 'The journals! I thought they were gone for ever!' She held the books out to her father. 'See, Dad, I told you I kept a journal of our time there. So did Agent B!'

'I'm so sorry we didn't believe you,' Joel apologized when he and Paelen found a moment alone with Emily. 'It was just such a wild story and honestly, you never disappeared.'

'I understand,' Emily said sadly as she looked at the two young men who had both admitted to loving her, but now didn't know she knew. 'I just wish you could remember so we could talk about it. We went through so much together.'

Joel stepped up to Pegasus and patted his side. 'If Paelen and Pegasus really did die, I don't want to remember any of it.'

Paelen grinned his crooked grin and shoved Joel. 'You just do not want to remember that I was a dragon-fighting hero!'

'I bet I was a hero too!'

'You were both my heroes,' Emily said. She smiled at Paelen. 'Even if you are still a thief.'

'I am not a thief!' Paelen insisted.

'Oh no?' Emily held up her hand and the sapphire ring. 'Vulcan told me you stole half the tools from the forge. And then you took this from Minerva to give to me.'

Paelen studied the ring. 'I do not remember this.'

'I do, Paelen,' she said as she kissed him on his cheek. 'I remember everything.'

With the horrors of the war still fresh in her mind, Emily was finding it impossible to sleep. Her dreams were filled with Shadow Titans, dragons and the death of Pegasus. Each night she would relive all the terrible things she'd seen in Tartarus.

With each nightmare, Pegasus would come to her. Emily would climb on his back and lift Mike up with her. Together they would fly to the silver beach beside the calm lake. As the stars shone, casting their diamond sparkles on the water, they would spend the long nights walking along the shore. Emily would toss a stick for Mike to fetch while telling Pegasus stories of the past and how thinking of him and this silver beach had freed her from the Energy Void.

Emily was grateful to have Pegasus back in her life. 'I missed you so much, Pegs. It was agony when you left me.'

Pegasus nickered softly and pressed his face to her.

They sat together in calm, peaceful silence until Emily reached into her tunic and pulled out Agent B's journal. Inside she found the agent's Pegasus pendant, right where she'd left it so long ago. She held it up to the stallion. 'He cared for you too, Pegs, and never took this off. I want you to know Agent B. I want you to understand what he did for us.'

She lit her hand and opened up the old, faded pages of Agent B's journal. Until now, she hadn't been able to look at it. But as she turned to the first page, she found a note to her.

My dear Emily,

If you are reading this and I am alive, shame on you! Close the book right now and put it away . . .

But if you are reading this because I am dead, please, keep going . . . Emily Jacobs, you are perhaps the most stubborn girl I

374

have ever met. You can be irritating beyond measure, irrational and infuriating. But you are also one of the most loyal and caring people I have had the pleasure to get to know.

We have fought side by side for months now. We have suffered together, bled together and at times, we've even laughed together.

As we are facing our toughest challenge yet, I have the strangest feeling I won't survive it. If I don't, if it's true that I am dead, I beg you, please find me in London. Find me and get me away from the CRU.

Let me know you again. Let me call you and Pegasus, Joel, the Olympians and that mangy mutt, Mike, my friends. Please Emily, find me and save me from myself.

Yours,

Benedict Richard Williams

P.S. Here is where you will find me.

Emily read the address in London. She looked at Pegasus. 'His name was Benedict. After all that time, I only ever called him Agent B.' She re-read his message. 'We'll do that, Pegs. We'll go back and find him and get him away from the CRU.'

Emily leafed through the pages of the journal. She saw that Agent B had not only made written entries in the book, he had also drawn beautiful pen and ink sketches. Emily started to smile.

Agent B had sketched a picture of the young and handsome Big Three, standing with Chiron. Another showed Paelen on Brue – the Mother of the Jungle had already started to change into her ferocious self and the picture showed her shaggy hair and long, sharp teeth. Yet another revealed Emily and Joel in battle against the Shadow Titans. Old Pegasus was standing on one side of her with Mike on the other. She held up the page for Pegasus to see. 'Look, it's full of pictures.'

Emily found another sketch that caught her heart. It was a quiet moment between her and elderly Pegasus. In it Emily held a brush in her hand and gently groomed the stallion. She remembered doing that not too long before he died. Emily caressed the picture and sighed sadly. She closed the book and looked up into the strong, youthful face of Pegasus.

'I was so scared I'd never see you again,' she said softly. 'I couldn't live without you. But Agent B was right; the reset button brought you back to me. No matter what happens next, Pegs, nothing will ever part us again!'

ALSO BY KATE O'HEARN

SHADOW OF THE DRAGON
PART ONE - KIRA

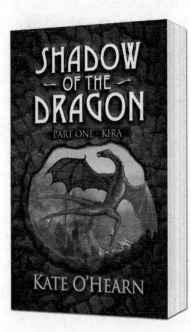

Kira is twelve, and strong willed. The daughter of a retired dragon knight, she yearns for adventure and dreams of following in her father's footsteps astride her own magnificent dragon. Then Lord Dorcon arrives in a whirl of destruction and fire and Kira knows the real fight is just beginning.

To stand a chance of seeing her family again, and to protect the life of her younger sister, she will need every bit of willpower she can find.

LET THE BATTLE COMMENCE...

Also available as an ebook

www.hodderchildrens.co.uk

Hodder Children's Books

WITH MORE TO FIGHT FOR THAN EVER, KIRA AND ELSPETH
MUST FACE THE NEXT PHASE OF THEIR ADVENTURE...

SHADOW OF THE DRAGON

PART TWO - ELSPETH

Strong and determined, Kira has done all that she can to protect and shield
her younger sister. But now it's time for Elspeth to grow up. When Paradon's
muddled magic sends them travelling through time to different eras, new
challenges and terrifying threats await the separated sisters. Especially to
Elspeth, left all alone to navigate a past world long before the rule of King
Ardon. And all the while in a strange, alien world of the future, Kira must find
a way to get back to Elspeth and reunite her family once again.

A prophecy to fulfil. A cruel monarchy to upend.

THE BATTLE CONTINUES...

www.hodderchildrens.co.uk

Hodder
Children's
Books